Charlotte

Jane Austen's
Charlotte

—⁕—

HER FRAGMENT OF A
LAST NOVEL, COMPLETED,
BY

Julia Barrett

—⁕—

M. EVANS AND COMPANY, INC.
New York

M. Evans and Company, Inc.
216 East 49th Street
New York, New York 10017

Library of Congress Cataloging-in Publication Data

Barrett, Julia.
    Jane Austen's Charlotte : Her fragment of a last novel, completed / by Julia Barrett.
        p.   cm.
    ISBN 0-87131-908-X
    I. Heywood, Charlotte (Ficticious character)—Fiction. 2. Young women—England—Sussex—Fiction. 3. Sussex (England)—Fiction. I. Austen, Jane, 1775-1817. Sanditon. II. Title
PS3552.A73463 C48 2000
813'.54—dc21   99-047961

Book design and typography by Rik Lain Schell

Printed in the United States of America

9   8   7   6   5   4   3   2   1

—◆◆◆—

To J. K.
Who listened lovingly, long,
and with impeccable ear,
through the whole of it.

—◆◆◆—

When Jane Austen died in 1817 at the age of forty-one, after a lingering illness thought to have been Addison's disease, she left behind the fragment of a novel that seems to mark a wholly new turn in her writing. Some decades later, her niece undertook to enlarge and complete those pages. In 1870, her nephew published a memoir in which he included some extracts, referring to the material as Sanditon, a title that remains attached to it, and it was not until 1925 that its text appeared. It is clear that Austen's story was to be told through the eyes of Charlotte Heywood, and that her subject was the southern coast of Sussex. In her own day, that region was not only a place of distinctive landscape and atmosphere, but one which could epitomize the economic forces rapidly altering her world. I have taken the liberty to continue where the writer abandoned a tale that is only at its beginning. Although completion of that story has been attempted before, it still waits to be told. This work is entitled Charlotte, after the young woman who is her implied heroine. Whether it might have been more faithful to her genius to have kept with Jane Austen's intended The Brothers, must be left to the reader's judgment. Yet, it is also to be considered that her niece, who had known the writer, did not herself use it, so indeterminate was the state of Austen's last effort.

In these pages, Sir Edward Denham quotes the poetry of Charlotte Smith. She was a Sussex-born novelist and poet, admired by Sir Walter Scott, who wrote a brief biography of her. Jane Austen knew her work, and I have taken the liberty here of characterizing her as Emmeline Turner.

Your prudent grandmammas, ye modern bells,
Content with Bristol, Bath and Tunbridge Wells,
When health required it, would consent to roam
Else more attached to pleasure found at home;

But now alike, gay widow, virgin, wife,
Ingenious to diversify dull life,
In coaches, chaises, caravans, and hoys,
Fly to the coast for daily, nightly joys,
And all, impatient of dry land, agree
With one consent to rush into the sea.

—William Cowper
"Retirement," ll. 515–524 (1782)

Part I

ONE

A gentleman and lady traveling from Tunbridge towards that part of the Sussex coast which lies between Hastings and Eastbourne, being induced by business to quit the high road and attempt a very rough lane, were overturned in toiling up its long ascent half-rock, half sand. The accident happened just beyond the only gentleman's house near the lane, a house, which their driver, on being first required to take that direction, had conceived to be necessarily their object, and had with most unwilling looks been constrained to pass by.

He had grumbled and shaken his shoulders so much indeed, and pitied and cut his horses so sharply, that he might have been open to the suspicion of overturning them on purpose (especially as the carriage was not his master's own) if the road had not indisputably become considerably worse than before, as soon as the premises of the said house were left behind—expressing with a most intelligent portentous countenance that beyond it no wheels but cart wheels could safely proceed.

The severity of the fall was broken by their slow pace and the narrowness of the lane, and the gentleman having scrambled out and helped out his companion, they neither of them at first felt more than shaken and bruised. But the gentleman had in the course of the extrication sprained his foot; and soon becoming sensible of it, was obliged in a few moments to cut short, both his remonstrance to the driver and his congratulations to his wife and himself and sit down on the bank, unable to stand.

"There is something wrong here," said he, putting his hand to his ankle. "But never mind, my dear," looking up at her with a smile, "it could not have happened, you know, in a better place. Good out of evil. The very thing perhaps to be wished for. We shall soon get relief. *There*, I fancy lies my cure," pointing to the neat-looking end of a cottage, which was seen romantically situated among woods on a high eminence at some little distance.

"Does not *that* promise to be the very place?!"

His wife fervently hoped it was, but stood, terrified and anxious, neither able to do or suggest anything, and receiving her first real comfort from the sight of several persons now coming to their assistance.

The accident had been discerned from a hayfield adjoining the house they had passed. And the persons who approached were a well-looking, hale, gentlemanlike man of middle age, the proprietor of the place, who happened to be among his haymakers at the time, and three or four of the ablest of them summoned to attend their master, to say nothing of all the rest of the field, men, women and children, not very far off.

Mr. Heywood, such was the name of the said proprietor, advanced with a very civil salutation, much concern for the accident, some surprise at anybody's attempting that road in a carriage, and ready offers of assistance.

His courtesies were received with good breeding and gratitude, and while one or two of the men lent their help to the driver in getting the carriage upright again, the traveller said, "You are extremely obliging, Sir, and I take you at your word. The injury to my leg is, I dare say, very trifling, but it is always best in these cases to have a surgeon's opinion without loss of time; and as the road does not seem at present in a favorable state for my getting up to his house myself, I will thank you to send off one of these good people for the surgeon."

"The surgeon, Sir!" replied Mr. Heywood, "I am afraid you will find no surgeon at hand here, but I dare say we shall do very well without him."

"Nay, Sir, if *he* is not in the way, his partner will do just as well, or rather better. I could rather see his partner indeed. I could prefer the attendance of his partner. One of these good people can be with him in three minutes, I am sure. I need not ask whether I see the house—looking towards the cottage—for, excepting your own' we have passed none in this place, which can be the abode of a gentleman."

Mr. Heywood looked very much astonished and replied, "What, Sir! are you expecting to find a surgeon in that cottage? We have neither surgeon nor partner in the parish, I assure you."

"Excuse me, Sir," replied the other, "I am sorry to have the appearance of contradicting you, but though from the extent of the parish or some other cause you may not be aware of the fact. Stay. Can I be mistaken in the place? Am I not in Willingden? Is not this Willingden?"

"Yes Sir, this is certainly Willingden."

"Then Sir, I can bring proof of your having a surgeon in the parish whether you may know it or not. Here Sir," taking out his pocketbook, "if you will do me the favor of casting your eye over these advertisements, which I cut out myself from the *Morning Post* and the *Kentish Gazette*, only yesterday morning in London, I think you will be convinced that I am not speaking at random. You will find in it an advertisement, Sir, of the dissolution of a partnership in the medical line in your own parish 'extensive business, undeniable character, respectable references, wishing to form a separate establishment.' You will find it at full length, Sir," offering him the two little oblong extracts.

"Sir," said Mr. Heywood, with a good-humored smile, "if you were to show me all the newspapers that are printed in one week throughout the kingdom, you could not persuade me of there being a surgeon in Willingden. For having lived here ever since I was born, man and boy, fifty-seven years, I think I must have *known* of such a person. At least I may venture to say that he has not *much business*. To be sure, if gentlemen were to be often attempting this lane in post-chaises, it might not be a bad speculation for a surgeon to get a house at the top of the hill. But as to that cottage, I can assure you, Sir, that in spite of its spruce air at this distance, it is as indifferent a double tenement as any in the parish, and that my shepherd lives at one end, and three old women at the other."

He took the pieces of paper as he spoke, and having looked them over, added, "I believe I can explain it, Sir. Your mistake is in the place. There are two Willingdens in this country, and your advertisements refer to the other, which is Great Willingden, or Willingden Abbots, and lies seven miles off, on the other side of Battle, quite down in the weald. And *we*, Sir," speaking rather proudly, "are not in the weald."

"Not *down* in the weald, of that I am sure Sir," replied the traveler, pleasantly. "It took us half an hour to climb your hill! Well, Sir, I dare say it is as you say, and I have made an abominably stupid blunder. All done in a moment. The advertisements did not catch my eye till the last half hour of our being in town; when everything was in the hurry and confusion which always attend a short stay there. One is never able to complete anything in the way of business, you know, till the carriage is at the door. And accordingly satisfying myself with a brief enquiry, and finding we were actually to pass within a mile or two of a *Willingden*, I sought no farther."

"My dear," to his wife, "I am very sorry to have brought you into this scrape, but do not be alarmed about my leg. It gives me no pain while I am quiet, and as soon as these good people have succeeded in setting the cargo to rights, and turning the horses round, the best thing we can do will be to measure back our steps into the turnpike road and proceed to Hailsham, and so home, without attempting anything farther. Two hours take us home, from Hailsham. And when once at home, we have our remedy at hand you know. A little of our own bracing sea air will soon set me on my feet again. Depend upon it, my dear, it is exactly a case for the sea. Saline air and immersion will be the very thing. My sensations tell me so already."

In a most friendly manner, Mr. Heywood here interposed, entreating them not to think of proceeding till the ankle had been examined, and some refreshment taken, and very cordially pressing them to make use of his house for both purposes.

"We are always well stocked," said he, "with all the common remedies for sprains and bruises. And I will answer for the pleasure it will give my wife and daughters to be of service to you and this lady in every way in their power."

A twinge or two, in trying to move his foot disposed the traveler to think rather more as he had done at first of the benefit of immediate assistance, and consulting his wife in the few words of, "Well my dear, I believe it will be better for us," turned again to Mr. Heywood and said, "Before we accept your hospitality, Sir, and in order to do away with any unfavorable impression which the sort of wild goose chase you find me in, may have given rise to, allow me to tell you who we are. My name is Parker, Mr. Parker of Sanditon; this lady, my wife, Mrs. Parker. We are on our road home from London. My name perhaps, though I am by no means the first of my family holding landed property in the parish of Sanditon, may be unknown at this distance from the coast. But Sanditon itself, everybody has heard of Sanditon, the favorite for a young and rising bathing-place, certainly the favorite spot of all that are to be found along the coast of Sussex; the most favored by nature, and promising to be the most chosen by man."

"Yes, I have heard of Sanditon," replied Mr. Heywood. "Every five years, one hears of some new place or other starting up by the sea, and growing the fashion. How they can half of them be filled, is the wonder! *Where* people can be found with money or time to go to them! Bad things for a country; sure to raise the price of provisions, and make the poor good for nothing, as I dare say you find, Sir."

"Not at all, Sir, not at all," cried Mr. Parker eagerly. "Quite the contrary, I assure you. A common idea, but a mistaken one. It may apply to your large, overgrown place, like Brighton, or Worthing, or Eastbourne, but not to a small village like Sanditon, precluded by its size from experiencing any of the evils of civilization, while the growth of the place, the buildings, the nursery grounds, the demand for every thing, and the sure resort of the very best company, those regular, steady, private families of thorough gentility and character, who are a blessing everywhere, excite the industry of the poor and diffuse comfort and improvement among them of every sort. No, Sir, I assure you, Sanditon is not a place. . . ."

"I do not mean to take exception to *any* place in particular Sir," answered Mr. Heywood, "I only think our coast is too full of them altogether. But had we not better try to get you. . . ."

"Our coast too full!" repeated Mr. Parker, "on that point perhaps we may not totally *disagree*, at least there are *enough*. Our coast is abundant enough; it demands no more. Everybody's taste and everybody's finances may be suited. And those good people who are trying to add to the number, are in my opinion excessively absurd, and must soon find themselves the dupes of their own fallacious calculations. Such a place as Sanditon, Sir, I may say was wanted, was called for. Nature had marked it out, had spoken in most intelligible characters. The finest, purest sea breeze on the coast, acknowledged to be so—excellent bathing, fine hard sand, deep water ten yards from the shore, no mud, no weeds, no slimy rocks. Never was there a place more palpably designed by nature for the resort of the invalid. The very spot which thousands seemed in need of. The most desirable distance from London! One complete, measured mile nearer than Eastbourne. Only conceive, Sir, the advantage of saving a whole mile, in a long journey. But Brinshore, Sir, which I dare say you have in your eye—the attempts of two or three speculating people about

Brinshore, this last year, to raise that paltry hamlet, lying as it does between a stagnant marsh, a bleak moor and the constant effluvia of a ridge of putrefying sea weed, can end in nothing but their own disappointment. What in the name of common sense is to *recommend* Brinshore? A most insalubrious air, roads proverbially detestable, water brackish beyond example, impossible to get a good dish of tea within three miles of the place. And as for the soil, it is so cold and ungrateful that it can hardly be made to yield a cabbage. Depend upon it, Sir, that this is a faithful description of Brinshore, not in the smallest degree exaggerated. And if you have heard it differently spoken of. . . ."

"Sir, I never heard it spoken of in my life before," said Mr. Heywood. "I did not know there was such a place in the world."

"You did not! There my dear," turning with exultation to his wife, "you see how it is. So much for the celebrity of Brinshore! This gentleman did not know there was such a place in the world. Why, in truth Sir, I fancy we may apply to Brinshore that line of the poet Cowper in his description of the religious cottager, as opposed to Voltaire. '*She*, never heard of half-mile from home.'"

"With all my heart Sir, apply any verses you like to it. But I want to see something applied to your leg. And I am sure by your lady's countenance that she is quite of my opinion and thinks it a pity to lose any more time. And here come my girls to speak for themselves and their mother."

Two or three genteel looking young women followed by as many maid servants, were now seen issuing from the house.

"I began to wonder the bustle should not have reached *them*. A thing of this kind soon makes a stir in a lonely place like ours. Now, Sir, let us see how you can be best be conveyed into the house."

The young ladies approached and said every thing that was proper to recommend their father's offers; and in an unaffected manner calculated to make the strangers easy. And, as Mrs. Parker was exceedingly anxious for relief, and her husband by this time, not much less disposed for it, a very few civil scruples were enough, especially as the carriage being now set up, was discovered to have received such injury on the fallen side as to be unfit for present use.

Mr. Parker was therefore carried into the house, and his carriage wheeled off to a vacant barn.

TWO

*T*he acquaintance, thus oddly begun, was neither short nor unimportant. For a whole fortnight the travelers were fixed at Willingden, Mr. Parker's sprain proving too serious for him to move sooner. He had fallen into very good hands. The Heywoods were a thoroughly respectable family, and every possible attention was paid in the kindest and most unpretending manner, to both husband and wife. *He* was waited on and nursed, and *she* cheered and comforted with unremitting kindness. And as every office of hospitality and friendliness was received as it ought, as there was not more good will on one side than gratitude on the other, nor any deficiency of generally pleasant manners on either, they grew to like each other in the course of that fortnight, exceedingly well.

Mr. Parker's character and history were soon unfolded. All that he understood of himself, he readily told, for he was very openhearted; and where he might be himself in the dark, his conversation was still giving information, to such of the Heywoods as could observe.

By such he was perceived to be an enthusiast; on the subject of Sanditon, a complete enthusiast. Sanditon, the success of Sanditon as a small, fashionable bathing place, was the object, for which he seemed to live. A very few years ago, and it had been a quiet village of no pretensions; but some natural advantages in its position and some accidental circumstances having suggested to himself, and the other principal land holder, the probability of its becoming a profitable speculation, they had engaged in it, and planned and built, and praised and puffed, and raised it to a something of young renown, and Mr. Parker could now think of very little besides.

The facts, which in more direct communication he laid before them, were that he was about five and thirty, had been married, very happily married seven years, and had four sweet children at home; that he was of a respectable family, and easy though not large fortune; no profession, succeeding as eldest son to the property which two or three generations had been holding and accumulating before him; that he had two brothers and two sisters, all single and all independent, the eldest of the two former indeed, by collateral inheritance, quite as well provided for as himself.

His object in quitting the high road, to hunt for an advertising surgeon, was also plainly stated. It had not proceeded from any intention of spraining his ankle or doing himself any other injury for the good of such surgeon, nor (as Mr. Heywood had been apt to suppose) from any design of entering into partnership with him. It was merely in consequence of a wish to establish some medical man at Sanditon, which the nature of the advertisement induced him to expect to accomplish in Willingden. He was convinced that the advantage of a medical man at hand could very materially promote the rise and prosperity of the place, could in fact tend to bring a prodigious influx; nothing else was wanting. He had *strong* reason to believe that *one* family had been deterred last year from trying Sanditon on that account and probably very many more. And his own sisters, who were sad invalids, and whom he was very anxious to get to Sanditon this summer, could hardly be expected to hazard themselves in a place where they could not have immediate medical advice.

Upon the whole, Mr. Parker was evidently an amiable family man, fond of wife, children, brothers and sisters, and generally kind-hearted; liberal, gentlemanlike, easy to please; of a sanguine turn of mind, with more imagination than judgment. And Mrs. Parker was as evidently a gentle, amiable, sweet tempered woman, the properest wife in the world for a man of strong understanding, but not of capacity to supply the cooler reflection which her own husband sometimes needed, and so entirely waiting to be guided on every occasion, that whether he were risking his fortune or spraining his ankle, she remained equally useless.

Sanditon was a second wife and four children to him, hardly less dear, and certainly more engrossing. He could talk of it forever. It had indeed the highest claims; not only those of birthplace, property, and home, it was his mine, his lottery, his speculation, and his hobby horse; his occupation, his hope and his futurity.

He was extremely desirous of drawing his good friends at Willingden thither; and his endeavors in the cause, were as grateful and disinterested as they were warm. He wanted to secure the promise of a visit, to get as many of the family as his own house could contain, to follow him to Sanditon as soon as possible, and healthy as they all undeniably were, foresaw that every one of them could be benefitted by the sea.

He held it indeed as certain, that no person could be really well, no person (however upheld for the present by fortuitous aids of exercise and spirits in a semblance of health) could be really in a state of secure and permanent health without spending at least six weeks by the sea every year. The sea air and sea bathing together were nearly infallible, one or the other of them being a match for every disorder of the stomach, the lungs or the blood. They were antispasmodic, antipulmonary, antiseptic, antibilious and antirheumatic. Nobody could catch cold by the sea. Nobody wanted appetite by the sea. Nobody wanted spirits. Nobody wanted strength. They were healing, softening, relaxing, fortifying and bracing, seemingly just as was wanted, sometimes one, sometimes the other. If the sea breeze failed, the sea-bath was the certain corrective; and where bathing disagreed, the sea breeze alone was evidently designed by nature for the cure.

His eloquence, however, could not prevail. Mr. and Mrs. Heywood never left home. Marrying early, and having a very numerous family, their movements had been long limited to one small circle; and they were older in habits than in age. Excepting two journeys to London in the year, to receive his dividends, Mr. Heywood went no farther than his feet or his well-tried old horse could carry him, and Mrs. Heywood's adventurings were only now and then to visit her neighbors, in the old coach which had been new when they married and fresh lined on their eldest son's coming of age ten years ago.

They had very pretty property; enough, had their family been of reasonable limits, to have allowed them a very gentlemanlike share of luxuries and change; enough for them to have indulged in a new carriage and better roads, an occasional month at Tunbridge Wells, and symptoms of the gout and a winter at Bath.

But the maintenance, education and fitting out of fourteen children demanded a very quiet, settled, careful course of life, and obliged them to be stationary and healthy at Willingden. What prudence had at first enjoined, was now rendered pleasant by habit. They never left home, and they had a gratification in saying so.

But very far from wishing their children to do the same, they were glad to promote *their* getting out into the world, as much as possible. *They* stayed at home, that their children *might* get out. And while making that home extremely comfortable, welcomed every change from it which could give useful connections or respectable acquaintance to sons or daughters.

When Mr. and Mrs. Parker, therefore, ceased from soliciting a family visit, and bounded their views to carrying back one daughter with them, no difficulties were started. It was general pleasure and consent.

Their invitation was to Miss Charlotte Heywood, a very pleasing young woman of two and twenty, the eldest of the daughters at home, and the one who under her mother's directions had been particularly useful and obliging to them; who had attended them most, and knew them best.

Charlotte was to go, with excellent health, to bathe, and be better if she could; to receive every possible pleasure which Sanditon could be made to supply by the gratitude of those she went with; and to buy new parasols, new gloves, and new brooches for her sisters and herself at the library, which Mr. Parker was anxiously wishing to support.

All that Mr. Heywood himself could be persuaded to promise was that he could send everyone to Sanditon who asked his advice, and that nothing should ever induce him (as far as the future could be answered for) to spend even five shillings at Brinshore.

THREE

Every neighborhood should have a great lady. The great lady of Sanditon was Lady Denham; and in their journey from Willingden to the coast, Mr. Parker gave Charlotte more detailed account of her than had been called for before.

She had been necessarily often mentioned at Willingden, for being his colleague in speculation. Sanditon itself could not be talked of long, without the introduction of Lady Denham, and that she was a very rich old lady, who had buried two husbands, who knew the value of money, was very much looked up to, and had a poor cousin living with her, were facts already well known, but some further particulars of her history and her character served to lighten the tediousness of a long hill, or a heavy bit of road, and to give the visiting young lady a suitable knowledge of the person with whom she might now expect to be daily associating.

Lady Denham had been a rich Miss Brereton, born to wealth but not to education. Her first husband had been a Mr. Hollis, a man of considerable property in the country, of which a large share of the parish of Sanditon, with manor and mansion house made a part. He had been an elderly man when she married him; her own age about thirty. Her motives for such a match could be little understood at the distance of forty years, but she had so well nursed and pleased Mr. Hollis, that at his death he left her everything—all his estates, and all at her disposal.

After a widowhood of some years, she had been induced to marry again. The late Sir Harry Denham, of Denham Park in the neighborhood of Sanditon had succeeded in removing her, and her large income to his own domains, but he could not succeed in the views of permanently enriching his family, which were attributed to him. She had been too wary to put anything out of her own power, and when on Sir Harry's decease she returned again to her own house at Sanditon, she was said to have made this boast to a friend, "that though she had *got* nothing but her title from the family, still she had *given* nothing for it."

For the title, it was to be supposed, she had married. And Mr. Parker acknowledged there being just such a degree of value for it apparent now, as to give her conduct that natural explanation.

"There is at times," said he, "a little self-importance, but it is not offensive; and there are moments, there are points, when her love of money is carried greatly too far. But she is a good natured woman, a very good natured woman, a very obliging, friendly neighbor; a cheerful, independent, valuable character, and her faults may be entirely imputed to her want of education. She has good natural sense, but quite uncultivated. She has a fine active mind, as well as a fine healthy frame for a woman of seventy, and enters into the improvement of Sanditon with a spirit truly admirable. Though now and then, a littleness *will* appear. She cannot look forward quite as I would have her, and takes alarm at a trifling present expense, without considering what returns it will make her in a year or two. That is, we think *differently*, we now and then, see things *differently*, Miss Heywood. Those who tell their own story, you know, must be listened to with caution. When you see us in contact, you will judge for yourself."

Lady Denham was indeed a great lady beyond the common wants of society, for she had many thousands a year to bequeath, and three distinct sets of people to be courted by; her own relations, who might very reasonably wish for her original thirty thousand pounds among them, the legal heirs of Mr. Hollis, who must hope to be more indebted to *her* sense of justice than he had allowed them to be to *his*, and those members of the Denham family, whom her second husband had hoped to make a good bargain for.

By all of these, or by branches of them, she had no doubt been long, and still continued to be, well attacked; and of these three divisions, Mr. Parker did not hesitate to say that Mr. Hollis's kindred were the *least* in favor and Sir Harry Denham's the *most*. The former he believed, had done themselves irremediable harm by expressions of very unwise and unjustifiable resentment at the time of Mr. Hollis's death; the latter, to the advantage of being the remnant of a connection which she certainly valued, joined those of having been known to her from their childhood, and of being always at hand to preserve their interest by reasonable attention.

Sir Edward, the present baronet, nephew to Sir Harry, resided constantly at Denham Park; and Mr. Parker had little doubt, that he and his sister Miss Denham, who lived with him, would be principally remembered in her will. He sincerely hoped it. Miss Denham had a very small provision, and her brother was a poor man for his rank in society.

"He is a warm friend to Sanditon," said Mr. Parker, "and his hand would be as liberal as his heart, had he the power. He would be a noble coadjutor! As it is, he does what he can, and is running up a tasteful little cottage orné on a strip of waste ground Lady Denham has granted him, which I have no doubt we shall have many a candidate for, before the end even of *this* season."

Till within the last twelvemonth, Mr. Parker had considered Sir Edward as standing without a rival, as having the fairest chance of succeeding to the greater part of all that she had to give, but there was now another person's claims to be taken into the account, those of the young female relation, whom Lady Denham had been induced to receive into her family.

After having always protested against any such addition, and long and often enjoyed the repeated defeats she had given to every attempt of her relations to introduce this young lady, or that young lady as a companion at Sanditon House, she had brought back with her from London last Michaelmas a Miss Brereton, who bid fair by her merits to vie in favor with Sir Edward, and to secure for herself and her family that share of the accumulated property which they had certainly the best right to inherit.

Mr. Parker spoke warmly of Clara Brereton, and the interest of his story increased very much with the introduction of such a character. Charlotte listened with more than amusement now; it was solicitude and enjoyment, as she heard her described to be lovely, amiable, gentle, unassuming, conducting herself uniformly with great good sense, and evidently gaining, by her innate worth, on the affections of her patroness. Beauty, sweetness, poverty and dependence do not want the imagination of a man to operate upon. With due exceptions, woman feels for woman very promptly and compassionately. He gave the particulars which had led to Clara's admission at Sanditon, as no bad exemplification of that mixture of character, that union of littleness with kindness with good sense, with even liberality, which he saw in Lady Denham.

After having avoided London for many years, principally on account of these very cousins, who were continually writing, inviting and tormenting her, and whom she was determined to keep at a distance, she had been obliged to go there last Michaelmas with the certainty of being detained at least a fortnight. She had gone to an hotel living by her own account as prudently as possible, to defy the reputed expensiveness of such a home, and at the end of three days calling for her bill, that she might judge of her state. Its amount was such as determined her on staying not another hour in the house, and she was preparing in all the anger and perturbation which a belief of very gross imposition there, and an ignorance of where to go for better usage, to leave the hotel at all hazards, when the cousins, the politic and lucky cousins, who seemed always to have a spy on her, introduced themselves at this important moment, and learning her situation, persuaded her to accept such a home for the rest of her stay as their humbler house in a very inferior part of London could offer.

She went; was delighted with her welcome, and the hospitality and attention she received from everybody; found her good cousins the Breretons beyond her expectation worthy people; and finally, was impelled by a personal knowledge of their narrow income and pecuniary difficulties, to invite one of the girls of the family to pass the winter with her.

The invitation was to *one*, for six months, with the probability of another being then to take her place; but in *selecting* the one, Lady Denham had shown the good part of her character. For passing by the actual *daughters* of the house, she had chosen Clara, a niece, more helpless, and more pitiable of course than any. A dependent on poverty, an additional burden on an encumbered circle, and one, who had been so low in every worldly view, as with all her natural endowments and powers, to have been preparing for a situation little better than a nursery maid.

Clara had returned with her, and by her good sense and merit had now, to all appearance, secured a very strong hold in Lady Denham's regard. The six months had long been over and not a syllable was breathed of any change, or exchange. She was a general favorite; influence of her steady conduct, and mild, gentle temper was felt by everybody.

The prejudices which had met her at first in some quarters, were all dissipated. She was felt to be worthy of trust, to be the very companion who would guide and soften Lady Denham, who would enlarge her mind and open her hand. She was as thoroughly amiable as she was lovely, and since having had the advantage of their Sanditon breezes, that loveliness was complete.

FOUR

And whose very snug-looking place is this?" said Charlotte, as in a sheltered dip within two miles of the sea, they passed close by a moderate-sized house, well fenced and planted, and rich in the garden, orchard and meadows which are the best embellishments of such a dwelling. "It seems to have as many comforts about it as Willingden."

"Ah," said Mr. Parker, "this is my old house, the house of my forefathers, the house where I, and all my brothers and sisters were born and bred, and where my own three eldest children born; where Mrs. Parker and I lived till within the last two years, till our new house was finished. I am glad you are pleased with it. It is an honest old place and Hillier keeps it in very good order. I have given it up you know to the man who occupies the chief of my land. *He* gets a better house by it, and I, a rather better situation!"

"One other hill brings us to Sanditon, modern Sanditon, a beautiful spot. Our ancestors, you know, always built in a hole. Here were we, pent down in this little contracted nook, without air or view, only one mile and three quarters from the noblest expanse of ocean between the south foreland and the land's end, and without the smallest advantage from it. You will not think I have made a bad exchange, when we reach Trafalgar House, which by the bye, I almost wish I had not named Trafalgar, for Waterloo is more the thing now. However, Waterloo is in reserve, and if we have encouragement enough this year for a little crescent to be ventured on (as I trust we shall) then, we shall be able to call it Waterloo

Crescent, and the name joined to the form of the building, which always takes, will give us the command of lodgers. In a good season, we should have more applications than we could attend to."

"It was always a very comfortable house," said Mrs. Parker, looking at it through the back window with something like the fondness of regret. "And such a nice garden, such an excellent garden."

"Yes, my love, but *that* we may be said to carry with us. *It* supplies us, as before, with all the fruit and vegetables we want; and we have in fact, all the comfort of an excellent kitchen garden without the constant eyesore of its formalities; or the yearly nuisance of its decaying vegetation. Who can endure a cabbage bed in October?"

"Oh! dear, yes. We are quite as well off for garden stuff as ever we were, for if it is forgot to be brought at any time, we can always buy what we want at Sanditon House. The gardener there is glad enough to supply us. But it was a nice place for the children to run about in. So shady in summer!"

"My dear, we shall have shade enough on the hill, and more than enough in the course of a very few years. The growth of my plantations is a general astonishment. In the meanwhile, we have the canvas awning, which gives us the most complete comfort within doors, and you can get a parasol at Whitby's for little Mary at any time, or a large bonnet at Jebb's, and as for the boys, I must say I would rather *them* run about in the sunshine than not. I am sure we agree my dear, in wishing our boys to be as hearty as possible."

"Yes indeed, I am sure we do, and I will get Mary a little parasol, which will make her as proud as can be. How grave she will walk about with it, and fancy herself quite a little woman. Oh! I have not the smallest doubt of our being a great deal better off where we are now. If we any of us want to bathe, we have not a quarter of a mile to go. But you know, still looking back, one loves to look at an old friend, at a place where one has been happy. The Hilliers did not seem to feel the storms last winter at all. I remember seeing Mrs. Hillier after one of those dreadful nights, when we had been literally rocked in our bed, and she did not seem at all aware of the wind being anything more than common."

"Yes, yes, that's likely enough. *We* have all the grandeur of the storm, with less real danger, because the wind meeting with nothing to oppose or confine it around our house, simply rages, and passes on, while down in this gutter, nothing is known of the state of the air below the tops of the trees, and the inhabitants may be taken totally unawares, by one of those dreadful currents which do more mischief in a valley, when they *do* arise, than an open country ever experiences in the heaviest gale."

"But my dear love, as to garden stuff; you were saying that any accidental omission is supplied in a moment by Lady Denham's gardener, but it occurs to me that we ought to go elsewhere upon such occasions, and that old Stringer and his son have a higher claim. I encouraged him to set up, and am afraid he does not do very well, that is, there has not been time enough yet. He *will* do very well beyond a doubt, but at first it is uphill work; and therefore we must give him what help we can, and when any vegetables or fruit happen to be wanted, and it will not be amiss to have them often wanted, to have something or other forgotten most days. Just to have a nominal supply you know, that poor old Andrew may not lose his daily job, but in fact to buy the chief of our consumption of the Stringers."

"Very well, my love, that can be easily done, and cook will be satisfied, which will be a great comfort, for she is always complaining of old Andrew now, and says he never brings her what she wants. There—now the old house is quite left behind. What is it your brother Sidney says about it's being a hospital?"

"Oh! my dear Mary, merely a joke of his. He pretends to advise me to make a hospital of it. He pretends to laugh at my improvements. Sidney says anything you know. He has always said what he chose of, and to us, all. Most families have such a member among them, I believe, Miss Heywood. There is a someone in most families privileged by superior abilities or spirits to say anything. In ours, it is Sidney; who is a very clever young man, and with great powers of pleasing. He lives too much in the world to be settled; that is his only fault. He is here and there and everywhere. I wish we may get him to Sanditon. I should like to have you acquainted with him. And it would be a fine thing for the place! Such a young man as Sidney, with his neat equipage and fashionable air, you and I Mary, know what effect it might have. Many a respectable family, many a careful mother, many a pretty daughter, might it secure us, to the prejudice of Eastbourne and Hastings."

They were now approaching the church and real village of Sanditon, which stood at the foot of the hill they were afterwards to ascend, a hill, whose side was covered with the woods and enclosures of Sanditon House and whose height ended in an open down where the new buildings might soon be looked for. A branch only of the valley, winding more obliquely towards the sea, gave a passage to an inconsiderable stream, and formed at its mouth, a third habitable division in a small cluster of fisherman's houses.

The village contained little more than cottages, but the spirit of the day had been caught, as Mr. Parker observed with delight to Charlotte, and two or three of the best of them were smartened up with a white curtain and "lodgings to let," and farther on, in the little green court of an old farm house, two females in elegant white were actually to be seen with their books and camp stools. And in turning the corner of the baker's shop, the sound of a harp might be heard through the upper casement.

Such sights and sounds were highly blissful to Mr. Parker. Not that he had any personal concern in the success of the village itself; for considering it as too remote from the beach, he had done nothing there, but it was a most valuable proof of the increasing fashion of the place altogether. If the *village* could attract, the hill might be nearly full.

He anticipated an amazing season. At the same time last year, late in July, there had not been a single lodger in the village! Nor did he remember any during the whole summer, excepting one family of children who came from London for sea air after the whooping cough, and whose mother would not let them be nearer the shore for fear of their tumbling in.

"Civilization, civilization indeed!" cried Mr. Parker, delighted. "Look, my dear Mary, look at William Heeley's windows. Blue shoes, and nankin boots! Who would have expected such a sight at a shoemakers in old Sanditon! This is new within the month. There was no blue shoe when we passed this way a month ago. Glorious indeed! Well, I think I *have* done something in my day. Now, for our hill, our health-breathing hill."

In ascending, they passed the lodge gates of Sanditon House and saw the top of the house itself among its groves. It was the last building of former days in that line of the parish. A little higher up, the modern began; and in crossing the down, a Prospect House, a Bellevue Cottage, and a Denham Place were to be looked at by Charlotte with the calmness of amused curiosity, and by Mr. Parker with the eager eye which hoped to see scarcely any empty houses.

More bills at the window than he had calculated on, and a smaller show of company on the hill. Fewer carriages, fewer walkers. He had fancied it just the time of day for them to be all returning from their airings to dinner. But the sands and the Terrace always attracted some, and the tide must be flowing, about half-tide now. He longed to be on the sands, the cliffs, at his own house, and everywhere out of his house at once. His spirits rose with the very sight of the sea and he could almost feel his ankle getting stronger already.

Trafalgar House, on the most elevated spot on the down was a light elegant building, standing in a small lawn with a very young plantation round it, about a hundred yards from the brow of a steep, but not very lofty cliff, and the nearest to it, of every building, excepting one short row of smart-looking houses, called the Terrace, with a broad walk in front, aspiring to be the Mall of the place. In this row were the best milliner's shop and the library; a little detached from it, the hotel and billiard room. Here began the descent to the beach and to the bathing machines, and this was therefore the favorite spot for beauty and fashion.

At Trafalgar House, rising at a little distance behind the Terrace, the travellers were safely set down, and all was happiness and joy between Papa and Mama and their children; while Charlotte, having received possession of her apartment, found amusement enough in standing at her ample Venetian window, and looking over the miscellaneous foreground of unfinished buildings, waving linen and tops of houses to the sea, dancing and sparkling in sunshine and freshness.

FIVE

When they met before dinner, Mr. Parker was looking over letters. "Not a line from Sidney!" said he. "He is an idle fellow. I sent him an account of my accident from Willingden, and thought he would have vouchsafed me an answer. But perhaps it implies that he is coming himself. I trust it may. But here is a letter from one of my sisters. *They* never fail me. Women are the only correspondents to be depended on.

"Now, Mary," smiling at his wife, "before I open it, what shall we guess as to the state of health of those it comes from, or rather what would Sidney say if he were here? Sidney is a saucy fellow, Miss Heywood. And you must know, he will have it there is a good deal of imagination in my two sisters' complaints, but it really is not so—or very little. They have wretched health, as you have heard us say frequently, and are subject to a variety of very serious disorders. Indeed, I do not believe they know what a day's health is. And at the same time, they are such excellent useful women, and have so much energy of character that, where any good is to be done, they force themselves on exertions which to those who do not thoroughly know them, have an extraordinary appearance. But there is really no affectation about them. They have only weaker constitutions, and stronger minds than are often met with, either separate or together."

"And our youngest brother, who lives with them, and who is not much above twenty, I am sorry to say, is almost as great an invalid as themselves. He is so delicate that he can engage in no profession. Sidney laughs at him but it really is no joke, though Sidney often makes me laugh at them all in spite of myself. Now, if he were here, I know he would be offering odds, that either Susan, Diana or Arthur would appear by this letter to have been at the point of death within the last month."

Having run his eye over the letter, he shook his head and began, "No chance of seeing them at Sanditon, I am sorry to say. A very indifferent account of them indeed. Seriously, a very indifferent account. Mary, you will be quite sorry to hear how ill they have been, and are. Miss Heywood, if you will give me leave, I will read Diana's letter aloud. I like to have my friends acquainted with each other, and I am afraid this is the only sort of acquaintance I shall have the means of accomplishing between you. And I can have no scruple on Diana's account, for her letters show her exactly as she is, the most active, friendly, warmhearted in existence; and therefore must give a good impression." He read,

"My dear Tom,

We were all much grieved at your accident, and if you had not described yourself as fallen into such very good hands, I should have been with you at all hazards the day after the receipt of your letter, though it found me suffering under a more severe attack than usual of my old grievance, spasmodic bile, and hardly able to crawl from my bed to the sofa. But how were you treated? Send me more particulars in your next. If indeed a simple sprain, as you denominate it, nothing would have been so judicious as friction, friction by the hand alone, supposing it could be applied instantly. Two years ago, I happened to be calling on Mrs. Sheldon when her coachman sprained his foot as he was cleaning the carriage and could hardly limp into the house, but by the immediate use of friction alone steadily persevered in, (and I rubbed his ankle with my own hand for six hours without intermission) he was well in three days.

Many thanks, my dear Tom, for the kindness with respect to us, which had so large a share in bringing on your accident But pray never run into peril again, in looking for an apothecary on our account, for had you the most experienced man in his line settled at Sanditon, it would be no recommendation to us. We have entirely done with the whole medical tribe. We have consulted physician after physician in vain, till we are quite convinced that they can do nothing for us and that we must trust to our own knowledge of our own wretched constitutions for any relief.

But if you think it advisable for the interest of the place, to get a medical man there, I will undertake the commission with pleasure, and have no doubt of succeeding. I could soon put the necessary irons in the fire. As for getting to Sanditon myself, it is quite an impossibility. I grieve to say that I dare not attempt it, but my feelings tell me too plainly that in my present state, the sea air would probably be the death of me. And neither of my dear companions will leave me, or I would promote their going down to you for a fortnight. But in truth, I doubt whether Susan's nerves would be equal to the effort, she has been suffering much from the headache, and six leeches a day for ten days together relieved her so little that we thought it right to change our measures, and being convinced on examination that much of the evil lay in her gum, I persuaded her to attack the disorder there. She has accordingly had three teeth drawn, and is decidedly better, but her nerves are a good deal deranged. She can only speak in a whisper, and fainted away twice this morning on poor Arthur's trying to suppress a cough. He, I am happy to say, is tolerably well, though more languid than I like, and I fear for his liver.

I have heard nothing of Sidney since your being together in town, but conclude his scheme to the Isle of Wight has not taken place, or we should have seen him in his way.

Most sincerely do we wish you a good season at Sanditon, and though we cannot contribute to your beau monde in person, we are doing our utmost to send you company worth having; and think we may safely reckon on securing you two large families, one a rich West Indian from Surrey, the other, a most respectable girls boarding school, or Academy, from Camberwell. I will not tell you how many people I have employed in the business—wheel within wheel. But success more than repays. Yours most affectionately, etcetera."

"Well," said Mr. Parker, as he finished. "Though I dare say Sidney might find something extremely entertaining in this letter and make us laugh for half an hour together, I declare, I, by myself, can see nothing in it but what is either very pitiable or very creditable. With all their sufferings you perceive how much they are occupied in promoting the good of others! So anxious for Sanditon! Two large families—one, for Prospect House probably, the other, for Number Two Denham Place or the end house of the Terrace, with extra beds at the hotel. I told you my sisters were excellent women, Miss Heywood."

"And I am sure they must be very extraordinary ones," said Charlotte, "I am astonished at the cheerful style of the letter, considering the state in which both sisters appear to be. Three teeth drawn at once—frightful! Your sister Diana seems almost as ill as possible, but those three teeth of your sister Susan's, are more distressing than all the rest."

"Oh, they are so used to the operation—to every operation—and have such fortitude!"

"Your sisters know what they are about, I dare say, but their measures seem to touch on extremes. I feel that in any illness, I should be so anxious for professional advice, so very little venturesome for myself, or any body I loved! But then, *we* have been so healthy a family, that I can be no judge of what the habit of self-doctoring may do."

"Why, to own the truth," said Mrs. Parker, "I *do* think the Miss Parkers carry it too far sometimes. And so do you my love, you know. You often think they would be better, if they would leave themselves more alone—and especially Arthur. I know you think it a great pity they should give *him* such a turn for being ill."

"Well, well, my dear Mary, I grant you, it *is* unfortunate for poor Arthur, that, at his time of life he should be encouraged to give way to indisposition. It *is* bad; it *is* bad that he should be fancying himself too sickly for any profession and sit down at one and twenty, on the interest of his own little fortune, without any idea of attempting to improve it, or of engaging in any occupation that may be of use to himself or others. But let us talk of pleasanter things. These two large families are just what we wanted. And here is something at hand, pleasanter still, Morgan, with his 'dinner on table.'"

SIX

*T*he party were very soon moving after dinner. Mr. Parker could not be satisfied without an early visit to the library, and the library subscription book, and Charlotte was glad to see as much, and as quickly as possible, where all was new.

They were out in the very quietest part of a watering-place day, when the important business of dinner or of sitting after dinner was going on in almost every inhabited lodging. Here and there, a solitary man might be seen, who was forced to move early and walk for health, but in general, it was a thorough pause of company, it was emptiness and tranquility on the Terrace, the cliffs, and the sands. The shops were deserted, the straw hats and pendant lace seemed left to their fate both within the house and without, and Mrs. Whitby at the library was sitting in her inner room, reading one of her own novels, for want of employment.

The list of subscribers was but commonplace. The Lady Denham, Miss Brereton, Mr. and Mrs. Parker, Sir Edward Denham and Miss Denham, whose names might be said to lead off the season, were followed by nothing better than: Mrs. Mathews, Miss Mathews, Miss E. Mathews, Miss H. Mathews. Doctor and Mrs. Brown, Mr. Richard Pratt, Lieutenant Smith, Royal Navy; Captain Little, Limehouse; Mrs. Jane Fisher, Miss Fisher; Miss Scroggs, Reverend Mr. Hanking, Mr. Beard, Solicitor, Grays Inn; Mr. Davis, and Miss Merryweather.

Mr. Parker could not but feel that the list was not only without distinction, but less numerous than he had hoped. It was but July however, and August and September were the months. And besides, the promised large families from Surrey and Camberwell were an ever-ready consolation.

Mrs. Whitby came forward without delay from her literary recess, delighted to see Mr. Parker again, whose manners recommended him to everybody. And they were fully occupied in their various civilities and communications, while Charlotte, having added her name to the list as the first offering to the success of the season, was busy in some immediate purchases for the further good of everybody, as soon as Miss Whitby could be hurried down from her toilette, with all her glossy curls and smart trinkets, to wait on her.

The library, of course, afforded everything; all the useless things in the world that could not be done without, and among so many pretty temptations, and with so much good will for Mr. Parker to encourage expenditure. Charlotte began to feel that she must check herself, or rather, she reflected that at two and twenty there could be no excuse for her doing otherwise, and that it would not do for her to be spending all her money the very first evening. She took up a book; it happened to be a volume of *Camilla*. She had not *Camilla's* youth, and had no intention of having her distress, so, she turned from the drawers of rings and brooches, repressed farther solicitation, and paid for what she bought.

For her particular gratification, they were then to take a turn on the cliff, but as they quitted the library they were met by two ladies whose arrival made an alteration necessary, Lady Denham and Miss Brereton. They had been to Trafalgar House, and been directed thence to the library, and though Lady Denham was a great deal too active to regard the walk of a mile as anything requiring rest, and talked of going home again directly, the Parkers knew that to be pressed into their house, and obliged to take her tea with them, would suit her best. And therefore the stroll on the cliff gave way to an immediate return home.

"No, no," said her Ladyship, "I will not have you hurry your tea on my account. I know you like your tea late. My early hours are not to put my neighbors to inconvenience. No, no, Miss Clara and I will get back to our own tea. We came out with no other thought. We wanted just to see you and make sure of your being really come, but we get back to our own tea."

She went on however towards Trafalgar House and took possession of the drawing room very quietly without seeming to hear a word of Mr. Parker's orders to the servant as they entered, to bring tea directly.

Charlotte was fully consoled for the loss of her walk, by finding herself in company with those whom the conversation of the morning had given her a great curiosity to see. She observed them well.

Lady Denham was of middle height, stout, upright and alert in her motions, with a shrewd eye, and self-satisfied air but not an unagreeable countenance; and though her manner was rather downright and abrupt, as of a person who valued herself on being free-spoken, there was a good humor and cordiality about her, a civility and readiness to be acquainted with Charlotte herself, and a heartiness of welcome towards her old friends, which was inspiring the good will, she seemed to feel.

And as for Miss Brereton, her appearance so completely justified Mr. Parker's praise that Charlotte thought she had never beheld a more lovely, or more interesting young woman. Elegantly tall, regularly handsome, with great delicacy of complexion, and soft blue eyes, a sweetly modest and yet naturally graceful address, Charlotte could see in her only the most perfect representation of whatever heroine might be most beautiful and bewitching, in all the numerous volumes they had left behind them on Mrs. Whitby's shelves.

Perhaps it might be partly owing to her having just issued from a circulating library, but she could not separate the idea of a complete heroine from Clara Brereton. Her situation with Lady Denham was so very much in favor of it! She seemed placed with her on purpose to be ill-used. Such poverty and dependence, joined to such beauty and merit, seemed to leave no choice in the business.

These feelings were not the result of any spirit of romance in Charlotte herself. No, she was a very sober-minded young lady, sufficiently well-read in novels to supply her imagination with amusement, but not at all unreasonably influenced by them; and while she pleased herself the first five minutes with fancying the persecutions which ought to be the lot of the interesting Clara, especially in the form of the most barbarous conduct on Lady Denham's side, she found no reluctance to admit from subsequent observation, that they appeared to be on very comfortable terms.

She could see nothing worse in Lady Denham than the sort of old fashioned formality of always calling her *Miss Clara*, nor anything objectionable in the degree of observance and attention which Clara paid. On one side, it seemed protecting kindness, on the other; grateful and affectionate respect.

The conversation turned entirely upon Sanditon, its present number of visitants, and the chances of a good season.

It was evident that Lady Denham had more anxiety, more fears of loss, than her coadjutor. She wanted to have the place fill faster, and seemed to have many harassing apprehensions of the lodgings being in some instances underlet. Miss Diana Parker's two large families were not forgotten.

"Very good, very good," said her ladyship. "A West Indian family and a school. That sounds well. That will bring money."

"No people spend more freely, I believe, than West Indians," observed Mr. Parker.

"Aye, so I have heard, and because they have full purses, fancy themselves equal, maybe, to your old country families. But then, they who scatter their money so freely, never think of whether they may not be doing mischief by raising the price of things. And I have heard that's very much the case with your West-Injines. And if they come among us to raise the price of our necessaries of life, we shall not much thank them, Mr. Parker."

"My dear Madam, they can only raise the price of consumable articles, by such an extraordinary demand for them and such a diffusion of money among us, as must do us more good than harm. Our butchers and bakers and traders in general cannot get rich without bringing prosperity to us. If *they* do not gain, our rents must be insecure; and in proportion to their profit must be ours eventually in the increased value of our houses."

"Oh, well! But I should not like to have butcher's meat raised, though. And I shall keep it down as long as I can. Aye, that young lady smiles, I see; I dare say she thinks me an odd sort of a creature, but *she* will come to care about such matters herself in time. Yes, yes, my dear, depend upon it, you will be thinking of the price of butcher's meat in time, though you may not happen to have quite such a servants' hall full to feed, as I have. And I do believe *those* are best off that have fewest servants. I am not a woman of parade, as all the world knows, and if it was not for what I owe to poor Mr. Hollis's memory, I should never keep up Sanditon House as I do. It is not for my own pleasure."

"Well, Mr. Parker, and the other is a boarding school, a French boarding school, is it? No harm in that. They'll stay their six weeks. And out of such a number, who knows but some may be consumptive and want asses milk, and I have two milch-asses at this present time. But perhaps the little misses may hurt the furniture. I hope they will have a good sharp governess to look after them."

Poor Mr. Parker got no more credit from Lady Denham than he had from his sisters, for the object which had taken him to Willingden.

"Lord! my dear Sir," she cried, "how could you think of such a thing? I am very sorry you met with your accident, but upon my word you deserved it. Going after a doctor! Why, what should we do with a doctor here? It would be only encouraging our servants and the poor to fancy themselves ill, if there was a doctor at hand. Oh! pray, let us have none of the tribe at Sanditon. We go on very well as we are. There is the sea and the downs, and my milch-asses. And I have told Mrs. Whitby that if anybody enquires for a chamber-horse, they may be supplied at a fair rate (poor Mr. Hollis's chamber-horse, as good as new)."

"And what can people want for more? Here have I lived seventy good years in the world and never took physic above twice and never saw the face of a doctor in all my life, on my *own* account. And I verily believe, if my poor dear Sir Harry had never seen one neither, he would have been alive now. Ten fees, one after another, did the man take who sent *him* out of the world. I beseech you, Mr. Parker, no doctors here."

The tea things were brought in.

"Oh! my dear Mrs. Parker, you should not indeed. Why would you do so? I was just upon the point of wishing you good evening. But since you are so very neighborly, I believe Miss Clara and I must stay."

SEVEN

The popularity of the Parkers brought them some visitors the very next morning, amongst them Sir Edward Denham and his sister, who, having been at Sanditon House, drove on to pay their compliments; and the duty of letter-writing being accomplished, Charlotte was settled with Mrs. Parker in the drawing room in time to see them all.

The Denhams were the only ones to excite particular attention. Charlotte was glad to complete her knowledge of the family by an introduction to them, and found them, the better half at least (for while single, the *gentleman* may sometimes be thought the better half of the pair) not unworthy of notice.

Miss Denham was a fine young woman, but cold and reserved, giving the idea of one who felt her consequence with pride and her poverty with discontent, and who was immediately gnawed by the want of an handsomer equipage than the simple gig in which they traveled, and which their groom was leading about still in her sight.

Sir Edward was much her superior in air and manner; certainly handsome, but yet more to be remarked for his very good address and wish of paying attention and giving pleasure. He came into the room remarkably well, talked much—and very much to Charlotte, by whom he chanced to be placed. And she soon perceived that he had a fine countenance, a most pleasing gentleness of voice, and a great deal of conversation. She liked him. Sober-minded as she was, she thought him agreeable, and did not quarrel with the suspicion of his finding her equally so, which *would* arise from his evident disregarding his sister's motion to go, and persisting in his station and his discourse.

I make no apologies for my heroine's vanity. If there are young ladies in the world at her time of life, more dull of fancy and more careless of pleasing, I know them not, and never wish to know them.

At last, from the low French windows of the drawing room which commanded the road and all the paths across the down, Charlotte and Sir Edward as they sat, could not but observe Lady Denham and Miss Brereton walking by; and there was instantly a slight change in Sir Edward's countenance with an anxious glance after them as they proceeded, followed by an early proposal to his sister not merely for moving, but for walking on together to the Terrace, which altogether gave a hasty turn to Charlotte's fancy, cured her of her half-hour's fever, and placed her in a more capable state of judging, when Sir Edward was gone, of *how* agreeable he had actually been.

"Perhaps there was a good deal in his air and address. And his title did him no harm," thought she.

She was very soon in his company again. The first object of the Parkers, when their house was cleared of morning visitors, was to get out themselves; the Terrace was the attraction to all; everybody who walked, must begin with the Terrace, and there, seated on one of the two green benches by the gravel walk, they found the united Denham party; but though united in the gross, very distinctly divided again: the two superior ladies being at one end of the bench, and Sir Edward and Miss Brereton at the other.

Charlotte's first glance told her that Sir Edward's air was that of a lover. There could be no doubt of his devotion to Clara. How Clara received it, was less obvious, but she was inclined to think not very favorably; for though sitting thus apart with him (which probably she might not have been able to prevent), her air was calm and grave.

That the young lady at the other end of the bench was doing penance, was indubitable. The difference in Miss Denham's countenance, the change from Miss Denham sitting in cold grandeur in Mrs. Parker's drawing-room to be kept from silence by the efforts of others, to Miss Denham at Lady Denham's elbow, listening and talking with smiling attention or solicitous eagerness, was very striking and very amusing or very melancholy, just as satire or morality might prevail. Miss Denham's character was pretty well decided with Charlotte, Sir Edward's required longer observation.

He surprised her by quitting Clara immediately on their all joining and agreeing to walk, and by addressing his attentions entirely to herself. Stationing himself close by her, he seemed to mean to detach her as much as possible from the rest of the party and to give her the whole of his conversation.

He began, in a tone of great taste and feeling, to talk of the sea and the sea shore; and ran with energy through all the usual phrases employed in praise of their sublimity, and descriptive of the *undescribable* emotions they excite in the mind of sensibility. The terrific grandeur of the ocean in a storm, its glassy surface in a calm, its gulls and its samphire, and the deep fathoms of its abysses, its quick vicissitudes, its direful deceptions, its mariners tempting it in sunshine, and overwhelmed by the sudden tempest—all were eagerly and fluently touched. Rather commonplace perhaps, but doing very well from the lips of a handsome Sir Edward, and she could not but think him a man of feeling till he began to stagger her by the number of his quotations, and the bewilderment of some of his sentences.

"Do you remember," said he, "Scott's beautiful lines on the sea? Oh! what a description they convey! They are never out of my thoughts when I walk here. That man who can read them unmoved must have the nerves of an assassin! Heaven defend me from meeting such a man unarmed."

"What description do you mean?" said Charlotte, "I remember none at this moment, of the sea, in either of Scott's poems."

"Do not you indeed? Nor can I exactly recall the beginning at this moment. But, you cannot have forgotten his description of woman—

"Oh! woman in our hours of ease"

"Delicious! Delicious! Had he written nothing more, he would have been immortal. And then again, that unequalled, unrivalled address to parental affection—

"Some feelings are to mortals given
With less of earth in them but heaven"
et cetera.

"But while we are on the subject of poetry, what think you, Miss Heywood, of Burns's lines to his Mary? Oh! there is pathos to madden one! If ever there was a man who felt, it was Burns. Montgomery has all the fire of poetry, Wordsworth has the true soul of it, Campbell in his pleasures of hope has touched the extreme of our sensations—

"Like angel's visits, few and far between."

"Can you conceive anything more subduing, more melting, more fraught with the deep sublime than that line? But Burns, I confess my sense of his pre-eminence, Miss Heywood. If Scott *has* a fault, it is the want of passion. Tender, elegant, descriptive, but *tame*. The man who cannot do justice to the attributes of woman is my contempt. Sometimes indeed a flash of feeling seems to irradiate him, as in the lines we were speaking of

"Oh! woman in our hours of ease"

"But Burns is always on fire. His soul was the altar in which lovely woman sat enshrined, his spirit truly breathed the immortal incense which is her due."

"I have read several of Burns's poems with great delight," said Charlotte, as soon as she had time to speak, "but I am not poetic enough to separate a man's poetry entirely from his character; and poor Burns's known irregularities greatly interrupt my enjoyment of his lines. I have difficulty in depending on the *truth* of his feelings as a lover. I have not faith in the *sincerity* of the affections of a man of his description. He felt and he wrote, and he forgot."

"Oh! no no," exclaimed Sir Edward in an ecstasy. "He was all ardor and truth! His genius and his susceptibilities might lead him into some aberrations. But who is perfect? It were hyper-criticism, it were pseudo-philosophy to expect from the soul of high-toned genius the grovelings of a common mind. The coruscations of talent, elicited by impassioned feeling in the breast of man, are perhaps incompatible with some of the prosaic decencies of life; nor can you, loveliest Miss Heywood," speaking with an air of deep sentiment, "nor can any woman be a fair judge of what a man may be propelled to say, write or do, by the sovereign impulses of illimitable ardor."

This was very fine; but if Charlotte understood it at all, not very moral; and being moreover by no means pleased with his extraordinary style of compliment, she gravely answered, "I really know nothing of the matter. This is a charming day. The wind I fancy must be southerly."

"Happy, happy wind, to engage Miss Heywood's thoughts!"

She began to think him downright silly. His choosing to walk with her, she had learnt to understand. It was done to pique Miss Brereton. She had read it, in an anxious glance or two on his side; but why he should talk so much nonsense, unless he could do no better, was unintelligible. He seemed very sentimental, very full of some feelings or other, and very much addicted to all the newest-fashioned hard words, had not a very clear brain she presumed, and talked a good deal by rote.

The future might explain him further.

But when there was a proposition for going into the library, she felt that she had had quite enough of Sir Edward for one morning, and very gladly accepted Lady Denham's invitation of remaining on the Terrace with her. The others all left them, Sir Edward with looks of very gallant despair in tearing himself away, and they united their agreeableness, that is, Lady Denham, like a true great lady, talked and talked only of her own concerns, and Charlotte listened, amused in considering the contrast between her two companions.

Certainly, there was no strain of doubtful sentiment, nor any phrase of difficult interpretation in Lady Denham's discourse. Taking hold of Charlotte's arm with the ease of one who felt that any notice from her was an honor, and communicative, from the influence of the same conscious importance or a natural love of talking, she immediately said in a tone of great satisfaction, and with a look of arch sagacity,

"Miss Esther wants me to invite her and her brother to spend a week with me at Sanditon House, as I did last summer. But I shan't. She has been trying to get round me every way, with her praise of this, and her praise of that; but I saw what she was about. I saw through it all. I am not very easily taken in, my dear."

Charlotte could think of nothing more harmless to be said, than the simple enquiry of, "Sir Edward and Miss Denham?"

"Yes, my dear. My *young folks*, as I call them sometimes, for I take them very much by the hand. I had them with me last summer about this time, for a week; from Monday to Monday; and very delighted and thankful they were. For they are very good young people, my dear. I would not have you think that I *only* notice them for poor dear Sir Harry's sake. No, no; they are very deserving themselves, or trust me, they would not be so much in *my* company. I am not the woman to help anybody blindfold. I always take care to know what I am about and who I have to deal with, before I stir a finger. I do not think I was ever over-reached in my life. And that is a good deal for a woman to say that has been married twice. Poor dear Sir Harry, between ourselves, thought at first to have got more. But," with a bit of a sigh, "he is gone, and we must not find fault with the dead. Nobody could live happier together than us—and he was a very honorable man, quite the gentleman of ancient family. And when he died, I gave Sir Edward his gold watch."

She said this with a look at her companion which implied its right to produce a great impression, and seeing no rapturous astonishment in Charlotte's countenance, added quickly, "He did not bequeath it to his nephew, my dear. It was no bequest. It was not in the will. He only told me, *and that* but once, that he should wish his nephew to have his watch but it need not have been binding, if I had not chose it."

"Very kind indeed! very handsome !" said Charlotte, absolutely forced to affect admiration.

"Yes, my dear, and it is not the *only* kind thing I have done by him. I have been a very liberal friend to Sir Edward. And poor young man, he needs it bad enough. For though I am *only* the *dowager* my dear, and he is the *heir*, things do not stand between us in the way they commonly do between those two parties. Not a shilling do I receive from the Denham Estate. Sir Edward has no payments to make *me*. He don't stand upper-most, believe me. It is I that help *him*."

"Indeed! He is a very fine young man, particularly elegant in his address."

This was said chiefly for the sake of saying something, but Charlotte directly saw that it was laying her open to suspicion by Lady Denham's giving a shrewd glance at her and replying, "Yes, yes, he is very well to look at. And it is to be hoped that some lady of large fortune will think so, for Sir Edward *must* marry for money. He and I often talk that matter over. A handsome young fellow like him will go smirking and smiling about and paying girls compliments, but he knows he must marry for money. And Sir Edward is a very steady young man in the main, and has got very good notions."

"Sir Edward Denham," said Charlotte, "with such personal advantages, may be almost sure of getting a woman of fortune, if he chooses it."

This glorious sentiment seemed quite to remove suspicion.

"Aye, my dear, that's very sensibly said," cried Lady Denham. "And if we could but get a young heiress to Sanditon! But heiresses are monstrous scarce! I do not think we have had an heiress here, or even a *co-*, since Sanditon has been a public place. Families come after families, but, as far as I can learn, it is not one in a hundred of them that have any real property, landed or funded. An income perhaps, but no property. Clergymen maybe, or lawyers from town, or half-pay officers, or widows with only a jointure. And what good can such people do anybody? Except just as they take our empty houses, and between ourselves, I think they are great fools for not staying at home. Now, if we could get a young heiress to be sent here for her health, and if she was ordered to drink asses milk I could supply her, and as soon as she got well, have her fall in love with Sir Edward!"

"That would be very fortunate indeed."

"And Miss Esther must marry somebody of fortune too. She must get a rich husband. Ah, young ladies that have no money are very much to be pitied! But," after a short pause, "if Miss Esther thinks to talk me into inviting them to come and stay at Sanditon House, she will find herself mistaken. Matters are altered with me since last summer, you know. I have Miss Clara with me now, which makes a great difference."

She spoke this so seriously that Charlotte instantly saw in it the evidence of real penetration and prepared for some fuller remarks; but it was followed only by, "I have no fancy for having my house as full as an hotel. I should not choose to have my two housemaids' time taken up all the morning in dusting out bedrooms. They have Miss Clara's room to put to rights as well as my own every day. If they had a hard place, they would want higher wages."

For objections of this nature, Charlotte was not prepared, and she found it so impossible even to affect sympathy, that she could say nothing. Lady Denham soon added, with great glee, "And besides all this, my dear, am I to be filling my house to the prejudice of Sanditon? If people want to be by the sea, why don't they take lodgings? Here are a great many empty houses, three on this very Terrace; no fewer than three lodging papers staring us in the face at this very moment, numbers three, four and eight. Eight, the corner house may be too large for them, but either of the two others are nice little snug houses, very fit for a young gentleman and his sister. And so, my dear, the next time Miss Esther begins talking about the dampness of Denham Park, and the good bathing always does her, I shall advise them to come and take one of these lodgings for a fortnight. Don't you think that will be very fair? Charity begins at home you know."

Charlotte's feelings were divided between amusement and indignation, but indignation had the larger and the increasing share. She kept her countenance and she kept a civil silence. She could not carry her forbearance farther; but without attempting to listen longer, and only conscious that Lady Denham was still talking on in the same way, allowed her thoughts to form themselves into such a meditation as this, "She is thoroughly mean. I had not expected anything so bad. Mr. Parker spoke too mildly of her. His judgment is evidently not to be trusted. His own good nature misleads him. He is too kind-hearted to see clearly. I must judge for myself. And their very *connection* prejudices him. He has persuaded her to engage in the same speculation, and because their object in that line is the same, he fancies she feels like him in others. But she is very, very mean. I can see no good in her. Poor Miss Brereton! And she makes everybody mean about her. This poor Sir Edward and his sister, how far nature meant them to be respectable, I cannot tell, but they are obliged to be mean in their servility to her. And I am mean too, in giving her my attention, with the appearance of coinciding with her. Thus it is, when rich people are sordid."

EIGHT

*T*he two ladies continued walking together till rejoined by the others, who, as they issued from the library, were followed by a young Whitby running off with five volumes under his arm to Sir Edward's gig. And Sir Edward approaching Charlotte said, "You may perceive what has been our occupation. My sister wanted my counsel in the selection of some books. We have many leisure hours, and read a great deal. I am no indiscriminate novel reader. The mere trash of the common circulating library, I hold in the highest contempt. You will never hear me advocating those puerile emanations which detail nothing but discordant principles incapable of amalgamation, or those vapid tissues of ordinary occurrences from which no useful deductions can be drawn. In vain may we put them into a literary alembic; we distill nothing which can add to science. You understand me I am sure?"

"I am not quite certain that I do. But if you will describe the sort of novels which you *do* approve, I dare say it will give me a clearer idea."

"Most willingly, fair questioner. The novels which I approve are such as display human nature with grandeur; such as show her in the sublimities of intense feeling; such as exhibit the progress of strong passion from the first germ of incipient susceptibility to the utmost energies of reason half-dethroned, where we see the strong spark of woman's captivations elicit such fire in the soul of man as leads him—though at the risk of some aberration from the strict line of primitive obligations—to hazard all, dare all, achieve all, to obtain her.

"Such are the works which I peruse with delight, and I hope I may say, with amelioration. They hold forth the most splendid portraitures of high conceptions, unbounded views, illimitable ardor, indomitable decision. And even when the event is mainly anti-prosperous to the high-toned machinations of the prime character, the potent, pervading hero of the story—it leaves us full of generous emotions for him; our hearts are paralyzed. It would be pseudo-philosophy to assert that we do not feel more enwrapt by the brilliancy of his career, than by the tranquil and morbid virtues of any opposing character. Our approbation of the latter is but eleemosynary. These are the novels which enlarge the primitive capabilities of the heart, and which it cannot impugn the sense or be any dereliction of the character of the most anti-puerile man, to be conversant with."

"If I understand you aright," said Charlotte, "our taste in novels is not at all the same."

And here they were obliged to part. Miss Denham being too much tired of them all to stay any longer.

The truth was that Sir Edward, whom circumstances had confined very much to one spot, had read more sentimental novels than agreed with him. His fancy had been early caught by all the impassioned, and most exceptionable parts of Richardson's; and such authors as have since appeared to tread in Richardson's steps, so far as man's determined pursuit of woman in defiance of every opposition of feeling and convenience is concerned, had since occupied the greater part of his literary hours, and formed his character.

With a perversity of judgment, which must be attributed to his not having by nature a very strong head, the graces, the spirit, the sagacity, and the perseverance of the villain of the story outweighed all his absurdities, and all his atrocities, with Sir Edward. With him, such conduct was genius, fire and feeling. It interested and inflamed him; and he was always more anxious for its success, and mourned over its discomfitures with more tenderness than could ever have been contemplated by the authors.

Though he owed many of his ideas to this sort of reading, it would be unjust to say that he read nothing else, or that his language was not formed on a more general knowledge of modern literature. He read all the essays, letters, tours and criticisms of the day with the same ill-luck which made him derive only false principles from lessons of morality, and incentives to vice from the history of its overthrow. He gathered only hard words and involved sentences from the style of our most approved writers.

Sir Edward's great object in life was to be seductive. With such personal advantages as he knew himself to possess, and such talents as he did also give himself credit for, he regarded it as his duty. He felt that he was formed to be a dangerous man, quite in the line of the Lovelaces. The very name of Sir Edward, he thought, carried some degree of fascination with it.

To be generally gallant and assiduous about the fair, to make fine speeches to every pretty girl, was but the inferior part of the character he had to play. Miss Heywood, or any other young woman with any pretensions to beauty, he was entitled (according to his own views of society) to approach with high compliment and rhapsody on the slightest acquaintance.

But it was Clara alone on whom he had serious designs; it was Clara whom he meant to seduce. Her seduction was quite determined on. Her situation in every way called for it. She was his rival in Lady Denham's favor; she was young, lovely and dependent. He had very early seen the necessity of the case, and had now been long trying with cautious assiduity to make an impression on her heart, and to undermine her principles.

Clara saw through him, and had not the least intention of being seduced. But she bore with him patiently enough to confirm the sort of attachment which her personal charms had raised. A greater degree of discouragement indeed would not have affected Sir Edward. He was armed against the highest pitch of disdain or aversion. If she could not be won by affection, he must carry her off. He knew his business.

Already had he had many musings on the subject. If he were constrained so to act, he must naturally wish to strike out something new, to exceed those who had gone before him, and he felt a strong curiosity to ascertain whether the neighborhood of Timbuctoo might not afford some solitary house adapted for Clara's reception.

But the expense, alas, of measures in that masterly style was ill-suited to his purse, and prudence obliged him to prefer the quietest sort of ruin and disgrace for the object of his affections to the more renowned.

Part II

NINE

O ne day, soon after Charlotte's arrival at Sanditon, she had the pleasure of seeing, just as she ascended from the sands to the Terrace, a gentleman's carriage with post horses standing at the door of the hotel, as very lately arrived, and, by the quantity of luggage being taken off, it might be hoped, some respectable family determined on a long residence.

Delighted to have such good news for Mr. and Mrs. Parker, who had both gone home some time before, she proceeded to Trafalgar House with as much alacrity as could remain, after having been contending for the last two hours with a very fine wind blowing directly on shore.

But she had not reached the little lawn, when she saw a lady walking nimbly behind her at no great distance; and convinced that it could be no acquaintance of her own, she resolved to hurry on and get into the house if possible before her.

But the stranger's pace did not allow this to be accomplished. Charlotte was on the steps and had rung, but the door was not opened when the other crossed the lawn; and when the servant appeared, they were just equally ready for entering the house.

The ease of the lady, her "How do you do Morgan?" and Morgan's looks on seeing her, were a moment's astonishment. But another moment brought Mr. Parker into the hall to welcome the sister he had seen from the drawing room, and she was soon introduced to Miss Diana Parker.

There was a great deal of surprise, but still more pleasure in seeing her. Nothing could be kinder than her reception from both husband and wife.

"How did she come? And with whom? And they were so glad to find her equal to the journey! And that she was to belong to *them*, was a thing of course."

Miss Diana Parker was about four and thirty, of middling height and slender; delicate looking rather than sickly; with an agreeable face, and a very animated eye; her manners resembling her brother's in their ease and frankness, though with more decision and less mildness in her tone.

She began an account of herself without delay. Thanking them for their invitation, but "*That* was quite out of the question, for they were all three come, and meant to get into lodgings and make some stay."

"All three come! What! Susan and Arthur! Susan able to come too! This was better and better."

"Yes, we are actually all come. Quite unavoidable. Nothing else to be done. You shall hear all about it. But my dear Mary, send for the children; I long to see them."

"And how has Susan born the journey? And how is Arthur? And why do not we see him here with you?"

"Susan has born it wonderfully. She had not a wink of sleep either the night before we set out, or last night at Chichester, and as this is not so common with her as with *me*, I have had a thousand fears for her, but she had kept up wonderful, had no hysterics of consequence till we came within sight of poor old Sanditon and the attack was not very violent, nearly over by the time we reached your hotel, so that we got her out of the carriage extremely well, with only Mr. Woodcock's assistance."

"And when I left her, she was directing the disposal of the luggage, and helping old Sam uncord the trunks. She desired her best love, with a thousand regrets at being so poor a creature that she could not come with me. And as for poor Arthur, he would not have been unwilling himself but there is so much wind that I did not think he could safely venture, for I am sure there is lumbago hanging about him, and so I helped him on with his greatcoat and sent him off to the Terrace, to take us lodgings."

"Miss Heywood must have seen our carriage standing at the hotel. I knew Miss Heywood the moment I saw her before me on the down. My dear Tom, I am so glad to see you walk so well. Let me feel your ankle. That's right; all right and clean. The play of your sinews a *very* little affected: barely perceptible."

"Well, now for the explanation of my being here. I told you in my letter, of the two considerable families, I was hoping to secure for you, the West Indians, and the Seminary."

Here Mr. Parker drew his chair still nearer to his sister, and took her hand again most affectionately as he answered, "Yes, yes, how active and how kind you have been!"

"The West Indians," she continued, "*whom* I look upon as the *most* desirable of the two—as the best of the good—prove to be a Mrs. Griffiths and her family. I know them only through others. You must have heard me mention Miss Capper, the particular friend of *my* very particular friend, Fanny Noyce. Now, Miss Capper is extremely intimate with a Mrs. Darling, who is on terms of constant correspondence with Mrs. Griffiths herself. Only a *short* chain, you see, between us, and not a wanting. Mrs. Griffiths meant to go to the sea, for her young people's benefit, had fixed on the coast of Sussex, but was undecided as to the where, wanted something private, and wrote to ask the opinion of her friend, Mrs. Darling. Miss Capper happened to be staying with Mrs. Darling when Mrs. Griffiths's letter arrived, and was consulted on the question; *she* wrote the same day to Fanny Noyce and mentioned it to her. And Fanny, all alive for *us*, instantly took up her pen and forwarded the circumstance to me except as to *names*, which have but lately transpired. There was but *one* thing for *me* to do. I answered Fanny's letter by the same post and pressed for the recommendation of Sanditon."

"Fanny had feared your having no house large enough to receive such a family. But I seem to be spinning out my story to an endless length. You see how it was all managed. I had the pleasure of hearing soon afterwards by the same simple link of connection that Sanditon *had been* recommended by Mrs. Darling, and that the West Indians were very much disposed to go thither. This was the state of the case when I wrote to you; but two days ago; yes, the day before yesterday, I heard again from Fanny Noyce, saying that *she* had heard from Miss Capper, who by a letter from Mrs. Darling, understood that Mrs. Griffiths has expressed herself in a letter to Mrs. Darling more doubtingly on the subject of Sanditon. Am I clear? I would be anything rather than not clear."

"Oh! perfectly, perfectly. Well?"

"The reason of this hesitation, was her having no connections in the place, and no means of ascertaining that she should have good accommodations on arriving there; and she was particularly careful and scrupulous on all those matters more on account of a certain Miss Lambe, a young lady (probably a niece) under her care, than on her own account or her daughters. Miss Lambe has an immense fortune, richer than all the rest, and very delicate health. One sees clearly enough by all this, the *sort* of woman Mrs. Griffiths must be: as helpless and indolent as wealth and a hot climate are apt to make us."

"But we are not all born to equal energy. What was to be done? I had a few moments indecision. Whether to offer to write to you, or to Mrs. Whitby to secure them a house? But neither pleased me. I hate to employ others, when I am equal to act myself, and my conscience told me that this was an occasion which called for me. Here was a family of helpless invalids whom I might essentially serve. I sounded Susan. The same thought had occurred to her. Arthur made no difficulties. Our plan was arranged immediately, we were off yesterday morning at six, left Chichester at the same hour today, and here we are."

"Excellent! Excellent!" cried Mr. Parker. "Diana, you are unequalled in serving your friends, and doing good to all the world. I know nobody like you. Mary, my love, is not she a wonderful creature? Well, and now, what house do you design to engage for them? What is the size of their family?"

"I do not at all know," replied his sister, "I have not the least idea; never heard any particulars; but I am very sure that the largest house at Sanditon cannot be *too* large. They are more likely to want a second. I shall take only one however, and that, but for a week certain. Miss Heywood, I astonish you. You hardly know what to make of me. I see by your looks, that you are not used to such quick measures."

The words, "unaccountable officiousness, activity run mad!" had just passed through Charlotte's mind, but a civil answer was easy.

"I dare say I do look surprised," said she, "because these are very great exertions, and I know what invalids both you and your sister are."

"Invalids indeed. I trust there are not three people in England who have so sad a right to that appellation! But my dear Miss Heywood, we are sent into this world to be as extensively useful as possible, and where some degree of strength of mind is given, it is not a feeble body which will excuse us or incline us to excuse ourselves. The world is pretty much divided between the weak of mind and the strong; between those who can act and those who can not; and it is the bounden duty of the capable to let no opportunity of being useful escape them. My sister's complaints and mine are happily not often of a nature to threaten existence *immediately*. And as long as we *can* exert ourselves to be of use of others, I am convinced that the body is the better for the refreshment the mind receives in doing its duty. While I have been traveling, with this object in view, I have been perfectly well."

The entrance of the children ended this little panegyric on her own disposition. And after having noticed, and caressed them all, she prepared to go.

"Cannot you dine with us? Is not it possible to prevail on you to dine with us?" was then the cry; and that being absolutely negatived, it was, "And when shall we see you again? And how can we be of use to you?"

And Mr. Parker warmly offered his assistance in taking the house for Mrs. Griffiths.

"I will come to you the moment I have dined," said he, "and we will go about together."

But this was immediately declined.

"No, my dear Tom, upon no account in the world, shall you stir a step on any business of mine. Your ankle wants rest. I see by the position of your foot, that you have used it too much already. No, I shall go about my house-taking directly. Our dinner is not ordered till six, and by that time I hope to have completed it. It is now only half past four. As to seeing *me* again today, I cannot answer for it; the others will be at the hotel all the evening, and delighted to see you at any time, but as soon as I get back, I shall hear what Arthur has done about our own lodgings, and probably the moment dinner is over, shall be out again on business relative to them, for we hope to get into some lodgings or other and be settled after breakfast tomorrow. "I have not much confidence in poor Arthur's skill for lodging taking, but he seemed to like the commission."

"I think you are doing too much," said Mr. Parker, "you will knock yourself up. You should not move again after dinner."

"No, indeed you should not," cried his wife, "for dinner is such a mere *name* with you all, that it can do you no good. I know what your appetites are."

"My appetite is very much mended, I assure you, lately. I have been taking some bitters of my own decocting, which have done wonders. Susan never eats, I grant you, and just at present, I shall want nothing; I never eat for about a week after a journey. But as for Arthur, he is only too much disposed for food. We are often obliged to check him."

"But you have not told me anything of the other family coming to

Sanditon," said Mr. Parker, as he walked with her to the door of the house. The Camberwell Seminary. Have we a good chance of *them?*"

"Oh! certain. Quite certain. I had forgotten them for the moment, but I had a letter three days ago from my friend Mrs. Charles Dupuis which assured me of Camberwell. Camberwell will be here to a certainty, and very soon. That good woman (I do not know her name), not being so wealthy and independent as Mrs. Griffiths, can travel and choose for herself. I will tell you how I got at her." Mrs. Charles Dupuis lives almost next door to a lady who has a relation lately settled at Clapham, who actually attends the Seminary and gives lessons on eloquence and belles lettres to some of the girls. I got that man a hare from one of Sidney's friends; and he recommended Sanditon. Without my appearing, however, Mrs. Charles Dupuis managed it all."

TEN

*I*t was not a week since Miss Diana Parker had been told by her feelings that the sea air would probably in her present state, be the death of her, and now she was at Sanditon, intending to make some stay, and without appearing to have the slightest recollection of having written or felt any such thing.

It was impossible for Charlotte not to suspect a good deal of fancy in such an extraordinary state of health. Disorders and recoveries so very much out of the common way seemed more like the amusement of eager minds in want of employment than of actual afflictions and relief.

The Parkers were no doubt a family of imagination and quick feelings, and while the eldest brother found vent for his superfluity of sensation as a projector, the sisters were perhaps driven to dissipate theirs in the invention of odd complaints. The *whole* of their mental vivacity was evidently not so employed; part was laid out in a zeal for being useful. It should seem that they must either be very busy for the good of others, or else extremely ill themselves.

Some natural delicacy of constitution in fact, with an unfortunate turn for medicine, especially quack medicine, had given them an early tendency at various times to various disorders; the rest of their sufferings was from fancy, the love of distinction, and the love of the wonderful. They had charitable hearts and many amiable feelings, but a spirit of restless activity, and the glory of doing more than anybody else had their share in every exertion of benevolence. And there was vanity in all they did, as well as in all they endured.

Mr. and Mrs. Parker spent a great part of the evening at the hotel; but Charlotte had only two or three views of Miss Diana posting over the down after a house for this lady whom she had never seen, and who had never employed her. She was not made acquainted with the others till the following day, when, being removed into lodgings and all the party continuing quite well, their brother and sister and herself were entreated to drink tea with them.

They were in one of the Terrace houses; and she found them arranged for the evening in a small neat drawing room, with a beautiful view of the sea, if they had chosen it, but though it had been a very fair English summer day, not only was there no open window, but the sofa and the table, and the establishment in general was all at the other end of the room by a brisk fire.

Miss Parker, whom, remembering the three teeth drawn in one day, Charlotte approached with a peculiar degree of respectful compassion, was not very unlike her sister in person or manner, though more thin and worn by illness and medicine, more relaxed in air, and more subdued in voice. She talked, however, the whole evening as incessantly as Diana; and excepting that she sat with salts in her hand, took drops two or three times from one, out of the several phials already at home on the mantelpiece, and made a great many odd faces and contortions, Charlotte could perceive no symptoms of illness which she, in the boldness of her own good health, would not have undertaken to cure by putting out the fire, opening the window, and disposing of the drops and the salts by means of one or the other.

She had had considerable curiosity to see Mr. Arthur Parker; and having fancied him a very puny, delicate-looking young man, the smallest very materially of not a robust family, was astonished to find him quite as tall as his brother, and a great deal stouter, broad made and lusty, and with no other look of an invalid than a sodden complexion.

Diana was evidently the chief of the family; principal mover and actor. She had been on her feet the whole morning, on Mrs Griffiths's business or their own, and was still the most alert of the three. Susan had only superintended their final removal from the hotel, bringing two heavy boxes herself, and Arthur had found the air so cold that he had merely walked from one house to the other as nimbly as he could and boasted much of sitting by the fire till he had cooked up a very good one.

Diana, whose exercise had been too domestic to admit of calculation, but who, by her own account, had not once sat down during the space of seven hours, confessed herself a little tired. She had been too successful, however, for much fatigue; for not only had she by walking and talking down a thousand difficulties at last secured a proper house at eight guineas per week for Mrs. Griffiths; she had also opened so many treaties with cooks, housemaids, washerwomen, and bathing women, that Mrs. Griffiths would have little more to do on her arrival than to wave her hand, and collect them around her for choice.

Her concluding effort in the cause had been a few polite lines of information to Mrs. Griffiths herself, time not allowing for the circuitous train of intelligence which had been hitherto kept up. And she was now regaling in the delight of opening the first trenches of an acquaintance with such a powerful discharge of unexpected obligation.

Mr. and Mrs. Parker and Charlotte had seen two post chaises crossing the down to the hotel as they were setting off, a joyful sight and full of speculation. The Miss Parkers and Arthur had also seen something; they could distinguish from their window that there was an arrival at the hotel, but not its amount. Their visitors answered for two hack chaises. Could it be the Camberwell Seminary? No, no. Had there been a third carriage, perhaps it might; but it was very generally agreed that two hack chaises could never contain a Seminary. Mr. Parker was confident of another new family.

When they were all finally seated, after some removals to look at the sea and the hotel, Charlotte's place was by Arthur, who was sitting next to the fire with a degree of enjoyment which gave a good deal of merit to his civility in wishing her to take his chair. There was nothing dubious in her manner of declining it, and he sat down again with much satisfaction. She drew back her chair to have all the advantage of his person as a screen, and was very thankful for every inch of back and shoulders beyond her preconceived idea.

Arthur was heavy in eye as well as figure, but by no means indisposed to talk; and while the other four were chiefly engaged together, he evidently felt it no penance to have a fine young woman next to him, requiring in common politeness some attention, as his brother, who felt the decided want of some motive for action, some powerful object of ani-

mation for him, observed with considerable pleasure. Such was the influence of youth and bloom that he began even to make a sort of apology
for having a fire.

"We should not have one at home," said he, "but the sea air is always
damp. I am not afraid of anything so much as damp."

"I am so fortunate," said Charlotte, "as never to know whether the air
is damp or dry. It has always some property that is wholesome and invig-
orating to me."

"I like the air too, as well as any body can," replied Arthur, "I am very
fond of standing at an open window when there is no wind, but unluck-
ily a damp air does not like me. It gives me the rheumatism. You are not
rheumatic, I suppose?"

"Not at all."

"That's a great blessing. But perhaps you are nervous."

"No, I believe not. I have no idea that I am."

"I am very nervous. To say the truth, nerves are the worst part of my
complaints in *my* opinion. My sisters think me bilious, but I doubt it."

"You are quite in the right to doubt it as long as you possibly can, I
am sure."

"If I were bilious," he continued, "you know wine would disagree with
me, but it always does me good. The more wine I drink in moderation
the better I am. I am always best of an evening. If you had seen me today
before dinner, you would have thought me a very poor creature."

Charlotte could believe it. She kept her countenance, however, and
said, "As far as I can understand what nervous complaints are, I have a
great idea of the efficacy of air and exercise for them, daily, regular exercise; and I should recommend rather more of it to you than I suspect you
are in the habit of taking."

"Oh! I am very fond of exercise myself," he replied, "and mean to walk
a great deal while I am here, if the weather is temperate. I shall be out
every morning before breakfast, and take several turns upon the Terrace,
and you will often see me at Trafalgar House."

"But you do not call a walk to Trafalgar House much exercise?"

"Not as to mere distance, but the hill is so steep! Walking up that hill,
in the middle of the day, would throw me into such a perspiration! You
would see me all in a bath by the time I got there! I am very subject to
perspiration, and there cannot be a surer sign of nervousness."

They were now advancing so deep in physics that Charlotte viewed the entrance of the servant with the tea things as a very fortunate interruption.

It produced a great and immediate change. The young man's attentions were instantly lost. He took his own cocoa from the tray, which seemed provided with almost as many teapots as there were persons in company, Miss Parker, drinking one sort of herb-tea, and Miss Diana another, and turning completely to the fire, sat coddling and cooking it to his own satisfaction, and toasting some slices of bread, brought up ready-prepared in the toast rack. And till it was all done, she heard nothing of his voice but the murmuring of a few broken sentences of self-approbation and success. When his toils were over, however, he moved back his chair into as gallant a line as ever, and proved that he had not been working only for himself, by his earnest invitation to her to take both cocoa and toast. She was already helped to tea, which surprised him, so totally self-engrossed had he been.

"I thought I should have been in time," said he, "but cocoa takes a great deal of boiling."

"I am much obliged to you," replied Charlotte, "but I prefer tea."

"Then I will help myself," said he. "A large dish of rather weak cocoa every evening agrees with me better than anything."

It struck her however, as he poured out this rather weak cocoa, that it came forth in a very fine, dark colored stream, and at the same moment his sisters both crying out, "Oh! Arthur, you get your cocoa stronger and stronger every evening," with Arthur's somewhat conscious reply of, "'Tis rather stronger than it should be tonight," convinced her that Arthur was by no means so fond of being starved as they could desire, or as he felt proper himself. He was certainly very happy to turn the conversation on dry toast, and hear no more of his sisters.

"I hope you will eat some of this toast," said he, "I reckon myself a very good toaster. I never burn my toasts. I never put them too near the fire at first, and yet, you see, there is not a corner but what is well browned. I hope you like dry toast."

"With a reasonable quantity of butter spread over it, very much," said Charlotte, "but not otherwise."

"No more do I," said he, exceedingly pleased. "We think quite alike there. So far from dry toast being wholesome, I think it a very bad thing for the stomach. Without a little butter to soften it, it hurts the coats of the stomach. I am sure it does. I will have the pleasure of spreading some for you directly, and afterwards I will spread some for myself. Very bad indeed for the coats of the stomach, but there is no convincing *some* people. It irritates and acts like a nutmeg grater."

He could not get command of the butter, however, without a struggle; his sisters accused him of eating a great deal too much, and he was not to be trusted; and he maintaining that he only ate enough to secure the coats of his stomach; and besides, he only wanted it now for Miss Heywood.

Such a plea must prevail. He got the butter and spread away for her with an accuracy of judgment which at least delighted himself; but when her toast was done, and he took his own in hand, Charlotte could hardly contain herself as she saw him watching his sisters, while he scrupulously scraped off almost as much butter as he put on, and then seizing an odd moment for adding a great dab just before it went into his mouth.

Certainly, Mr. Arthur Parker's enjoyments in invalidism were very different from his sisters—by no means so spiritualized. A good deal of earthy dross hung about him. Charlotte could not but suspect him of adopting that line of life, principally for the indulgence of an indolent temper, and to be determined on having no disorders but such as called for warm rooms and good nourishment. In one particular, however, she soon found that he had caught something from *them*.

"What!" said he, "Do you venture upon two dishes of strong green tea in one evening? What nerves you must have! How I envy you. Now, if I were to swallow only one such dish, what do you think its effect would be upon me?"

"Keep you awake perhaps all night," replied Charlotte meaning to overthrow his attempts at surprise, by the grandeur of her own conceptions.

"Oh ! if that were all!" he exclaimed. "No, it acts on me like poison and would entirely take away the use of my right side, before I had swallowed it five minutes. It sounds almost incredible, but it has happened to me so often that I cannot doubt it. The use of my right side is entirely taken away for several hours!"

"It sounds rather odd, to be sure," answered Charlotte coolly, "but I dare say it would be proved to be the simplest thing in the world, by those who have studied right sides and green tea scientifically and thoroughly understand all the possibilities of their action on each other."

Soon after tea, a letter was brought to Miss Diana Parker from the hotel.

"From Mrs. Charles Dupuis," said she, "some private hand."

And having read a few lines, exclaimed aloud, "Well, this is very extraordinary! Very extraordinary indeed! That both should have the same name. Two Mrs. Griffiths! This is a letter of recommendation and introduction to me, of the lady from Camberwell and *her* name happens to be Griffiths too."

A few lines more, however, and the color rushed into her cheeks, and with much perturbation she added, "The oddest thing that ever was! A Miss Lambe too! A young West Indian of large fortune. But it *cannot* be the same. Impossible that it should be the same."

She read the letter aloud for comfort. It was merely to "introduce the bearer, Mrs. Griffiths from Camberwell, and the three young ladies under her care to Miss Diana Parker's notice. Mrs. Griffiths, being a stranger at Sanditon, was anxious for a respectable introduction, and Mrs. Charles Dupuis, therefore, at the instance of the intermediate friend, provided her with this letter, knowing that she could not do her dear Diana a greater kindness than by giving her the means of being useful. Mrs. Griffiths's chief solicitude would be for the accommodation and comfort of one of the young ladies under her care, a Miss Lambe, a young West Indian of large fortune, in delicate health."

It was very strange! very remarkable! very extraordinary! But they were all agreed in determining it to be *impossible* that there should not be two families; such a totally distinct set of people as were concerned in the reports of each made that matter quite certain. There *must* be two families. Impossible to be otherwise.

"Impossible" and "impossible" were repeated over and over again with great fervor. An accidental resemblance of names and circumstances, however striking at first, involved nothing really incredible—and so it was settled.

Miss Diana herself derived an immediate advantage to counterbalance her perplexity. She must put her shawl over her shoulders, and be running about again. Tired as she was, she must instantly repair to the hotel, to investigate the truth and offer her services.

ELEVEN

*I*t would not do. Not all that the whole Parker race could say among themselves could produce a happier catastrophe than that the family from Surrey and the family from Camberwell were one and the same.

The rich West Indians, and the young ladies Seminary had all entered Sanditon in those two hack chaises. The Mrs. Griffiths who in her friend Mrs. Darling's hands had wavered as to coming and been unequal to the journey, was the very same Mrs. Griffiths whose plans were at the same period (under another representation) perfectly decided, and who was without fears or difficulties.

All that had the appearance of incongruity in the reports of the two, might very fairly be placed to the account of the vanity, the ignorance, or the blunders of the many engaged in the cause by the vigilance and caution of Miss Diana Parker. *Her* intimate friends must be officious like herself, and the subject had supplied letters and extracts and messages enough to make everything appear what it was not.

Miss Diana probably felt a little awkward on being first obliged to admit her mistake. A long journey from Hampshire taken for nothing, a brother disappointed, an expensive house on her hands for a week, must have been some of her immediate reflections.

And much worse than all the rest, must have been the sort of sensation of being less clear-sighted and infallible than she had believed herself. No part of it, however, seemed to trouble her long. There were so many to share in the shame and the blame, that probably when she had divided out their proper portions to Mrs. Darling, Miss Capper, Fanny Noyce, Mrs. Charles Dupuis, and Mrs. Charles Dupuis's neighbor, there might be a mere trifle of reproach remaining for herself. At any rate, she was seen all the following mornings walking about after lodgings with Mrs. Griffiths as alert as ever.

Mrs. Griffiths was a very well-behaved, genteel kind of woman, who supported herself by receiving such great girls and young ladies as wanted either masters for finishing their education, or a home for beginning their displays. She had several more under her care than the three who were now come to Sanditon, but the others all happened to be absent. Of these three, and indeed of all, Miss Lambe was beyond comparison the most important and precious, as she paid in proportion to her fortune. She was about seventeen, half-mulatto, chilly and tender, had a maid of her own, was to have the best room in the lodgings, and was always of the first consequence in every plan of Mrs. Griffiths.

The other girls, two Miss Beauforts, were just such young ladies as may be met with, in at least one family out of three, throughout the kingdom. They had tolerable complexions, showy figures, an upright decided carriage, and an assured look; they were very accomplished and very ignorant, their time being divided between such pursuits as might attract admiration, and those labors and expedients of dexterous ingenuity, by which they could dress in a style much beyond what they ought to have afforded. They were some of the first in every change of fashion. And the object of all was to captivate some man of much better fortune than their own.

Mrs. Griffiths had preferred a small, retired place, like Sanditon, on Miss Lambe's account and the Miss Beauforts, though naturally preferring anything to smallness and retirement, yet having in the course of the spring been involved in the inevitable expense of six new dresses each for a three days visit, were constrained to be satisfied with Sanditon also, till their circumstances were retrieved.

There, with the hire of a harp for one, and the purchase of some drawing paper for the other and all the finery they could already command, they meant to be very economical, very elegant, and very secluded; with the hope on Miss Beaufort's side, of praise and celebrity from all who walked within the sound of her instrument, and on Miss

Letitia's, of curiosity and rapture in all who came near her while she sketched; and to both, the consolation of meaning to be the most stylish girls in the place.

The particular introduction of Mrs. Griffiths to Miss Diana Parker, secured them immediately an acquaintance with the Trafalgar House family, and with the Denhams; and the Miss Beauforts were soon satisfied with "the circle in which they moved in Sanditon," to use a proper phrase, for everybody must now "move in a circle," to the prevalence of which rotatory motion is perhaps to be attributed the giddiness and false steps of many.

Lady Denham had other motives for calling on Mrs. Griffiths besides attention to the Parkers. In Miss Lambe, here was the very young lady, sickly and rich, whom she had been asking for, and she made the acquaintance for Sir Edward's sake, and the sake of her milch asses.

How it might answer with regard to the baronet, remained to be proved, but, as to the animals, she soon found that all her calculations of profit would be vain. Mrs. Griffiths would not allow Miss Lambe to have the smallest symptom of a decline, or any complaint which asses milk could possibly relieve.

"Miss Lambe was under the constant care of an experienced physician; and his prescriptions must be their rule." And except in favor of some tonic pills, which a cousin of her own had a property in, Mrs. Griffiths did never deviate from the strict medicinal page.

The corner house of the Terrace was the one in which Miss Diana Parker had the pleasure of settling her new friends; and considering that it commanded in front the favorite lounge of all the visitors at Sanditon, and on one side whatever might be going on at the hotel, there could not have been a more favorable spot for the seclusions of the Miss Beauforts.

And accordingly, long before they had suited themselves with an instrument, or with drawing paper, they had, by the frequency of their appearance at the low windows upstairs, in order to close the blinds, or open the blinds, to arrange a flower pot on the balcony, or look at nothing through a telescope, attracted many an eye upwards, and made many a gazer gaze again.

A little novelty has a great effect in so small a place; the Miss Beauforts, who would have been nothing at Brighton, could not move here without notice.

And even Mr. Arthur Parker, though little disposed for supernumerary exertion, always quitted the Terrace in his way to his brother's by this corner house, for the sake of a glimpse of the Miss Beauforts—though it was half a quarter of a mile round about, and added two steps to the ascent of the hill.

TWELVE

Charlotte had been ten days at Sanditon without seeing Sanditon House, every attempt at calling on Lady Denham having been defeated by meeting with her beforehand. But now it was to be more resolutely undertaken, at a more early hour, that nothing might be neglected of attention to Lady Denham or amusement to Charlotte.

"And if you should find a favorable opening, my love," said Mr. Parker, who did not mean to go with them, "I think you had better mention the poor Mullins's situation, and sound her Ladyship as to a subscription for them. I am not fond of charitable subscriptions in a place of this kind— it is a sort of tax upon all that come. Yet as their distress is very great and I almost promised the poor woman yesterday to get something done for her, I believe we must set a subscription on foot, and therefore, the sooner the better; and Lady Denham's name at the head of the list will be a very necessary beginning. You will not dislike speaking to her about it, Mary?"

"I will do whatever you wish me," replied his wife, "but you would do it so much better yourself. I shall not know what to say."

"My dear Mary," cried he, "it is impossible you can be really at a loss. Nothing can be more simple. You have only to state the present afflicted situation of the family, their earnest application to me, and my being willing to promote a little subscription for their relief, provided it meet with her approbation."

"The easiest thing in the world," cried Miss Diana Parker, who happened to be calling on them at the moment. "All said and done, in less time than you have been talking of it now. And while you are on the subject of subscriptions, Mary, I will thank you to mention a very melancholy case to Lady Denham which has been represented to me in the most affecting terms. There is a poor woman in Worcestershire, whom some friends of mine are exceedingly interested about, and I have undertaken to collect whatever I can for her. If you would mention the circumstance to Lady Denham! Lady Denham *can* give, if she is properly attacked. I look upon her to be the sort of person who, when once she is prevailed on to undraw her purse, would as readily give ten guineas as five. And therefore, if you find her in a giving mood, you might as well speak in favor of another charity which I and a few more have very much at heart, the establishment of a charitable repository at Burton-on-Trent. And then, there is the family of the poor man who was hung last assizes at York, though we really *have* raised the sum we wanted for putting them all out. Yet if you *can* get a guinea from her on their behalf, it may as well be done."

"My dear Diana!" exclaimed Mrs. Parker, "I could no more mention these things to Lady Denham than I could fly."

"Where's the difficulty? I wish I could go with you myself. But in five minutes I must be at Mrs. Griffiths to encourage Miss Lambe in taking her first dip. She is so frightened, poor thing, that I promised to come and keep up her spirits, and go in the machine with her if she wished it. And as soon as that is over, I must hurry home, for Susan is to have leeches at one o'clock, which will be a three hours business. Therefore, I really have not a moment to spare besides that, between ourselves, I ought to be in bed myself at this present time, for I am hardly able to stand and when the leeches have done, I dare say we shall both go to our rooms for the rest of the day."

"I am sorry to hear it, indeed; but if this is the case, I hope Arthur will come to us."

"If Arthur takes my advice, he will go to bed too, for if he stays up by himself, he will certainly eat and drink more than he ought. But you see, Mary, how impossible it is for me to go with you to Lady Denham's."

"Upon second thoughts, Mary," said her husband, "I will not trouble you to speak about the Mullins. I will take an opportunity of seeing Lady Denham myself. I know how little it suits you to be pressing matters upon a mind at all unwilling."

His application thus withdrawn, his sister could say no more in support of hers, which was his object, as he felt all their impropriety and all the certainty of their ill effect upon his own better claim. Mrs. Parker was delighted at this release, and set off very happy with her friend and her little girl, on this walk to Sanditon House.

It was a close, misty morning, and when they reached the brow of the hill, they could not for some time make out what sort of carriage it was which they saw coming up. It appeared at different moments to be everything from the gig to the phaeton, from one horse to four; and just as they were concluding in favor of a tandem, little Mary's young eyes distinguished the coachman, and she eagerly called out, "It is Uncle Sidney, Mama, it is indeed."

And so it proved. Mr. Sidney Parker, driving his servant in a very neat carriage was soon opposite to them, and they all stopped for a few minutes. The manners of the Parkers were always pleasant among themselves, and it was a very friendly meeting between Sidney and his sister in law, who was most kindly taking it for granted that he was on his way to Trafalgar House.

This he declined, however. He was just come from Eastbourne, proposing to spend two or three days, as it might happen, at Sanditon. But the hotel must be his quarters. He was expecting to be joined there by a friend or two.

The rest was common enquiries, and remarks, with kind notice of little Mary, and a very well-bred bow and proper address to Miss Heywood on her being named to him. And they parted, to meet again within a few hours.

Sidney Parker was about seven or eight and twenty, very good looking, with a decided air of ease and fashion, and a lively countenance.

This adventure afforded agreeable discussion for some time. Mrs. Parker entered into all her joy on the occasion, and exulted in the credit which Sidney's arrival would give to the place.

The road to Sanditon House was a broad, handsome, planted approach between fields, and conducting at the end of a quarter a mile through second gates into the grounds, which though not extensive had all the beauty and respectability which an abundance of very fine timber could give. These entrance gates were so much in a corner of the grounds or paddock, so near one of its boundaries, that an outside fence was at first almost pressing on the road till an angle *here*, and a curve *there* threw them to a better distance.

The fence was a proper park paling in excellent condition; with clusters of fine elms, or rows of old thorns following its line almost everywhere. *Almost* must be stipulated, for there were vacant spaces, and through one of these, Charlotte, as soon as they entered the enclosure, caught a glimpse over the pales of something white and womanish in the field on the other side.

It was something which immediately brought Miss Brereton into her head; and stepping to the pales, she saw indeed and very decidedly, in spite of the mist, Miss Brereton seated not far before her, at the foot of the bank which sloped down from the outside of the paling and which a narrow path seemed to skirt along—Miss Brereton seated, apparently very composedly, and Sir Edward Denham by her side.

They were sitting so near each other and appeared so closely engaged in gentle conversation, that Charlotte had instantly felt she had nothing to do but to step back again, and say not a word. Privacy was certainly their object. It could not but strike her rather unfavorably with regard to Clara; but hers was a situation which must not be judged with severity.

She was glad to perceive that nothing had been discerned by Mrs. Parker. If Charlotte had not been considerably the taller of the two, Miss Brereton's white ribbons might not have fallen within the ken of *her* more observant eyes.

Among other points of moralizing reflection which the sight of this tête a tête produced, Charlotte could not but think of the extreme difficulty which secret lovers must have in finding a proper spot for their stolen interviews. Here perhaps they had thought themselves so perfectly secure from observation! The whole field open before them, a steep bank and pales never crossed by the foot of man at their back, and a great thickness of air to aid them as well. Yet, here she had seen them. They were really ill-used.

The house was large and handsome. Two servants appeared, to admit them, and every thing had a suitable air of property and order. Lady Denham valued herself upon her liberal establishment, and had great enjoyment in the order and the importance of her style of living. They were shown into the usual sitting room, well-proportioned and well-furnished; though it was furniture rather originally good and extremely well kept, than new or showy.

And as Lady Denham was not there, Charlotte had leisure to look about, and to be told by Mrs. Parker that the whole length portrait of a stately gentleman, which, placed over the mantlepiece, caught the eye immediately, was the picture of Sir Henry Denham; and that one among many miniatures in another part of the room, little conspicuous, represented Mr. Hollis. Poor Mr. Hollis! It was impossible not to feel him hardly used; to be obliged to stand back in his own house and see the best place by the fire constantly occupied by Sir Henry Denham.

In the silence of that stately room, amid its fine appointments, Charlotte stood gazing around her. And, for the first time since her coming among her many new acquaintances at Sanditon, she found herself openly voicing her thoughts. There could be no harm in it, after all. Were they not, the sweet-natured Mrs. Parker, young Mary and herself quite private at that moment in the grand edifice?

"Dear Madam," she asked, "were you then privileged to know the gentleman of this gracious house whilst still he walked these venerable halls? And what manner of man might Mr. Hollis have been? Surely, no pygmy among his peers? Neither so small nor of so little account as to be now interspersed thus among the miniatures," she added with a half-smile, "along with all the others here in this, his own former home?"

The genial Mrs. Parker, despite herself, was cheered by her young friend's jaunty manner, and only tittered while the two ladies were briefly united in their little amusement. Charlotte had at least succeeded in relieving her own anxiety concerning their present intrusion upon the great lady as the three stood unattended in her elegant chamber.

Yet, what neither of them had observed, while they huddled thus together, was the arrival of their hostess herself, Lady Denham. Nor was there any doubt that she had come upon the scene just a moment too soon.

She approached swiftly enough, and pronounced without ceremony, "How obliging you are to take such an interest in my dear Mr. Hollis, Miss Heywood! And how definitively you do speak for one so young and untried. I believe you must come of a respectable, a very large family. And are *all* of your brothers and sisters equally encouraged in their insolence?"

Abruptly turning from her now towards Mrs. Parker, her greeting was less reproachful, if not altogether convincing or warm.

"My good Mrs. Parker, sweet little Mary, I am delighted to see *you* here, she continued. "Your young protegée, it would seem, has cannier thoughts than most, and some, apparently, are even designed to contribute to our general merriment. How elevating that must be proving for yourself and your family."

Upon hearing Lady Denham's reproof, Mrs. Parker's discomfort intensified. This good woman was incapable of giving offense to any being, and could hardly be associated with such an indiscretion during her long life. Most certainly, never to her husband's closest ally and benefactor! She was immediately ready, entirely eager to mend any slight, no matter how small, and now did everything in her power to accomplish this.

"Dear Lady Denham, as ever so very gracious in your welcome. Our young lady—protegée—as you would name her, is merely overwhelmed by the beauty of such surroundings; the splendor of the view your house commands above the ocean, even the very special position in which it sits—all have staggered her from the start. Charlotte, my child," now addressing our subdued heroine, "Have we not stood here together in awe at the grandeur before us these many moments as we awaited her Ladyship's coming?"

Charlotte Heywood could feel the color rising to her cheeks. She was hardly able to manage a deferential response. How chagrined she now felt. She saw that she had presumed upon her good hosts, and had disappointed them in their expectation. The good Mr. and Mrs. Parker had taken her in their generosity upon trust alone. They had brought her from home, shown her a new and utterly diverting world, indulged her, delighted her, and made her as comfortable as she might be with her own family. Yet, she—who had so prided herself on her understanding—she had ridiculed, she had criticized, and above everything—she had judged. It was humiliation that she felt! In effect, she had disappointed them; perhaps even ruined her chance to answer their hopes for her emergence.

Miss Heywood found herself heartily ashamed. Quite suddenly, she longed for her dear family and the simplicity of her earlier life at Willingden. However, here she stood, and Lady Denham awaited her reply. She must speak.

"Madam," she rallied, "Mrs. Parker has just been good enough to introduce me to, and display the intricacies of your many artful appurtenances, to point out the finest paintings on your walls, and to show me your glorious position over the sea. Be assured that I am only eager to know of their history. Nothing more. I see across the chamber a remarkable pianoforte, for example, and trust that it is you, yourself alone, who can tell us of the origins of your precious musical instrument and just how it made its way to you here in Sanditon?"

Lady Denham was something surprised by this application, but diverted she was, even sufficiently appeased, it would seem to launch as a consequence into her recitation about the *provenance* of the pianoforte directly, and to lecture them contentedly for all the rest of the hour they remained at Sanditon House.

Part III

THIRTEEN

*T*hat Charlotte should often find herself out of spirits can hardly be wondered at. It was not so much because she had given offense to her friends—first in her thoughts and finally in her playful speech—for while she remained among them she stood resolute in her determination to check herself in every *future* encounter—but that she could not succeed in putting from her mind her first impressions. How persistent they had become! She *would* recall what she had espied in her new acquaintances—the indolence, the displays of indulgence, and the folly.

Yet silence is ever a prudent course, when one is unsure of any thought or observation. And now, at Sanditon, how much more could it serve our heroine when feelings of certainty prevailed!

To compose herself, and set her mind at rest, Miss Heywood's recollections turned toward happier times with her own dear family. She pictured them all, and reimagined the pleasures she had enjoyed in the countryside with her sisters and brothers so near to their farm. Those days of dazzling light, with the sunshine falling on the hedgerows, the meadows fresh after a spring shower. Such days as were made for dances on the green or country weddings. She delighted in remembering the scattered cottages covered with roses, the orchards in bloom, and how the cherry trees tossed their fragrant flowers up to the wind.

She had come away so full of cheer, so given to thinking her thoughts unchecked. There at home in Willingden, whatever was said amongst them brought only laughter and jollity, never great consequence. And within her own family, such sallies were of daily occurrence. In truth, in their conviviality, her brothers and sisters considered the whole of the county their dominion, their special entertainment, even, their plaything.

Their good-willed father was seldom discomfited or provoked by any of his children's harmless tale-telling, or even their antics; in effect, he was known to be encouraging for their every enterprise. Mr. Heywood, a hearty man of middle age enjoying excellent health, was universally modest, not only in means but in his thought and action. This was true in his business dealings as much as it was so in his daily intercourse with his neighbors.

His expectations therefore for his offspring were exactly the same. He remained as confident of *their* continued judiciousness and superiority as any on earth. He saw them only as he would suppose them to be, and always in the guise of full-fledged adults. Moderation had been his standard; and so far in his life, it had served him admirably. He saw no cause, therefore, for admonishment for any childish transgressions.

Not that there hadn't been moments when youthful exuberance tried his patience any less than another man's. But Mr. Heywood was of such even temperament as to regard them not at all. He simply entrusted these minor divergences and infractions to the attention of his good wife.

In many families, this delegation of duties could have proved the ideal solution for any such particulars. For is it not the female of the line whom we traditionally regard suited for such a charge? Surely, we must look to her as the more intense, the more firm, the more ready to be importuned in all such pairings? Not so, alas, amongst the Heywoods.

The lady of this house was, it would seem, of even more sanguine a disposition than her husband, and could contentedly permit her children their digressions, whether they consisted of mischief with their pets and the farm animals, and even with the children of the nearby parish.

Parents so entirely unmindful, and benevolent, as these, in fact, so oblivious to their children's pranks—and there were as many as fourteen young Heywoods in all—must suffer consequences. Woe to them if they do not mend their ways, and that at the soonest!

Fortunately for all the tribe, rescue came quite naturally, without their having so much as an awareness of it. Mr. and Mrs. Heywood scarcely took notice. The source of relief was from within the family itself.

It was the eldest amongst them who promptly took to managing the household. And as each grew to maturity and left the post, such duties fell to the next of the line. For many years, so it proceeded. Though none of these growing children could remember *when* they had been deputized for this formidable chore, neither could they recall any other pattern for daily conduct. In her turn, when her older sisters married, Charlotte, along with their next brother, Henry, soon learned to keep order at the Heywoods, if not the most perfect peace.

Indeed, new sisters or brothers continued to appear with every year—their mother herself, more and more preoccupied, and thus less likely to be engaged in such elemental matters of deportment—so did each of their offspring perform yet even more arduous commissions to ensure uninterrupted family harmony.

It had fallen to Charlotte, in truth, to look to the younger ones among them, almost before she had reached herself a very reasonable age. Henry, sensible lad that he was, must still turn for guidance to his sister when it came his time, though willingly did he wish to assist her in every way he knew how. And while he proved apt for the little boys' pastimes—the bird-nesting, pony-riding and rough shooting over stubble and pasture, she undertook to maintain the little girls' samplers, their music, and their household tasks. Above everything, however, she it was who command-ed. She arbitrated in each quarrel, overruled any bravado or bullying, and punished the practical jokers. She alone brought tranquility and order to the house.

Of all their daughters, Charlotte had not only been the most oblig-ing, but of the greatest service to them. She understood her dear, gentle, ineffectual parents better than all who had come before.

Was it just possible, as consequence, that our heroine had grown a touch *too* knowing and—to speak candidly—a little *too* certain in herself? Had she developed, perhaps, a somewhat exalted notion of her own powers of discernment? Her promotion, after all, *had* come so soon! And though it is maintained that duty, and great diligence in its performance, will, of necessity, have made her wise early in life, could it not also be put forward that it might as well embolden a young lady to excess, even set her apart?

At home, she had willingly discharged all these many awesome tasks, and gently seen to it that each of their sisters and brothers, if playful and full of the devil, were kept firmly within the boundaries of good fellow-ship. But, dear reader, scrupulous we need be. Thus it must here be acknowledged that until her accidental reprieve by Mr. and Mrs. Parker, and her consequent departure for Sanditon, the authority of Miss Charlotte Heywood had gone wholly unchallenged! In one so empowered beyond her brothers and sisters, never questioned (or pausing to look back)—there had perhaps grown a disposition too ready to castigate, to admonish, to dismiss others, just as she might her juvenile charges. In truth, *our* young Charlotte *could* be seen as one much given to her own way.

But, was there still more to consider? Could such early approbation have brought it about that some gifts were denied to our spirited young lady? For at the age of twenty-two—unlike her good sisters before her—she stood precariously unattached, and moreover, peculiarly unreceptive to the several suitors who had already come to seek her out. A young person, it was apparent, who had notions!

Sober minded, cool headed, and no more astute than her particular circumstances had made her, Charlotte, in sum, would not contemplate any man whom she did not esteem or regard. And to hear her laughingly tell it to her older sisters, what she had seen before her hitherto were the rough boys of their county—boys akin to her own brothers, but who, unlike them, went simply unchallenged in their country ways, in their boisterous preoccupations with the local sports competitions, their seasonal fixation upon the hunt, or, in all the other wholesome games available.

Charlotte's estimable father observed hardly anything of this in all that while; even had he done so, most surely would have held fast. Never could *he* be troubled by mere circumstance. Whatever his daughter chose or *did not* choose was never a question. She knew her mind, and he cheered her for it!

Sweet-tempered, Mr. Heywood was, in fact, preoccupied most days, gone from home, out for service with his tenants, to assist his workmen in their labors, and, if not that, to attending his neighbors' needs. Such duties took him up the week round. As a gentleman proprietor of his good establishment at Willingden, a not inconsiderable domain, he felt himself obliged to a participation as energetic as it was exemplary.

Whether it be in overseeing the attendance of his cows, pigs, geese or chickens, instructing the carpenter in the repair of his barn, engaging the blacksmith for reshoeing a limping horse, or in his frequent trips to the village shop and local public house, he had little leisure for domestic stratagem of any sort. His obligation, he saw, was to remain vigilant over his inherited land, his developing crops, and even more, over the many whose welfare and livelihood depended upon his continuing devotion.

If it is true that over the years Mr. Heywood had never known want— even to this day his wife kept a good table—this was, he believed, precisely *because* of his unrelenting exertions for the properties to which he had been fortunate enough, as the eldest of a fine family, to have been entitled. Thus had he maintained his prosperous position in society, and understood early the limits of any benefits bestowed upon him. His own husbandry, his natural disdain for ostentation of any sort, and the cultivation in his good wife of a stalwart resistance to extravagance in the face of all temptation, had sustained him handsomely. And, better even, he had purveyed these same principles to an ever growing family.

His own ambitions simply never deviated. They were neither exorbitant nor adventurous; designed merely for preserving that which his father had made possible, and which his own father's father had provided before that. Despite all the current stylishness of it, he had seen little reason to consider any speculations other. His trips up to London were infrequent, yet steady. He made them twice a year, and then but for the purpose of collecting what was due him in dividends. Never had another plan invaded his pleasant life.

This country gentleman, in his tailed double-breasted, riding-coat, his white linen stock wound about his throat and tied in a bulky bow, with his tall hat and curly brim, such a splendid figure, was pleased to be saluted genially wherever he went. And since he had always shown compassion for all his tenants, in his services on the bench as Justice of the Peace, as an Officer of the Yeomanry, as well as acted the protective patron, generous enough to ensure their use of small patches of garden and pasture lands during the worst of times, he was indeed respected and loved, in the whole of the surrounding county.

Yet, as he listened to the latest outcries about him, even a Mr. Heywood must see the change that was upon them. It was but lately, with the war's end on the Continent and on the high seas, that such disparate notions had so much as entered his enclosed world. Still, those anxieties grew large with the surprising discovery of desperate retrenchments among his neighboring families, their need to let or even sell their ancestral properties. Such, it would seem, were now altogether to be driven from their homes and the countryside of their fathers!

Alarming this was to him. And even more so the arrival of new own-ers to supplant them, those who had bought such distressed estates of the gentry. Mostly from London, they presented themselves eagerly at Willingden. Pure strangers they seemed, gentlemen such as he could know nothing of.

"That man is a fool," he explained to his wife, "who cannot duly esti-mate the difference between those attached to the soil and known to every farmer from childhood—the good man who frequents their com-pany, practices hospitality without ceremony from lifelong habit—and the interloper with no relish for the countryside, and who himself is haughty in behavior. Are such upstarts then to displace us all? I cannot but think, dear Mrs. Heywood, they come not to live among us but in search of rents and other rewards from the land."

His distaste was further provoked when he saw the "improvements" to their houses these new squires promptly undertook. Indeed, it was as though they saw such alteration vital to their future welfare within the country. Mr. Heywood watched in wonder as the most unprepossessing of such country establishments were contemplated and then again reex-amined by fine gentlemen brought down especially from the City—young architects of distinction—who studied every angle, toured the park, and expounded upon extended plans for rectifications.

Moreover, in these days he found himself tutored regularly by such incoming neighbors.

"Good Heywood," intoned a certain Colonel Fraser, newly arrived, and fitted in his stylishly long and loose Cossack pantaloons, "surely you are alerted to the news that rebuilding in these days is the *requirement*, to be sure, even is it *à la mode*."

Thus was each structure, however modest, enhanced into elegance; and soon the simplest appeared to loom over them wherever they looked, as if spiritual in its nature—a cathedral, more like—its gothic arches superimposed—to suggest magnificence at once and piety.

Of this much, Mr. Heywood was certain. Their efforts were a disser-vice to the countryside. Taste must surely be wanting in such restorations. And this said nothing of what he saw as the pretension to nobility imposed upon what were once simple estates.

Worse still, with these "improvers" came other troubling alterations. In these latter days, Mr. Heywood could not but notice the departure of some of his prized craftsmen. With the loss of their finest families—

those they so long regarded as their own patrons—several cottagers now reluctantly packed their own scant possessions. Uncertainty for their futures was the cause, and even more particularly, several were tempted by the possibility of carriage to the Americas, and even more distant parts. Tenants decided now to take passage and emigrate.

All these persistent developments left Mr. Heywood aghast. He could hardly fathom such defections, they struck him to his heart. When the artisan, William Birkbeck, a favorite of his family, came to make his farewells, the young fellow had explained sadly, "There must be a need for the like of me somewhere, Mr. Heywood, if I could but find me the place! I could keep on with my clock-making right here in Willingden; but, with my landlord of old himself gone off to the seaside, to return who knows when, and a new proprietor just arrived from London, I know I would better go now myself. And nightly, at the Brotherly Society's meeting, I hear told how I could manage it. Good Sir," he now added ruefully, "this looks to be the only way for me, if I would do well by my family."

The very disposition of Thomas Heywood would not allow it; yet he must own that life around him *was* in flux. More and more, he would repent that with England at peace, he must begin to acknowledge that even a country life was no guarantee against change.

Despite those ancient assurances when a boy, that the greatest of men looked to his own, fixed his station where best he could do for his family what was right and proper, he pondered. What after all did such principles come to in times such as these? Even the prospects for his own heirs did not seem to have meaning, as once they did in his own coming of age.

But, when one of his own sons, just grown to manhood, came forward with similar designs, the poor gentleman felt altogether shaken, he must retreat into himself. He had always favored, openly encouraged his children's venturing into the greater world, to see and to learn. That his own offspring should turn from the country of their ancestors, that *his* son's view of life could be contrary to his own parents'! It was such a concept as this that seemed against his upbringing, against his breeding, yes, his very being. To Mr. Heywood it was untenable.

Yet even so had his young Henry Heywood determined. No longer could he dream, as he had done as a boy, of position in glorious naval battles. Now the war was at an end, *he* would look instead to London for his future. In Willingden, he explained to his father, what he now saw was the past—and a past that held within it merely the silence and the tedium of each seasonal change. For his own growing ambition, he could imagine no means amidst the county's farms or the craftsmen of the town. It was to London that *he* must turn.

This last announcement left Mr. Heywood, together with his ever placid wife, stunned. They could but nod their heads in despondency and wish him well.

FOURTEEN

While it was Mr. Parker whose eloquence was to be steadily relied upon to captivate eager comers—to incline them towards their excellent seaside enterprise at Sanditon—it was Lady Denham alone who was entrusted with its emergent social observances. *She* understood what such engagements must embrace; could artfully descry what elegant families might expect; in effect, she it was who comprehended what *any* proper society must regard infallible for its elevation, and its pleasure.

Since her triumph in the organization of a Library at Sanditon, a splendid purveyor of more than books and periodicals, and the station of any number of curiosities to be sampled and gossiped over—and that, accomplished so early as to be currently admired by all—she had not been idle. She had turned to her more particular aspiration, her own favorite notion of how to secure about her true grace and civility; a state, she believed, to be achieved only by the acquisition of a fine and public space for the town's social assembly. The need was pressing, she understood, especially with the new season almost upon them.

Immediately enlisting for this valiant pursuit her admirer and ally from the Library, Mrs. Whitby, she made plain the urgency, "Dear lady, you must see that as fine young ladies and gentlemen continue to make their appearance among us in our community, as they assemble daily to take the waters, as they commence to imbibe of our good sea air, to feel more comfortable and at their ease, to make such steady advances in heartiness," and here she sighed with genuine pleasure, "surely, it is evident that we cannot brook delay. No, Mrs. Whitby, there shall be no more hesitation for us. Is it not plain to you that with such new currents soaring through them, energizing them in breath and scope, animating their life's force, that they will be in immediate want of festivity, of dance, of gaiety? Every variety *must* be provided—promptly and in the grandest manner, akin to Brighton, to Weymouth, or to Scarborough—to any of your best spas. I must assure you, there is simply no time to be lost."

The two thereupon dedicated themselves in earnest. It was a mission whose outcome is hardly be doubted. Sanditon, like any other important watering place *would* endow its families!

Soon enough followed the awaited, the triumphant announcement. A celebration to be held at the newly expanded and tidied quarters. An Initiation Ball. A Most Gala Evening in Tribute to Each New Addition to the Township.

Nor did industry cease with the mere acquisition of such a beautifully enlarged hall. Superb musicians were solicited and discovered to be ready to make a journey from as far away as Tunbridge Wells. Immediately was that too widely broadcast. A particular group of traveling instrumentalists, it would seem, gentlemen of some account in that they had already been said to have performed for the Regent himself at Brighton, had at once taken special note of the reputation of the rising resort at Sanditon, and would—if, indeed, at no inconsiderable expense to that new center—be proudly at their service for the upcoming ball.

Such tidings were greeted with jubilation in all quarters. Just arrived families were honored; longtime residents, exhilarated. And what followed next in that flurry was very much to be anticipated. Every lady within miles must now be absorbed by the proprieties for dress for such a sparkling occasion.

Deliberations without cease were to be heard in each drawing room amongst young and old. As for Lady Denham herself, she had made it known that a dressmaker was to be especially brought down from London to see to *her* attire for the evening. Moreover, in all her goodness, she allowed that Mrs. Parker might also undertake to engage this same lady's talents in the design of her own gown.

"My sweet Mary," she granted, "there is little question that your position as the wife of my coadjutor will demand of you a strikingly modish appearance at our festivity. For there, all eyes must certainly be upon the founders of Sanditon. To be sure, I myself am accustomed to such attentions; but *you* too might well be noticed in your rising situation. Dear lady, you will understand that without such impeccability, we can little hope to excite in all others the passions that we ourselves already embrace, that ultimate faith in our designs for an Olympian society at Sanditon."

Diverse preparations continued through an entire fortnight, and as Lady Denham discovered such business overwhelming, she was able in her condescension to further grace Mrs. Parker by delegating to her the task of looking to the late night service at their revelry. There, she explained, elegance must certainly depend upon cuisine of the most delicate.

"What importance can any evening of festivity make claim to if there is no sitting down to supper? Conviviality, yes; but without a superb understanding of such nuance, there can be little hope of Sanditon's being seen in a serious light. I feel, however, that I *can* entrust you, Mrs. Parker, to oversee the cooks in their accomplishments," and here she thought for a moment before continuing—to look to such as the cold meats, the sweetbreads, the fricassees, the salmon in its shrimp sauce, along with the blanc manges, the jellies, pastries, and even the celery. Indeed, they must *all* be artfully displayed."

Lady Denham clearly took pride in such exertion, concluding her recommendation with, "As for the whipped syllabub, you will doubtless see to its decoration with violets all over. And do you not suppose, dear friend, that a sizable pineapple in conspicuous view ought to be contemplated as well? Hospitality, after all, is foremost, and commands us all. No expense may be spared. I myself, you may depend upon it, shall inspect the choice of wines."

Mr. Parker's own delight at this latest enrichment was undisputable. He had begun to witness his dream for ideal living at last in point of realization! Over these many years, *his* devotion had been to a species of wholesomeness; a faith that placed him firmly into regions where the latest concepts of healthful maintenance reigned. It was such a certainty alone that had brought him now to this extraordinary moment. It seemed all he had wished for—everything lay before him distinctly in its potential.

What joy! Only to recall the exquisite privilege of seeing to it that his children could be favored in their own futures with such a salubrious way of life! These were benefits long hoped for, the reward for persistence and more, a victory for all imaginative thought and deed.

Mr. Parker promptly made it his business to inform his new neighbors. They too must be made cognizant of their good fortune, the imminence of a Utopian circumstance. Mrs. Griffiths and the young ladies of her school, particularly, should be alerted to its wondrous prospect.

However, if Mrs. Griffiths herself had as yet not arrived at the appreciation of her fortunate choice for the favored refuge, she had at least discovered its advantages in simpler terms. Her dear girls could be noticed properly, seen here and presented at their elegant best.

"How might you doubt, Mr. Parker," she pronounced, "that our Miss Lambe alone would grace any society? And as for the Miss Beauforts, they do not dawdle behind her. The splendor of any of these young ladies' gowns would serve them were they to enter Carleton House itself. Why, only this afternoon, Lady Denham herself sent word requesting of Miss Beaufort a performance upon her harp for your evening's gala. She has graciously accepted; even now you may find her dutifully at practice. You must own that the sight of our sweet Augusta at her instrument will make any young man in love."

Thomas Parker came away reassured. There could, he felt, be every expectation of the success of his grand venture now. As he strolled the Terrace, he remembered that his own brother, the dashing Sidney Parker, was newly installed in rooms at the hotel, and soon to be joined by one or more of his distinguished London cohorts. No lack of suitable young men present for the gaiety.

The county was preoccupied by the coming event. Sanditon had often been reported to have enlarged its importance, even to prosperity, but it had not before aspired to celebrity. With word spreading, attendance for their evening might prove more general than first anticipated. In truth, many of the near neighborhoods had become curious to see for themselves what eminence there was by now.

Nor did stir subside when the evening arrived; people came from afar to glimpse the display. In the exuberance of the occasion, Lady Denham's every effort during these many months seemed to come to fruition in the jaunty milieu. How could any doubt for their beloved resort the accrual of benefits and bounty?

When, on the appointed night, she made her entrance into the ballroom the debonair lady was lauded by gentlemen and ladies alike—she might have been royalty itself. Such as had come were eager to see, curious to observe, if perhaps not quite so ready to subscribe their families or relocate. Their number was large, greater as the hours passed; and, of them, few could be thought to be unworthy in their aspect, bedecked as they were in their finest.

The Parker contingent had appeared before most others. Mr. and Mrs. Parker were warmly welcomed by their radiant collaborator, then instantly delegated to key posts about the room to manage the arriving guests, to squire them further into the hall, and to complete them in their introductions to the party at hand. All of this, to be sure, after the grand hostess of the occasion had ushered them in with her own courtly greetings.

When espying Charlotte Heywood among their party, on the other hand, Lady Denham took little interest. Dismissing her instead, *she* was summarily dispatched to the ailing Misses Parker, where she might make herself useful. An obedient Charlotte had no recourse but to cross the chamber to take up an inconspicuous position beside them.

Greatly improved, however, was the first lady of Sanditon's demeanor upon the entry soon after of Mr. Sidney Parker, with another young gentleman in his company. To these, Lady Denham was affability itself.

"I had indeed been informed, Sir," she declared with an emphasis, "that you had already arrived in Sanditon; but as you neglected to present yourself at Sanditon House," and here nodding towards the gentleman at his side, "or your companion, I gave little credence to the report. I see that I was in error. No matter. I welcome you despite such a shameful slighting."

Young Parker, in his bemused way, was much diverted by her reproof, and countered her genially, "Dear Madam, I confess it, this was a serious lapse from the civility I owe your Ladyship. My excuse is merely that in my compunction to be dutiful to my indisposed sisters and brothers, I was inevitably detained. I can only wish that you might find it in your heart to indulge me, for I promise that I shall make up for every courtesy lacking."

He turned to his friend, Lord Collinsworth, and presented him now to the grand lady. The manners of that gentleman were in every way so appealing that Lady Denham stood engaged and the occasion was miraculously rescued.

Collinsworth was not only well spoken; he was truly at his ease. In his compliments upon the brilliance of the evening, his enthusiasm was, perhaps, excessive. His admiration surmounted all that came before him—

the charm of Sanditon's avenues, the views embraced by the position of their beach, its scintillant sands—his offerings were balm to her, almost as though she herself were the particular object of his adulation.

That happy circumstance allowed young Parker to go the while in search of his sisters to pay his respects. He circled the room seeking them out, until there they were, comfortably seated at the far end of the grand chamber. Arthur was to be seen just a little apart, much engaged in conversation with a remarkably attractive young lady.

Scarcely had he approached to embrace them before Diana took up her incessant lament. To see him again tonight, she began, was clearly fine—their having so oddly encountered one another—so by chance and without expectation here at Sanditon—of all possible places, where not one of them had intended the visit.

"But I can only wonder," continued she, "that you do not find yourself overcome with fatigue and illness. The abandon with which you do wander about from place to place, young man, thinking nothing about draughts and change of air! I can assure you, such wildness shall not serve you. We take care to see that poor Arthur's encounters are far more economical, you may be certain of that!"

Sidney Parker was accustomed to his sister's forebodings, her perpetual anxieties for his welfare. Sometimes, he even regarded her disquiet as alarm for the entire generation—in truth, for all those young now populating the world. With regularity, he found himself able to laugh heartily at her insistent malaise.

"Yet from the sound of it, dear sister, my own health is not nearly in such jeopardy as stood our brother Thomas's lately. Nor does *he* gallivant through the universe! Even so, Diana," and here he checked an impulse to laugh aloud, "his most recent excursion in search of medical assistance—that carriage—might have overturned his every scheme, even carried him off without ceremony and entirely! Still, here tonight we see him stand squarely upon that tender ankle, and welcoming the world at large!"

With this he went in search of the dear man himself to offer his compliments. For so engaged had his brother been with a party of ladies just then announced, that Sidney had but managed the merest gesture of fond greeting to him when he entered. But, perusing the crowded room, he could not find him and approached Mrs. Parker instead. To her he made his inquiry for his brother's recovery.

Fortunately, when his sister Mary reviewed their recent adventures in Willingden there was another tone. With her usual cheerful manner, she beamed, "Yes, for this glorious moment Thomas is stalwart! He manages despite his injured ankle. But, my dear Sidney, it *is* just as Thomas has said, *good out of evil* indeed; for we were rescued and nursed in the most loving fashion by a fine family of that county. And we are now favored to have with us one of their daughters, our delightful Miss Heywood. That young lady you see engaged with your brother Arthur."

Sidney Parker glanced about the room in search of the pair he had glimpsed earlier. It was true. Seldom had he known his younger brother to seem so engrossed, so lively, before. He found himself curious.

Arthur's animation stemmed, in fact, from an earlier conversation with Charlotte Heywood. He had eagerly awaited their next encounter for the chance to tell her so.

"You see, Miss Heywood, I have been considering and reconsidering your remonstrances, especially pertaining my continuing susceptibilities. Our presence here at the seaside forces me to rethink my constitutional failings, my biliousness and rheumatic propensity. Surely, here in the damp air, they could be the end of me. Nevertheless, I have taken your advice and attempted the routines you recommend. As you can see, because of them I do not expire. Even I stand perplexed by my curious rally."

As Sidney approached, he could not but overhear the last, and quipped to his brother, "Surely, you will not yet expire so young, dear Arthur. It will not do for you entirely, or for any of us. As your elder brother, I quite forbid it!" And now turning towards his charming companion, he demanded to be presented.

"You are kind, Sir," was Miss Heywood's immediate response, "but we have already met; indeed, we have before this encountered one another, and that was not many days ago."

His own answer came with eagerness. "Madame, if that were the case, how might I have forgotten you? Do you suggest that such delights are everywhere to be seen? No, Miss Heywood, you are mistaken. Such a sight as I now look upon is neither usual nor expected. And, how can I not wonder at Arthur thus enlivened? It would seem that our brother Thomas's late misadventure has brought forth a hidden treasure."

Charlotte could but muse over that family's propensity for hyperbole. Still, by now she knew better than to let any such thoughts of her own find expression. Instead, she kept her countenance, responding in all politeness.

"Sir, I do assure you of our having met upon the road immediately you entered Sanditon itself. Your sister, Mrs. Thomas Parker, most graciously saw to that introduction as we strolled to Sanditon House. It is of little consequence, I assure you, for I am quite ready to comprehend how every distraction will have allowed yourself to overlook it. Then, too," she asked, "how, Sir, might you have recognized so promptly such excellence as you now seem to discern," adding with a laugh, "and this especially since I have never till this moment uttered so much as a word!"

Young Parker's was an arch expression; his amusement would, however, conceal a perplexity at the nicety of her distinctions. Piqued he was and would say more, but as she was promised to the smartly-attired Sir Edward Denham for the reel just striking up, there was no opportunity. That gentleman was already bowing before them to conduct her to the crowded dance floor as the music commenced. Charlotte was gone before he could summon another word.

FIFTEEN

The handsome aspect of his person rendered Sidney Parker a man whose presence in any room would not long go unnoticed. His easy manners, his gaiety, caught the eye of every lady in the room, so that he soon discovered himself surrounded by admirers.

Charlotte, the meanwhile, joined the dance willingly with the partner who had come to claim her. Tonight, Sir Edward Denham's gallantry was especially notable. He could extemporize for his companion as charmingly upon the radiance of each lady attending, as he did delight in her movements. And he could also, as they paused to wait for the next round, philosophize in dark enough tones.

Revolving now through the chamber and glancing at the young hopeful misses engaged in the dance, he pronounced upon the inevitability of their unfortunate disappointments in life—those betrayals each *must* expect to contend with.

"I know that you cannot but agree, Miss Heywood—for our poets have always known it—it is the fairer sex that is the more daring. *She,* is ever audacious, impetuous."

Here he turned pensive, "And dear Lord Byron understood this better than any, did he not—when he spoke of 'woman, lovely woman! thou, my hope, my comforter, my all!' I, too, in my modest way, dear lady, am given to pondering, in moments of quiet contemplation—for such higher thoughts will intrude to taunt us—this venerable question: who might conceivably answer for woman's power over us?"

He continued, gazing penetratingly into her eyes, "Ah yet, how well did the poet see the fearful consequence of all of it, think upon it. For is it not ever the valiant heroine, as Goldsmith has so touchingly depicted her for us, that lady whose devotion knows no bounds, that same *she* who stoops to folly, and then, alas, in the thorny business that must succeed, must bear the burden of her passion forever after?"

This last display of brilliance brought Sir Edward's image entirely into the light. Here before our Charlotte stood *the man of feeling* himself! And yet, as she observed the expression of torment his face assumed, our heroine could not resist thinking how well it suited that resplendently self-sufficient countenance!

Miss Heywood would not, could not, permit herself to laugh, yet the inclination *must* present itself. Only their brief separation for a fortunate moment during the procession of the dance could provide her rescue, for she was able to compose herself and return to him with serene aspect.

"My compliments, Sir," she then ventured. "Your admirable skill for hearing poetry in each occasion does you credit. And your thought speaks to your erudition—but *that*, I had already seen elegantly on display when last we met. As to our delight in motion—you *are* sensitive. Dance gives us such elevation of spirit, how can it not be thought of as neighboring on the sublime and even as music's own particular poetry?"

He smiled broadly, was emboldened by her praise, and would go further. But Charlotte checked at once this impulse by continuing.

"Yet, will you allow me to wonder, Sir Edward, over your touching concern for the ladies here assembled? Even as I willingly commend your tender sentiments, I can not suppose them to be brooding about sadnesses to come. Young ladies, to be philosophizing?' Come, come, good Sir, surely, you are not serious. I myself question whether any so much as are concerned to ponder about the future."

But Sir Edward was not to be put off. His determination to idolize— to see a heroine in every pretty girl resembling the part—and this evening the room seemed equipped to surfeit with such—demanded that he persist in such heroic rumination.

Fortunately for her, the dance had by then concluded and he need escort his partner back to her party. As they made their way towards the Parker sisters, Charlotte chanced in the moment, once more, to face their elusive brother, Sidney. He had managed in the interim to separate himself from his circle, ostensibly for the recovery of his friend Lord

Collinsworth from Lady Denham's unwavering attention, and to draw him away for presentation to his brother and host.

But, catching her eye momentarily as they passed, he changed his course as if a sudden gust had put a breeze in his sail. For once, inquisitiveness had taken hold of this scoffer, and he went tacking about like a coastal trader to put in for port. Now right beside him he descried his brother. As to Lord Collinsworth, the poor fellow could surely await rescue a bit longer.

Mr. Thomas Parker was as ever surrounded by eager young ladies and their escort, Mrs. Griffiths. As his brother approached him, and after an exchange of civilities all around, Sidney commenced with no further hesitation. He would consult with his brother, question him about the intriguing young woman whom he had brought with him from the country.

"Indeed, Thomas, though you certainly described for me at some length your mishap upon the road, you neglected to reveal anything of the family you befriended there. Yet here I see accompanying you tonight one of their number! If she show an example of their excellence, there should be more—in truth, I understand there are many more Heywoods—why did you not fetch them *all* with you here in your seaside Olympia?"

"Ah, you are off again, are you, dear Sidney! I do recognize *that* in your tone. It reminds me, had there been a doubt, that you are once more among us—and as ever ready to mock at even the most respectable of families. Need I tell over again of the remarkable warmth, the hospitality my dear Mary and I were fortunate enough to be favored with in the company of the Heywoods of Willingden? I assure you, I have spoken of nothing else these many months. Yes, they *are a* large and prosperous clan, with a fine establishment in the country. Though I will confess the property to be at the very center of nowhere—in a hamlet of no account, and certainly without a roadway to assure safe passage to any passerby. And good brother, you can imagine the position we might have faced without the help of that valiant gentleman and his family."

Sidney was engaged, and quite ready to hear more. His brother now described their open ways, the simplicity of their country life, their playfulness and delight in one another, and especially the generosity that persisted during the long fortnight they spent as the Heywoods' unexpected, nay, uninvited, guests.

"Depend upon it, brother, I did propose, cajole, and finally urge upon Mr. Heywood that very thing, for he is himself a man of some age. I *would* convince him that the conservation of his health yearned for a change of air, demanded an awakening of spirit," he concluded, "yet he attended this not at all. Even now, he comprehends nothing of the marvels that seaside cures can bestow. I fear there are still some, like Mr. Heywood, who remain immovable concerning such advancements to our well-being. Those who refuse, in the obstinacy of their understanding, to entertain such notions, even were they delivered them from God, if they should hint of progress. Alas, dear Sidney, my efforts were of no avail."

"Still," laughed his brother, "he was willing enough to part with his daughter, was he not? But perhaps this was for other than her health's sake. You must agree that such a gesture might still imply forward thinking, of a sort? Such a charming creature as she, and here amid the many, many seekers with their comings and goings? Yes, very politic, to be sure."

"Mr. Heywood, politic? Not likely, dear Sidney, merely a country gentleman, and an innocent, he. Yet, we are fortunate to be able to count Charlotte among us. We consider her our jewel. A someone of qualities, and altogether receptive to every innovation she can discover at Sanditon. Why, she has already proved a great asset to our Mary, and you must know that, as for Lady Denham herself, she has taken a fancy to the splendid girl. Miss Heywood does, I understand, attend to her so astutely in her every discourse."

"It would not surprise me. I merely overlook in awe the miracle she works upon our Arthur. Nor can I recollect him ever as animated as I see him; in truth, not since his first wail at the hour of his birth."

Here he looked out over the room, where he saw Charlotte as she stepped comfortably with Sir Edward to their sisters and younger brother. "Yes, to be sure, a presence, and her manner forthright."

Finally did Sidney make his way back to his friend Collinsworth, to bring about his release, and present him to Thomas and his familiars for engagement in the pleasures of the dance.

This duty accomplished, he found himself, as it were, instinctively drawn again toward his sisters' post, where Miss Heywood perched.

She, still much engaged in her conversation, did not so much as notice his reappearance. Sir Edward, however, who had not yet saluted the gentleman this evening, was more than cordial in his welcome.

"Your presence here, Mr. Parker, has much been missed. You stand accused, particularly by your good family, of not often enough appearing at the seaside, of neglecting us entirely. They, your good brothers and sisters, fret endlessly over the state of your health. I am happy to see you come tonight."

"Yes, Thomas especially foresees my demise, an imminent doom, if only for the foul air of London."

He wished now to address the young lady; but found instead that Sir Edward was not to be deterred.

"Yet, it is in excellent time, Mr. Parker, that you that do come among us, for a man such as you, in short, a man of the world, will, I am certain, attest to, indeed confirm, the assertions I have lately been making to Miss Heywood. The lady, you see, does contest me my every presentiment."

"Good sir, I put the question to you—can *you* doubt that it is womankind who after all leads us gentlemen astray? With all its glorious subtleties, the sex, I submit, *is* most frequently the whole cause of our destruction and despair. What think you, Mr. Parker, on the subject? Every admirer, each cavalier, yourself among them, must accept this truth to be inescapable! We ourselves are, are we not, but what poor creatures nature makes of us, forever at the mercy of the fair?"

That Sidney Parker listened amused was apparent; yet he seemed, at least in the moment, unwilling to take up the badinage. He shook his head merrily, displaying a dubious air at such a choice of converse.

"How strenuous does your talk seem, good sir, and here at these festivities. It can only weary your companion, I fear."

Here, he attempted once more to address the lady. But Sir Edward's expression never altered, nor did his attitude change. Sidney Parker could hardly have guessed that his position as hero might be genuinely compromised—yet he knew there was no escaping from the question. Therefore offering a discernible detachment in his look, he made his reply at his most sanguine.

"Sir Edward, little may we question the importance of the ladies to us all. *Their* presences are ever felt. Yet, earnest as such engagements may be, they can never become the serious business of our life. That must be reserved for our own duty as men. There can be no confusing, dear Sir, thought and valor in heroic deed—the conquest of nations, or rule upon the high seas—with the frivolity of an amorous hour. No, Sir, I cannot think that whilst the ladies, all our dear ladies, might be our fate—and this delightful in itself—they are the sole determiners of our fortune as well."

Charlotte had overseen the gentlemen's exchange, and considered it sufficiently preposterous. Surprised she found herself, however, by

Sidney Parker's agility in escaping the overflow of that maudlin tenderness. Unquestionably here was clarity of mind, and the wit to convey it. And in her current circumstance, she most certainly welcomed that discovery as rare pleasure.

Beyond that, what struck her, was that young man's careless disregard for *every* attempt at seriousness. This evening, his demeanor could not conceal—had revealed for her—a certain deficiency of his own. He seemed immune to the society about him. Young Parker, it became apparent, was perfectly capable of making ruthless sport not just of Sir Edward's pretensions, but of the *entire* corps of revelers in his brother's seaside wonderland.

She said nothing. No longer would she speak her mind at Sanditon. Still, try as she might, these perceptions could not be suppressed. In the charming Mr. Parker, there was decidedly a lack.

She smiled pleasantly, nodded to both gentlemen, and returned her attention to a waiting Arthur, who must instantly take up again the boasts of an improved regimen to recover his health.

SIXTEEN

"Fear not, dear Miss Lambe," was Diana Parker's encouragement to that hesitant participant as she ascended the hook-ladder into the bathing chariot. "In Sanditon, you need not be plagued by prying eyes from on shore. Here no one might, even in stealth, undertake to observe *your* trembling, or floundering before the plunge. Not at this, my brother Thomas's own excellent establishment! *He* would have none of those machines—the like of designs at Brighton—which, we so often hear it whispered, allow such excesses! Shocking, is it not?"

And, then looking properly abashed over these proceedings, she turned her eyes up at the splendid new canvas device so amply shielding each of their halting motions. It provided her the comfort of assurance.

Even so, her young companion's disquiet persisted. Miss Lambe, it began to seem, was incapable of calming herself. She scarcely was concerned over prospects of being indecently overseen, knew little enough of such affairs. Her own distress, in fact, stemmed from trepidation itself. The child was fragile, a delicate young thing who could in no way be supposed to enjoy robust health; moreover, she was altogether unused to exertions.

Still, when Mrs. Griffiths received the proposals of Miss Parker to assist at her seaside initiation, the young innocent had perforce acquiesced. As always, Miss Lambe would prove herself compliant with whatever her companion thought fit to arrange. Ever since having left her home—to be placed under the tutelage of this good lady—she had been submissive in her adherence to the careful engagements chosen for her by her attentive mistress. She remembered—could not be allowed to for-get—that her family had every confidence in her mentor. Mrs. Griffiths's ingenuity was the very means, they supposed, for the finding of success-ful entry to excellent society. Was it not in these isles, after all, that cul-tivation resided? Miss Lambe therefore, had been given to understand herself, particularly chosen to be her parents' emissary, to lead her younger sisters the way to genteel and suitable husbands.

This indulged eldest of a family endowed with a fine property in the Indies, and, descendant as she was of an English father together with a prepotent Antiguan mother, had only newly emerged from a part of the world fortunate in its clime, and more gentle in its surrounding seas. It was not surprising that young lady should be intimidated by the frigid adventure she faced this morning.

Her enterprising friend Mrs. Griffiths took no notice of such qualms. She had as a matter of course assumed that their good helper, as sister to the founder of Sanditon, spoke as adept in *all* matters relating to its salubrious functions. She must lose no time in her campaign to strength-en her charge's character by the improvement of her condition.

"Our great good fortune, child, you will soon appreciate," she explained, "for, as special disciples of Miss Parker, we are chosen to be in the forefront of Sanditon's emergence among fashionable spas. And, my love, I know *you* to be up to its every rigor."

The sweet girl could but assent.

And how might Diana Parker herself disappoint such worthy confi-dence in her own capabilities? Hence, here they were out early of a morn-ing; despite an advancing season, there was little doubt that the sea air was brisk, even cutting. As to the sea itself, Miss Lambe—in proving the little test of dipping her toe in it—had already discovered its bite. How bitter immersion itself was going to prove!

The delicate miss resisted whimpering, even as faithful Miss Parker exquisitely reassured her by holding forth upon the benefits to be gained from sacrifice, foolhardy as it could seem to her in the present moment.

"As you shall see, dreams are to be realized in the marvels of a resilient body. You will find first an increase of appetite, and later, better still, of spirits. No more habits of lassitude will be yours. Such warrants we our-selves have heard from the lips of Dr. Relhan. Now, come, my child, let us for it, and do as the good practitioner demands—take the plunge. If we are to effect a true transformation, it is the whole body, you understand, that is required to be submerged!"

So did she prevail, ordering the dipper to proceed, while yet again repeating how despite its first shock such a temperature must prove bracing! Unquestionably, she concluded, here was the very remedy they sought.

Given the urgency of the moment—and the despair felt by both ladies confronting the test—there remained no room for hesitation, certainly no opportunity for candor from the older of them. Yet should exactitude be sought, it must be acknowledged that Miss Parker's pertinacity during those first minutes derived from her need to cheer *herself* in this work.

Nor will astute observers have forgotten the lady's initial posture. Had we not, after all, been unequivocally advised that, during those interminable years when her brother regaled her with his beliefs in these dramatic potentials, urging their immediate practice, even proselytizing, all for true conversion, she had refused any trial? To the contrary, she had held such doctrine ever distant, and securely within the realm of the impossible.

Her views, together with those of both sister and brother, both similarly recusant, were categorically averse to cures. These miracle recoveries held no attraction for them! What could nostrums effect for the likes of a rheumatic Arthur, a headachy and nerve-wracked Susan, or, for that matter, her own recurrence of acute spasmodic bile? Even to entertain those notions were idle. Only a worrisome future could thereby be assured for their dainty constitutions. Fortunate for all three, the invalid in Miss Diana Parker, ever vigilant, had checked such false hopes. She remained staunchly infirm. Superior was her dyspeptic urge than any other, and far too tenacious to allow any swift remedy. To even convincing evidence she had given no credence; that is, until now.

So when one afternoon, her gullible younger sister Susan had returned home with a tale of just one such marvel, her patience was short.

"Dear Diana," began she in breathless recital, "I have only now seen the most extraordinary demonstration! It so unexpected as to make the phenomenon all the more wonderful. Our sweet friend, Mrs. Addison, newly returned from Brighton, partook there of Dr. Awsiter's recipe for dipping and drinking, then dipping and drinking again. The results must be seen, lest you, Sister, believe them not. I promise you, she not only can move about, but moves like a gazelle! No more the swollen feet we looked upon with pity before she took up her regimen. Altogether renewed is she! Yes, and a partisan for seaside restoration! She is a convert to the recovery of youth itself."

Miss Parker's response at that time was predictable enough. Said she, "You *will* go on, Susan, so like our Thomas. *He* has elevated the rank of sea-water above all elixirs, beyond even the rare mud of the River Nile! No, Sister, I for one remain unregenerate; I shall never subscribe."

That from Diana, and not so very long ago!

Yet here stood she this morning, shivering together with pitiful Miss Lambe. Well might we wonder what could have brought such reversal? Was she grown demented? It would seem unlikely. Despite the good lady's hard skepticism, and her lack of experience with the sea cures, there was, as she now apprehended it, *sufficient* motive.

Consider the predicament in which she found herself. Had *she* herself not been the director of Mrs. Griffiths and her party towards fair Sanditon? And did not her brother's welfare now depend upon her strenuous action to keep this lady's group, and others like hers, happily in place there?

Her *volte-face* came of her eagerness to serve Thomas's own interests, while at the same time, she longed to be of true assistance to these good ladies. The valiant Miss Parker had, in short found ample ground to suspend her doubts and look to it herself that *each* would be enriched in her expectations.

Miss Parker had sometimes reflected upon her own conduct in critical moments. She would savor the sentiment excited in her breast by a daring rescue. When she served, then only did she sense her worth. A brave act supported her best opinion of her own character; it sanctified her complacence, her self-gratulation; it afforded her occasion even for self-applause. A commission requiring valor proclaimed her allegiance not merely to family but to a higher power—to a level reached at such a height as she deemed divine in service to her neighbor. To aspire to the greater good, would realize for Miss Diana Parker an approach to the angels.

Perhaps the most peculiar effect was, that here at the shore—once believed lethal to her welfare, all agues suddenly were as none. She felt them not. So employed, as Miss Parker continued, so occupied in duty from that recent day when she had come to make herself useful in her brother's cause, her complaints ebbed. For only at such labors could she cherish a finer feeling—that delicate silken rope uniting mankind—and at the same time strengthen thereby affection between brother and sister.

Admittedly, it was she who had erred in the earlier effort on his behalf. In her enthusiasm, she had overly estimated the numbers engaged, anticipating a far larger company to manifest itself than had actually arrived. Her own disappointment, she could bear; for her brother's sake, she continued uneasy for the oncoming season, with its threats of vacancies unfilled. For the few takers she had herself enticed thither, she felt only mortification.

Miss Parker vowed to make good that error. She pondered upon the means. Her competence in such affairs was not to be contended. More than once, she had thought with clarity, or found a path for them; always, she had acted with dispatch.

What she now saw plainly enough—was that if such an enterprise as Sanditon was to be understood in its potential for future prominence, *she* must now take a hand. The elegant Lady Denham and her coadjutor, Miss Parker's dear brother, may have *dreamt* of expansion—in the complacency of their confidence that position alone must earn them the attention of the larger world. Convinced of the importance of their new venture, they would rely on the beauty and varying delights of its surroundings in any season, to accomplish that success.

Diana Parker's mind was made of a firmer stuff; she knew more determined advocacy must be her part, their cause hers. She alone comprehended just what was to be undertaken. More innovational measures must therefore be devised, if they hoped to cut a broader swath. Ambition need enlist expert minds, ingenious developers of novel attractions, in short, true gentlemen of business—such as were schooled in the process. To ensure the attention of fashionable London would require that she seek out sources.

Oddly enough, it was by a chance encounter that very morning, as she and her companion were returning from Sanditon beach, when her inspiration took flight. As they were being escorted from the chariot, before them there had appeared young Sir Edward Denham, preparing to take to the waters.

As ever his gracious self, his greeting was of the most cordial. His ease, the spontaneous recital of his latest ditty, but more especially in recognizing these ladies, he immediately enchanted—

> "Is't true, what ancient Bards suppose," began he,
> "That Venus from the ocean rose,
> Before she did ascend the skies
> To dwell among the deities?"

Then laughingly concluding with—

> "Yes, sure: Why not? Since here you see
> Nymphs full as beautiful as she,
> Emerging daily from the sea."

Young Miss Lambe stood still shivering so violently with cold that her blush was scarcely visible. As for Miss Parker, she delighted in this gallantry. Here, it occurred to her, was an honest Bacchanalian, a true admirer of the fair sex; and, *why not?* a most suitable ally.

Of course. She must enlist him in the expediting of her plans, such a forward-looking fellow as he was; in fact, one whose indeterminate fortune was dependent upon the good will of relatives. He could only prove receptive.

As she enunciated her notion for advancing the prospects for their community and set out her proposal to enhance its popularity, to advertise its curative powers, he heeded, most attentive.

"*You* will comprehend," she explained, "that natural beauties, positioning, any or all of Sanditon's general perfections, will not insure us its success. We need advance our own steps. Let us take a lead, set trends, influence fashion. The best of London society alone can provide selective adherents. All this, dear Sir, requires other enthusiasm than merely our own."

Sir Edward could have not more agreed. "Madam, you *are* astute. Until the moment all London speaks of superior society to be encountered in Sussex, and the most well-spoken of them sing its praises—few will elect to be seen here. All your brother's lovely lodgings, his fine terraces, his elegant shops and library, will continue vacant, and his assemblies go unheralded."

In his own hands, however, matters could take a better turn. He would himself provide the very London connections to the purpose.

"If ever you condescend to look again at those newly built rooms at Almack's, you might note that there, Madam, are the very *exclusives* we seek—those whose *ton* is stamped by it. This is where every young *debutante* of fashion *must* seek as her object admission—as much as any politician needs a seat upon the Privy Council Board to flourish. My good Miss Parker, my assurances upon the matter, should *I* choose to enlist the people of rank who seek their dances at the Club, we might indeed have inspiration for many takers."

"Your Sanditon can soon stamp its own *bon ton!* A considerable noise in the interests of the cause; indeed, and that, to be discreetly inserted at that very place, the new assembly rooms at Almack's, or at the tables at Brooke's. You shall then see the effects. As the Duke of Wellington favors his Cheltenham, so shall we select our own distinguished champions. Why, but the other night, in chatting with your dear brother's London friend, Lord Collinsworth, was I brought to attention on that very subject; for he is, you will know, an accepted favorite of the best set there, or at White's, and any other, to come to think upon it."

Miss Parker was heartened by his knowledgeable recitation. The young gentleman understood her brother's cause. In concert, they two could act. So, in their name, she would dispatch him, lest Thomas's hope of a seaside haven be altogether dissipated.

Part IV

SEVENTEEN

*T*he regard in which Lady Denham held her relation was not idly come by. But in the short time since Clara Brereton had arrived to serve the exacting lady, that impoverished young kinswoman had repeatedly demonstrated superiority in suiting her deliverer's every whim, together with a distinct adaptability in the task.

So if it *must* yet be acknowledged that her aunt had invited Clara to spend the winter only at Sanditon House—in a guarded gesture that had confined itself to obligations, she felt could answer to the kindness of that family during her stay in London—and if it need be further conceded that, in offering hospitality to this reduced clan she had chosen, not among the several needy Brereton daughters, but a remoter relation and the one most *helpless* of them all, Lady Denham could at least now congratulate herself upon foresight in her selection.

Long ago had her disinclination towards involvement with these cousins faded, her reluctance for entanglement turned instead to a tolerant acceptance of their reconciliation. And by this time, she had dispensed too with *any* notion of sending Clara home, and away from her—not in a few short months—or even at all. Clara Brereton she observed to be as thoroughly amiable as she was lovely. Her various virtues—warmth of heart, an open disposition, fitting modesty—had shown themselves regularly in her present situation. There can be no contesting her claim to every such excellence. Her steadiness alone had brought a new continuity to the Denham household, enlivening allegiances from both servants and tenants alike; Miss Brereton's unassuming manner had proved tonic for everyone. These good efforts were visible to its imperious proprietor.

Withal—and here we mean no reprimand to an untried young being—what might possibly give pause—even raise an eyebrow with this observer—was her hour of dalliance with Sir Edward, so inadvertently come upon by an unsuspecting Charlotte.

Without question it need be allowed that Miss Brereton's actions must be of her own choosing, and altogether free. This, whatever her station. Still, to be discovered as she was, secreted and in such an attitude, startled our Miss Heywood.

Why, we must wonder, would a sensible Clara Brereton have placed herself in jeopardy? Had not her benevolent patroness expressed her own expectation and determination in that quarter? And could Miss Brereton not have imagined the danger of arousing her mistress to ire? Surely, so obliging, and so forebearing a person as she was, she could have seen that hazards enough there were in these vagaries.

Lady Denham had made herself plain often enough, and expressed a staunch opposition to such foolery. Two people of the same broader family, daily within reach of one another, intimate? Unseemly! There could be little doubt of that. Well-born this young man might have been, but impoverished he remained. Nor can it be denied that in this particular acquaintance, each was not only penniless, but entirely at the disposition of a capricious relation.

Are we to surmise then that Clara Brereton's *rendezvous* with Sir Edward was abandonment to an irresistible attraction for that gentleman? And if so, in all fairness, can we fault a young lady for such acknowledgment of his gallantries?

"Sir Edward can strut and simper as well as the best of his sex," Lady Denham had proffered, "for he is exquisitely studied in the intricacies of pleasing a lady. Yet, oh yet, he needs look more plainly into the bleakness of a future without the benefit of elemental comforts. It is not in him, I do assure you, despite his lyrical flights into the higher regions of poesy, to suffer any genuine deprivation, all in the cause of love."

His aunt was ever astute when she suspected her own interest to be even slightly imperiled; she long ago had taken the measure of her husband's dashing, prospective heir. A dedicated-enough fellow she found him, firmly at her service, of a serious cast as well. Was not young Sir

Edward—albeit self-acclaimed—a discerning reader, attached to his studies, and devoted to his books?

For herself, she had given little enough attention to such fanciful undertakings, and shown less patience with those who themselves subscribed. What after all could be garnered from novels that life did not already illuminate? Many another such as this young votary would do better instead to look about, to see a harsher force, with all of its reality, at work both in nature and society. Wisdom was there to be sought—everywhere hidden in event—in the countryside, as well as in the brutalities of great cities—even here with us in the quiet of the seaside. The practiced Lady Denham would proclaim these conclusions to her associates. And as she would rehearse it, the cultivation of such insights, the development of true vision, was *the* lifelong study.

"All is before us, we need but to look in order to see what may be uncovered—in a canny reading of cause and effect, and further still in a nimble interpretation of sequence and its consequence."

Her long experience proved this. From youth, Lady Denham's concentration had remained firm. She had never rested until she had assessed the intricacies of her position in life, had studied the proprieties of condescension; and, having brilliantly sought out and affixed that proper place, could allow herself to enjoy the regard shown her by the highest of society, together with the natural deference of those less worthy. Most important, she had determined upon preserving such order in all of good society.

How then might it not occur to this successful ascendant, recently the innovator of a sparkling township, that her husband's nephew's profound immersion in novels, in the dramas and romances of the day, would not advance his future prospects, or promote his rise? The overbearing Lady Denham faulted not his intellectual prowess, but his cherished books instead—unlike Mr. Parker's young visitor, Charlotte Heywood, who had found appealing Sir Edward's ventures into literature, only to be taken aback by his odd assumptions, ruefully concluding that understanding itself did not appear to be a priority.

As unsuited to want as the gentleman seemed, and less able even to imagine its possibilities, *he* continued secure in the certainty that he was never meant to suffer deprivation. Fortunate then, that the Lady better comprehended the exigencies. She recognized that with his bravado, his fashionable attitudes—his absurd efforts to charm the fairer sex—he could achieve the reverse of his aims and deprive himself instead of whatever chance might be seized for a comfortable subsistence.

"As for his sister, Esther," was the still less tolerant judgment she rendered to the attentive Mrs. Parker, "*she* would do best to put herself squarely in line of potential, at the very center of good society, and instantly, too. You must know, my friend, that one may not, no matter how it is to be wished, remain either young or handsome beyond the time appointed. And, to my view, her own attractions are, unlike others more fortunate, minimal, even in the splendor of these, her salad days."

Alas! All those supplicants everywhere about her. Must Lady Denham forever be plagued by persons who had no prospects of their own? The very idea repelled her, and she had determined to put such inconsequentiality from her mind. Time enough was there for somber thoughts. She had herself too long labored to see to it that her own situation in life should be securely graceful, and would certainly refuse these distractions today.

For solace, she preferred to turn towards her own creation, the biddable, mindful, malleable Miss Clara. Presently, this young woman altogether better suited the pleasure of the mistress of Sanditon House, who had never been looked to so punctiliously before. The more curious fact was, that little as she was inclined to ponder the disposition of her wealth—for it after all entailed the necessity of her own demise—she found, that she was given to contemplating a potential for *her*, having discerned something of herself in this efficient young thing.

Such had been distant from the Lady's thoughts at their tentative beginning. The helpless relation's arrival had caused inconvenience enough. Where might she be installed in the great house? How regarded? A serving girl, she surely was not. Yet, her hostess had never pictured her as family. As for intimate or equal, eminent personage that *she* was, she had sought no pitiful child companion. It was by virtue of such added commissions, that Lady Denham felt herself put out upon the girl's first appearance.

Even so, duties there were, and their exacting execution would most assuredly be demanded of her. How else make her worthy of acceptance in this fine household? We may be certain that Miss Brereton fell promptly to mastering her assigned chores, to making her presence felt, to providing comfort and security for everyone about her.

Yet how little considered in that entry has been her own state of mind,

her turmoil whilst she wandered through the long halls of her new surroundings. To have left what people she knew, the closest of her living
relatives, the loneliness she now felt, and this isolation from all she was
formerly attached to, was distressful to her.

True, she felt gratitude toward Lady Denham. Overwhelmingly, however, her sensations were of awe. Had she not been taken from poverty
to settle here in an estate grandly facing the sea? Above everything, had
she not been salvaged from the prospect of a joyless life—a future of
service in some wretched, alien household, nursemaid at best, or, worse
even, to continue as the dependent of her distant relations, whose own
financial woes were constant? The Breretons she knew to be kind people.
They would never have deserted her; yet, there was so little to be shared
amongst them, and so many awaiting receipt of it.

Clara must always feel her imposition, the burden placed upon the
patience of the lady by her appearance at Sanditon; for it was thus that
she understood her cousin's benevolence. Whatever the obstacles it presented, she determined in her freshness and youth to be hopeful, to turn
her agile thoughts toward making way in her new home,

In consequence, how much, and so finely too, was altered in her favor.
Still, no matter how she was presently valued by the lady, she would
remember that coldness; that censorious tone upon her arrival, when,
knowing so little of the habits of her mentor, she had for the briefest
moments allowed every fearful feeling to recede in joy—those instants
when she first looked upon the luxurious quarters of her mistress, that
happiness in the sense of rescue, of being in safe harbor. There was a
dance in her step, a liveliness of demeanor, almost a skipping, and an
involuntary crooning in celebration of such good fortune, as she went
from room to room. Then it was those sobering words from her cousin
brought her up sharp.

"Child, such display! I am little accustomed to the wildness of young
people. Calm yourself—your clatter will endanger my cherished crystal
ware—do you mean to shatter it all to crumble with this shrillness? Here
you will soon understand gentility. My tutelage can acquaint you with
the obedience expected from your superiors. At Sanditon House, such is
the cardinal rule. Never is it to be violated by associates of mine own."

Her reproof had rung out, first freezing the young lady into an
uncharacteristic solemnity; then chastening her into complete silence.
From that time, she assessed her situation: were she to be tolerated at all,

she must mind her place. So did young Clara Brereton retreat into herself. Vigilant, she allowed nothing of her true emotion to be seen again. She was there on sufferance; only to please.

It was, however, a comfort that came to her not long after in the appearance of a stalwart young visitor to Sanditon House. Sir Edward Denham befriended the girl. He was courtly; he was flirtatious; he was dedicated. How could he not have been admirable?

Lonely, and despairing, she relished his every kind word. Is it any wonder that she inclined to believe the romantic Sir Edward as he levelled his dark eyes upon her and recited endlessly from his store of verse?

Why then make little, or much of the "white and womanish" scene our Charlotte had glimpsed? How think it surprising, or to be judged as improper? The pair was young; the attractions between them considerable, the lady's own charms entirely sufficing to make more of it than was seemly.

She could attend enchanted to his recitations. She could delight in his passion for poetry. Hers was boundless wonder at such erudition. How often had she not dreamt of such a man? What young woman has not? A sensitive, spirited hero, whose love of study, whose admirations reached so much further beyond the humdrum and the mundane, who sought the adventurous, glorious life she too had found only in books. So had Sir Edward, in those first days of her somber coming, appeared to her.

It was true Miss Brereton was then little aware of the lavish attentions the young fellow bestowed upon every lady of his acquaintance, and the zeal he squandered upon each. As the irresistible Lovelace, his pose must never be challenged! That determination had he made early on. Foolish, or what should be more than foolish—unseeing—she was not. She accounted his foibles merely young man's notions—minor fancies thrown off by the vigor of an ambitious nature, such as authentic heroism might engender. A Lovelace, and ruthless? Plainly, he was not of that metal.

Besides, *she* could love him. She would *see* him turned towards sense. Had not those worthy of such—in the past, great women of imagination—always served that aim? Then, too, she remembered her namesake, that indomitable undaunted Clarissa. Just see what an effect upon that unscrupulous gentleman *she* had wrought. But why not? Through Clara's love, he should discover what was possible, whatever can be brought to happy conclusion, just as much as in his own treasured novels and poems.

Clara Brereton saw few choices open for herself. Understanding then her quarry, she would think ahead for them both, and pursue him to the end.

On his part, this capricious fantasist and impractical imaginer kept surprises of his own in store. He had thought more upon his welfare of late, more than his aunt might suspect, weighed each possibility, and uncovered ingenious, worldly schemes. What struck his notice was his good aunt's growing devotion to the young lady. He studied its unpromising warmth. Might it alter his prospects? His title—even his claim to distinction—he already possessed; but ever since this lady's marriage years ago to his dear uncle, he had felt himself encouraged toward grander expectation. She should, as a matter of right, see to his fortune. Of course she would! Yet here she was admirably attended of late; perhaps so content with her superb discovery as to redirect her course. Suddenly both himself and his sister had begun to seem almost superfluous to her society.

Trying Lady Denham upon this very matter but recently, he had sensed palpable danger.

"I see, Madam, that your young invention is the flower in your garden," he had offered, "a bloom most brilliant in your eyes—such a decorative creature, indeed, a perfect handmaiden."

Lady Denham's response was generous.

"Admiration for my cousin seems to be as pervasive as the sea air, so much do I hear her praises sung. Justly so. I confess she does manage the servants, and oversees my household with striking ease—my table is supplied to perfection itself. I will not deny that I have come to look upon her favorably, as one of mine own; for indeed, at her work she is an apt young person."

He heard her well and saw he must attend.

EIGHTEEN

*U*pon a morning soon after, so extraordinary a stir was there in the neighborhood upon the arrival at the Inn of a smartly-liveried chaise, that it might have signalled a progress of royalty. The carriage bore the party of Emmeline Turner, a lady of some reputation.

That she had elected Sanditon was surprising; all yet the more so that she had made the excursion without preliminaries.

Thomas Parker, instantly informed, was observed rushing to the scene for welcome. He admonished his wife with the importance of this dramatic addition.

"Sweet Mary, if you could but conceive of what such an appearance signifies? The accomplished Mrs. Turner, here to take a place with us! Surely, we can do no better! She, who already commands the ear of all London society. Only consider the popularity of her last opus, *Celestina*, and before that, the inspiring *Ethelinde*."

With that he readied himself for audience before that lady.

It was in hopes of *escaping* celebrity that Emmeline Turner had made her journey. Seeking a needed cure, she preferred to come and go quietly amongst her party of assistants. For this reason alone, she had repaired to Sanditon. Of Brighton and of Weymouth she had seen quite enough; that she felt no attraction for Bath was a conclusion foregone.

Furthermore, this was to come sweetly home to her native country, with its turbulent shore and its rugged headlands. For the lady had been born at nearby Lewes and reared there for the better part of her young life. How she did yearn to breathe its air, so moist and fresh, and to look upon her Sussex altogether, its fields and gardens and their blaze of color in any season. Even, with greater nostalgia, had she pictured the familiar delight in watching a game of bowls of an afternoon in her own LewesHigh Street. If Mrs. Turner was to regain that peace, along with her health, she welcomed now those gentler sounds; and beyond them, the roar of the sea's fierce pounding; but most, the sweetest silences of her home country.

For in all her accomplishment until now, she recollected her debt to this Norman corner of England, with its ancient timber framed structures yet preserved. Its beauty resided comfortably inside her head, and thoughts of its simple pleasures never abandoned her, when daily she wrestled with mud and dirt in the London streets she knew all too well now.

Why should she not seek replenishment? As a girl, she had clambered about in the coves, strolled on the beaches, and wandered further inland. She had so delighted in these solitary rambles—her parents never objecting even in bad weather. Her city existence deprived her of that quiet of mind her home country fostered. Moreover, in her lately discovered Sanditon, she had chanced upon an unfashionable, unattended bit of shore where, without distraction, she might recover something of her former self. Or so at least was her anticipation.

Indeed, her London physicians had already thrown up their hands at her condition, her state having declined under continued pressure of mental labor and the anxiety attendant upon her maintaining an independence. The most eminent of a series of them, a Dr. Harris Long in Harley Street, had succeeded in isolating those acrid humors which derange the functions or destroy the structure of those organs upon which vital action depend. He had pronounced her to be exhausted; her system in disarray; he wondered at her persistence despite such debilitating circumstances and care.

The great specialist's fear for her continued subsistence resulted in the prescription of his own phenomenal new remedial agent, an application that could extract and remove such disease. He promised her complete recovery; that there could be little doubt of it, within good time, was his confident appraisal.

His concoction, whose simple base came from mere cabbage leaves, to be imbibed each morning and night as instructed, was accompanied by the doctor's own cheerful overseeing of his inhalation therapy from the immense vaporizing machines installed in his elegant rooms. To those treatments, Mrs. Turner was wholly faithful. Were such, after all, not regarded by every fashionable Londoner as the current panacea for improvement? The effective cure all. Yet as the long winter months progressed, and despite her adherence to rigid regime, scant headway was made. The lady did not rally. Mrs. Turner continued listless and in despair, a shadow of her former self.

It was with some degree of desperation, then, that her thoughts turned towards the sea. She had been aware of all the proponents for sea-bathing cures, eminent believers in the miracle of salt water drink, a congregation of swearers to the qualities of the Creator's primordial substance, those who saw it as the remedy sovereign against "hypochondriac melancholy and windiness."

Yet, till now, she had given no credence to this mania; and could scarcely fathom the near-religious dedication to it. In truth, she found such conversions more apt as the object of ridicule. Were these folk not exemplars of folly, willing victims to superb humbug?

Ah, the healing wonders described by adherents. After the prodigious upheaval of being hurled down into the sea—the surprise, the fear of being engulfed—came a miraculous result, a soothing modification in the organs of thought and throughout the whole nervous system. Often she heard too, good Dr. Russell's quoting the ancients, that "the sea washes away and cleanses *every* human stain." How might it be doubted?

Withal, Mrs. Turner was herself now in need. At this crucial time of her life, she must seek relief. If her own impetus was distinct from those at whom she had formerly scoffed, she, like them, would return to the elements she had known once so well, anxious to retrieve health and spirits. There had remained in her a pull towards the sea, although rather more in search of mystery than miracle. She remembered the days of her youth, those hours she sat about idly contemplating the vast, unknown deep and its chaos. She could only wonder at her recollection, vividly attached now to a longing for lost vitality. It was akin to a search for Eden, the paradise that was before the Flood.

With her fortuitous discovery of the faltering Sussex enterprise set so newly near to her own native scenes, she could barely delay the hours to take herself back home again. In short, she had determined to give to that cure its moment. Who knows, she allowed, might not it touch upon her own unrelenting malaise, her crippling inability to proceed in her work and thought?

The paradox was, that even as she went forward with her plan, she would make sport of herself; indeed, it amused the lady to see herself reborn, like Aphrodite emerging from the sea. Further release came in another more immediate notion: "What entertainment," she thought, "in *not* encountering all those significant people, along with their displays of obligatory wit and wisdom, their show of elegant fashion, their parade of wealth. And how sweet, to find none of the demand for special court of the highborn, ever so wearisome at Weymouth."

At *her* modest choice of spa, there would be no such preening and prancing. She looked forward to wild beauty, to simplicity, to country calm.

But her sunny hope dimmed. Mr. Parker's appearance, his prompt attendance upon her, was a surprise. To be sure the gentleman's greetings were altogether cordial, his person agreeable. The lady, if not yet alarmed, was dismayed.

She was content to greet him. And yes, she responded to his happy questions. She *had* indeed elected to spend her time with them at Sanditon; and yes, absolutely, she found herself delighted by what she had been able to see thus far! As to the matter of inadequacy in her lodgings at the Inn, in what might such consist? No, she thanked him again, she could imagine no need to improve upon them. All services seemed agreeable enough for the moment; and, once more, no,—there was hardly cause to accept his kind offer to secure for her one of the grander houses overlooking the sea, an edifice still awaiting its suitable summer tenant.

"Good Sir," she continued warmly, "you may be easy on that score. My needs are simple, and though I am sure the company at large is as delightful as you declare, I shall require little entertainment during my residence with you. I come, you see, intending to devote myself entirely to my restoration—to reclamation of a quiet mind, to the purity that will emerge after intervals of looking out upon the sea and breathing its salty fragrance."

What a pity the lady's protest was heard too late. The news of Mrs. Turner's arrival was already abroad, and she, much the subject of curiosity. Lady Denham, when advised of the honor paid them, would not be deterred in her own generous offer of hospitality. Within the hour, her servant was dispatched to deliver her greeting, and more particularly, her expectation of enjoying their late arrival's presence at Sanditon House at week's end as her dinner guest.

Lady Denham that very afternoon had welcomed this delightful intelligence, following directly upon a trying encounter with her newly-engaged young parson. She had found this gentleman zealous in his wish to enlist her support for what the Lady apprehended as grandiose notions of religion. Demonstration of these excesses of fervor, as her confidants informed her, were already to be seen daily in his nearby parish. Hence she was today singularly arch in her delivery.

When, for example, she deputized her disciple, Miss Brereton, to organize her soaring event, she addressed the able child as follows: "I myself vouch for it, Miss Clara. Our dear England suffers from the jibe that she supports one hundred religions—a variety to accommodate any and every want—yet, to this day, alas, even at her grandest tables or at Carleton House itself, she can boast but one sauce alone. This is an accusation that remains more than just! For my taste, the reverse condition should have served all of us much better! Dear girl, would not our countrymen have been better off, far better indeed with more sauces, and one simple faith? Culinary variety, it is what we lack; that something we live desperately in need of!

"I leave us now in *your* capable hands, and hope to inspire such elegance for our evening, for I cannot but observe that our temperamental French cook can be wooed by you alone. All that is vital to our pleasure, and you, my child, shall seek it for us."

"For myself, I have undertaken to arrange a party worthy of our distinguished new guest. It behooves us, you understand, to entice, to cosset the lady, to provide a brilliance of company and a wit to which she is accustomed. We shall enchant her in our magical landscape by the sea. The lady's former life must pale amongst us by comparison; an encounter with the pick of Sanditon's society may even prove an enrichment for the fantastical world of her books!"

How might Emmeline Turner decline such overtures? Reluctant as she was, she contemplated the alternative, and determined that her own pursuit of tranquility could not permit offence to the well-meaning. She sent forward her patient acceptance.

The evening proved grand. Miss Brereton, charged to spare no expense in pleasing their valued guest, devoted herself to its perfection. The frenzy in the kitchen at Sanditon House testified to her industry; while the table was itself a triumph in artistry, laid as it was with a sprinkling of rose petals and seasonal flowers.

The company itself was not large. Select, is the more apposite description. Mr. Parker, Sanditon's co-founder, and his lady done in her finest, along with his brothers, his sisters, and Charlotte Heywood, their charge. There, to represent the hostess'. exalted Denham connections, was Sir Edward as well, accompanied by his sister, Esther. The group was as well complemented by Mrs. Griffiths' attractive party of young heiresses.

Emmeline Turner had determined to be equal to such festivities. It seemed to her that by enduring such an initiation, she might be guaranteed privacy within her new circumstance. Little did she suspect the consequence Sanditon's residents put upon her implied approbation, let alone the prosperity they anticipated from obtaining such a blessing.

Once assembled in the drawing room, the beauty of the house properly admired, they could advance with all formality to the dining hall, Lady Denham to lead the party's way, upon the arm of the well-favored Sidney Parker.

All was as hoped for; the converse continued agreeable over a magnificent dinner of salmon trout, followed by a fricando of veal and giblet pie, done to perfection. The removals continued—many and long, sustaining the elegance of the occasion, even to the relaying of table with fresh linen for exquisitely pyramided fruits set upon an epergne, and a train of incoming jellies and sweetmeats. Such glorious fixings, to flaunt Lady Denham's wealth, could but make an impression.

Place at table had been given serious contemplation by the mistress of the house. She had had no hesitation in settling the eligible young gentlemen beside herself and her new friend, Mrs. Turner. The lesser company must, simply make do.

As for our heroine, she had been situated at a little distance, thus had no need of speech; in truth, was unheard from most of their time at dinner. Arthur Parker, dispensable himself, had been relegated to join her, where he found himself ensconced happily among the other young ladies, Miss Lambe, the Misses Beaufort, Miss Brereton, and Miss Heywood. Quite properly, then, did he wax eloquent to this audience. He had not been remiss with further investigation into health regimens. His delivery pronounced that recent verve which had been noticed privately in the young man. Tonight, it was on display.

Charlotte tried to attend to his disquisition. Yet must it be acknowledged, that her mind would wander as he discoursed, her gaze inevitably moving towards the company assembled at the other end of the table. She could not but overhear some of the exchange there in progress. As much wine was poured out and continued to be consumed, particularly by the waggish young Sir Edward, his performance grew ever louder. Seeing it as duty to his aunt to engage her eminent guest by a rehearsal of his learning, he had begun in bravado early.

Charlotte's eye fell upon Sidney Parker, in his customary hang back posture, that of an Epicurean listener, an attendant with raised eyebrow, who wore an expression to denote hearty enjoyment of Sir Edward's poetic delectations. While noticeably amused, he remained himself something aloof, withdrawn, much as she had seen him before. While nodding in a necessary civility, he contributed little.

As for Mrs. Turner, she now welcomed each diversion, preferring to listen, unready to speak. She confessed astonishment at Sir Edward's performance. He had recited ably his choice poets—his Scott, his Byron, his Burns—the lionized poets of the day—quoting liberally from his favorite pieces. It was then—with his listener so complimentary for his aptitude—that he seized the moment. Dumbfounded, she heard her own words uttered, and splendidly.

"Dear Lady," he commenced, "even among such bards as these—who has given us more of truth than yourself. I cherish your *To My Lyre!* How you did depict our—nay, every man's fate in the presence of pulchritude!" He then spoke more softly, yet with feeling,

> *"Who that has heard thy silver tones*
> *Who that the Muse's influence owns,*
> *Can at my fond attachment wonder*
> *That still my heart should own thy power?*
> *Thou—who hast soothed each adverse hour,*
> *So thou and I will never sunder."*

And on he continued, all rapturous admiration. Every fantasy Sir Edward had read was now before him in the lady herself. He saw the very soul of romance in the author, a true intimacy with hidden delights. Here he looked upon an explorer into the heart of human nature! Did she not each hour live in her art?

Mrs. Turner heard him with growing discomfort. She was, to be sure, as eager as any author to enjoy praise, as willing as any to hear her own work again from the lips of such a reader! Yet, that adulation as was here offered seemed to her even excessive—it verged on the preposterous. How little did this young man understand!

For the most part what she had written, she had done in melancholy, in disappointment, in loss. Her sense of the true had little to do with the escaping ladies of her own novels. Rather, nothing at all. And were the case to be properly set forth, there might remain more to be heard. And now, her admirer looked expectant. She could only accept his ardent tribute.

"You are too kind," said she warmly, "I make no claim to these laurels. Were I, alas, more often summoned to literary labor from artistic ambition, than from necessity, I should gladly wish to make that boast. Ingenious I may be, yet I am simply obliged to produce for the supply of the obdurate daily press. This, I fear, allows me to devise no more than those rough-hewn stories of distressed ladies who live yet in hope, to trace their anguish, and then to salvage them in good time, oh, miraculously! from disaster. I do, I confess, I *see* their suffering, and *feel* their distress. Secretly, can I even weep for them. Yet depend upon it, rescue my charges I shall—that, before too long—whatever their doleful circumstance.

"For so it must be in all my opera, wherein the sky, though it uniformly lours upon us in such narrations, will break forth on the conclusion, to cheer the scene. Yes, at that moment, at least, when we are about to part from it! Good Sir, I promise you, I *do* my share to gladden my ardent readers in what seems to be a virtually hopeless horizon for them; indeed, perhaps uniformly dismal for us all as well. So far, I may quite agree with you."

And she left off, looking dejected.

Emmeline Turner felt she need hardly go further; this was not the forum for subtle distinctions. Of her art, her hopes, she would not speak. And we must, in candor, question whether such discourse might not have proved something too far above the young man's comprehension.

Fortunately, there sat other listeners at table who were discerning. Charlotte Heywood particularly, finding herself touched by the author's protest, could not abstain—even from the distance at which she sat. Despite her resolution to guard herself from expressing any opinion upon the subject, she spoke up.

"But then, dear lady, what use of plot could be more apt than to bring in fine things, those rare attainments we await from a true artist? An accomplished storyteller, such as you are, need not provide us with runaways, abductions, pursuits, to assure us of her genius. Surely, your characterizations, your subtleties, allow your artistry to reign, whatever the vagaries of story may be. And too, for your own elevation, there is your poetry: no false note therein, and the allowance of that very melancholy that overshadows each of us. There, your path is free entirely of commerce, is it not?"

Mrs. Turner, looking down the table for the first time during the long evening, focussed her gaze upon this young lady. She was startled, and visibly gratified, to hear a fresh voice, and one with implicit sympathy with her plight as author. After so continuous chatter and empty talk, it sounded like enlightenment itself.

But Mr. Thomas Parker, who could evidently abide little serious exchange, intercepted cheerily. He remembered his youthful days as a student, "Was it not," said he, proudly, "ever the poet's reminder, 'that he, who casts to write a living line must sweat . . . upon the Muse's anvil— or some such advice?" This alerted even the dispassionate Sidney Parker to intercede in the lady's favor, "No, no, dear brother, Mrs. Turner does not speak of her toil, of labors, but of her artistic results. And Miss Heywood alone has heard her!"

He had early noted Charlotte at table; but, seated far from her, had not to this moment found his opportunity to salute her.

"Art, Madam," said he, turning towards Miss Heywood now, "is our great good fortune—we are its beholders, we are its listeners, its readers, its contemplators, its beneficiaries. Yet at what cost to those who create it? We seldom give thought to its demands, to the deprivation and the hardship—in short, the suffering—that contributes to our benefit. The price our creator pays is often heavy indeed, far too heavy."

Charlotte Heywood and Mrs. Turner could applaud the young man for such sympathies. And the former, again startled by him, was even more elated at hearing his words.

NINETEEN

Well it might be asked: What could better charge the imagination of a young man than the damsel in distress? What more admirably suit his heroic impulse? What serve to enhance the sense of his importance? In our enlightened days, when ladies abducted by tyrants who rule them without pity are little in view, such romantically inclined gentlemen need the more resort to ingenuity. Our valiant Sir Edward, for example, *could* do battle—even glimpse glory—in the rescue of a newfound community, a worthy seaside land rife with speculation.

Can we wonder then, that he was aflame with the passion to insure the future of Sanditon? His good aunt, and, better still—the lovely ladies of his acquaintance—should admire and salute his enterprise. Everywhere he turned, he could anticipate applause as the reward for his acumen. And little time was there to be lost. He must make his adieus and set out promptly for London.

Pressing as his errand was, the desire to advertise his mission before his departure proved more immediate. He would willingly confess to it. His urgent purpose was to be noticed by his latest admirer, the fair Clara Brereton. He should see to it that his devout idolater and potential *inamorata* had intelligence of it.

Private farewell with the lady, he could little hope for. Her duties at Sanditon House required her constant attention. These made a tender interval unlikely. What pretext might offer itself within the next hours to provide him opportunity? Desperate as he felt he was, he *would* find her, if but to alert her to this sudden desertion—a leave-taking demanding an indeterminate absence from his chosen.

As is wont with lovers, a means was promptly found. The gentleman determined to make his way to the Terrace, where each evening he knew her to take her stroll in the company of their relative. Somehow, there he must contrive a diversion to take Miss Brereton aside and speak to her.

Fortunately, the evening was accommodating. Strollers were about, ambling between the shops or settling upon benches to take the fine, brisk air. Miss Brereton, as usual, was to be found at the service of her mistress's arm, ready for whatever command. It seemed today that the whole of Sanditon society was illuminated in the splendid light of a waning sun.

Lady Denham, as she proceeded, greeted her ubiquitous acquaintance. Always she could relay something of importance to one or another, together with exacting instructions for acquisition and most effective management of Sanditon property.

That circumstance provided the eager Sir Edward opening for momentary, ample, if guarded, converse with his lady.

"Miss Brereton," he whispered, "Reluctant as I am, I must take leave of you, for our urgent business takes me off to London! Alas, dear lady, our fate is to be parted. How long such separation must be endured, I can not say. Yet such duty as I am charged to perform is of the most vital. Upon it rests all hope for the future, for the concerns of my dear aunt, and those we here cherish."

With this he paused, directing at her a look, solemn, pained; it seemed dejection almost overcame his courtly manner of elegant speech.

"When I might return to our friends in Sussex, and to you, I can not tell. By no means, before I have set to rights the economic ailments beset-ting our community; in short, when I can boast of my achievement. To reappear in triumph as this little Eden of ours takes its place in greater society! There can be no better consummation to be wished for Sanditon."

Clara Brereton looked upon that young hero in full silence. What on earth, she could wonder, accounted for this passionate posture; what, in this new cause? In truth, she had no understanding of what had so agi-tated him. This display was quite unlike his customary flutter, his store of excitement over the daring ventures of the idols he read in his novels. No longer was it Sir Walter Scottish ladies awaiting their reprieve, or Sir Charles Grandison, or occupants of Headlong Hall and Crotchet Castle.

Here was a genuine impetus for dramatic action. Reality had gripped him and seized hold, to the extent that he had come to recognize the cir-cumstance around him. Here he saw himself in the role he had ever searched for. The Baronet—a modern man of quality and connection—felt the importance of his superb gifts to his intimates; he foresaw the value they now promised for their future.

Miss Brereton checked herself, imperturbable. The dear, foolhardy defender; what drama in his anguish! To be gone from her now, without an idea of the duration of their parting? What could he mean by it? How should such wanton temperament serve Sanditon? Of what practical use would this champion be to his aunt's enterprise?

She looked about her, and saw the customary faces of residents, of cottages, shop keepers, heads of business establishments, the town's craftsmen, and a scattering of their visitors—all taking the evening air. In this peaceable view, there seemed little to urge a dash toward glorious deeds. What purpose might be satisfied? Would he have the royal party decamp from nearby Brighton, that they might uncover their little cove? What could be sweeter than the open beaches, the very absence of crowds? Tranquil spaces they now looked upon would have sufficed another.

She barely succeeded in uttering an assurance under her breath, when Lady Denham called her to heel.

As the group approached the milliner's shop, emerging from it, they could see Mrs. Parker and Miss Heywood. Sir Edward, having communicated his news, broke off and addressed this pair. Miss Brereton, somewhat surprised at his abrupt dismissal, looked on as he announced this latest boast to them.

"Ah, Mrs. Parker," he began proudly, "I come to assure you and your good husband both that the errand upon which your sister had dispatched me will ensure profitable expansion here upon the coast. You need no longer fret upon that account. The very grandest of your houses will soon be let for seasons to come. I shall be the means of that!"

He glanced the while at the young lady beside her. It gave him a certain air. "Our Sanditon, Miss Heywood, how little thought till now, or true attention has rested upon its future! It will soon be *ton;* yes, the very thing for discerning society. I have made it my business to look to its reputation among the arbiters of taste."

Charlotte heard him in good humor, even smiled to hear his boast, though, in truth, naught she knew of what he might possibly have had in his mind. She thought it best to nod as if with approval of the gentleman's flamboyance, but say little more.

Sir Edward not only found too perfunctory her response, he was put out to see her impassive. Did the young lady care nothing for strategy? Would she ignore brilliance and achievement?

No, it could not be left to stand thus. He would commence again his explanation of his great charge. But that moment espying their friends strolling nearby, he turned to the good gentlemen before him for support.

"Sirs," said he, greeting them and calling Sidney Parker and Lord Collinsworth closer, "you arrive in the very nick! Expose, if you will, to this young person the importance of my mission to preserve our dear Sanditon—more, to bring it into the real world."

The pair had been idling upon the Terrace to view the several other parties in their finery. They seemed without a care, and certainly innocent of the matter that now pressed hard upon Sir Edward.

"I can immediately rush, you see, to advertise our seaworthy charms among the fashionable clubs of London. I am to look to the image of our post here in Sussex, so little is it known, so little talked of; while its neighbors at Eastbourne and Brighton are much in the converse of the least wag in London, touted for miraculous cures, and commended to heiresses in search of the proper husbands. We are left behind, left far behind, while the season progresses apace. Miss Heywood will not understand, neither the necessity of planning, nor yet of action!"

Sidney Parker thought his performance hilarious. He addressed the lady with an assumed gravity of mien, suitable to the subject, "Miss Heywood, you would not deny Sanditon its proper place in the discourse of fashionable thinkers of our day? Only Denham, here, apprehends the means by which they can be seduced hither."

"Hardly, Sir," said she, keeping countenance. "I enjoy the sea air as well as the next, and would recommend it to every soul as wishes to breathe of it; but, to rush to London? Solicit comers? I am unaware what such an errantry must achieve. But then, my notions are merely of a practical nature. I agreed with your brother Thomas, in the matter of his search for an apothecary for Sanditon—a far more pressing need, to my mind, for his growing community. When those with every ailment shall come to seek salubrity hither, who will safeguard their infirmities? Of your smart world, I know nothing, nothing whatever."

"Do you then, Miss Heywood see only catastrophe for visitors who take the cure?" chided Sidney Parker. "And, here in Sanditon, will you speak in the mode of Cassandra, that we are to expect only illness and misery? Come, dear lady, are you then no believer in miracles?"

"You may," replied she, "make sport of the current fashion for cure. I do enjoy the good fortune of my own healthful constitution yet think myself as hopeful as any other, and can see much profit for those whose ailments suit the treatments. But, what of those ill-advised souls who convince themselves that Sanditon is apt for every other affliction? They are unguided, nay, destined for harm. A practitioner who is acquainted with the true possibilities ought to serve as the guarantor against excess, to prevent further injury, rather than securing from it pecuniary benefit. No, Sir, I consider self-regulation and care only as good as its author."

"My own sister will have it merely the fearful nature of our brother Thomas to think so. Diana will be first to tell you of his just punishment in being rushed off to search one out. Moreover, Lady Denham is herself of her view entirely. And for all his efforts, poor Thomas to this day limps. Yet, I will grant that it is indeed folly to expect cheerful faces about one, when invitations are abroad to every invalid in the land to bring himself to Sussex particularly for water cure? Somewhere in this puzzle, Miss Heywood, there lurks faulty thinking, I fear, though I myself cannot break it out."

With this, he laughed heartily. But Miss Heywood would not join with him. She enjoyed mirth, was drawn to the good-natured smile he turned upon her; but would not applaud his disinterest and its mockery—a sophistication that could only vex her.

He was something bemused to find her unwilling to engage in his gentle raillery. Could the serious young lady be right after all? His brother, soliciting the *invalides*, the wealthy, the genteel, the debilitated, the infirm—was he not inviting, as well, the most difficult, compromising, and worrisome in all of society? And would that not soon enough come to grief? Miss Heywood's anxiety for Sanditon's welfare, he must own, was perhaps not unfounded?

Sidney Parker returned to address his fair adversary in a sobered mood.

"I take your meaning, Miss Heywood. My brother's quest for an apothecary was wiser than its consequences. His is but an ankle, after all. The matter must be attended to, and soon."

It struck him that his family's folly had so long been a source of diversion to him, that he had lost a decent sense of responsibility towards his kin. So much in a different world to theirs had he lived, he had grown merely to relish their failings, and neglect any dangers they were too likely to engender. He felt himself chastened.

TWENTY

Neither rank nor riches affords ground for envy. So it is commonly contended. Yet, how avidly are means towards them sought! Far from idling in such enterprise had been our Esther Denham. This young person discovered even profounder dedication to the business, immediately she detected disaffection in the lady whose fortunes must determine her own.

So given to perpetual jealousy, and combining a suspicious temper with a cold eye, Miss Denham could not but sense the faintest of alteration in the atmosphere about her. Soon enough did she recognize at Sanditon House a darkening cloud.

Once—not too long ago—she would anticipate her own visits to their formidable relative, together with the dashing baronet her brother. They were solicited to attendance at the seaside estate. There Miss Denham's expectations were both cordially and elegantly met, if indeed with sometimes inadequate grace by her then newly-elevated aunt, a lady still anxious to secure her position in the line of that superior family.

Our Miss Denham had, in short, permitted herself to expect esteem from her aunt. During her early journeys into Sussex following the death of their uncle, Sir Harry, she had been as consistent in her duty as she was vigorous in the necessary rituals. After each arrival at Sanditon House, she awaited her aunt's latest overtures, giving them scrupulous consideration, to accommodate herself to every purpose.

Whilst her uncle lived, long had she sat in patience, silently watching as her dear, dramatic Sir Edward made his own distracted approaches to the unvoiced question. Though she regarded her brother able, even adept with the ladies—young or old—and was confident that he could, when at his best pitch, captivate, she instinctively apprehended that his ministration here should never succeed. Not with their canny relation. His good efforts, for all the flourish that framed them, could only come to nought. Alas, in the company of his aunt, sweet Edward's citations of poetic texts, his romantic persona that commanded such admiration elsewhere—all, stood stubbornly in his own way.

No, if there *were* to be hope, *she* must take into her own hands the courtship of her aunt. She had labored mightily in their cause at each visit to the seaside. And to whatever courtesies and valiant adulation, crooned with ohs, and ahs directed towards her aunt's person, the great lady had by degrees grown susceptible, and at last, even it seemed, hospitable. Miss Denham had cultivated an unwilling subject for her energetic blandishments. Her aunt was persuaded to accept compliments with an open mind.

Indeed, Lady Denham *had* wanted fair speech. Esther Denham's offerings were then as balm to the new widow. Brought soon after the unfortunate loss of her dear Harry, they both assuaged and confirmed her station. She welcomed to her side these young people of quality; she entertained them; she fussed over their comfort; set them forth on display; and almost regretted their eventual departures to Denham Park. Did they not exhibit elegant breeding? Bearing her name, did they not assure and affirm her claim to that distinction—to which she had aspired in effecting her second marriage? She was as reluctant to have them part from her; they seemed to take away with them the greater portion of that nobility.

It could not hold. Lady Denham was lately become mistress of a society, albeit one of her own invention. Here now was a woman of consequence, an assessor of tastes. The great lady of Sanditon, she it was to whom the community looked for such stateliness, and such occasional lavishings of pomp as she cared to expend. No more a person whose standing was ever dubious! Thus her earlier anxiety had faded into vague recollection.

In Esther Denham's return this year, she was at once struck by a sea change. Her aunt's disposition loomed in the giant form of ostentation.

Rudeness, shortness of temper, from that lady she was used to expect; but such unresponsiveness and indifference to her warmest words? Too much! She saw someone who seemed even disposed to slight their superior rank.

The Lady Denham received coldly her niece's various attempts at engagement, manifesting a distaste. No matter how the young Miss Denham now strove to strike at her fancy, appeal to her vanity, in short, to flatter, she was unable to regain Lady Denham's attention, let alone recover her former position of indispensability. What she was offered instead were shows of impatience; indeed more often, outright irritability.

Her own mortification by such a reception was depthless. And how little should it have required to bring Esther to confess it aloud! She, who had given so much of herself and so generously! It appeared ingratitude itself. Was that woman not the late-comer to their eminent family, a merest relation by marriage? Absolutely a woman of no distinction whatsoever? Yet, how accepting had been she and her brother, first to their uncle's ambitious lady wife, and then to his bereaved widow? How willing to welcome the novice into their superior society, to act in her interests, to sponsor, to tutor, to polish.

Suddenly, amidst her swarm of fresh associates—these transient lords and ladies, an Emmeline Turner, her Misters and Misses Parkers, her Misses Lambe and Beaufort, she could not acknowledge former friends. Did she need them not at all? Had they become merely relics of some ancient attachment, today's hangers on, excesses to be abandoned altogether?

There was yet more. As from nowhere, Clara Brereton had appeared to overshadow Miss Denham's ascendancy. Who was this creature, how might *she* merit attention from their aunt? Surely no more than an onlooker to good society; worse, the emissary of an impoverished London family. Even so, she had discovered this intruder installed in Sanditon House, to serve in *her* place as youthful mistress, and to displace her own wise counsel.

Of this turn, Miss Denham had determined to take no notice, at least at first. Since she had come to know her aunt, the lady was given to spontaneous enthusiasms. Miss Denham had watched these wane as quickly. Lady Denham's ever unsatisfied nature, her continuing restlessness, rendered her as easily disaffected as excited. Soon bored with those who would please her, she must fault all efforts to woo her too. She demonstrated crisply and liberally her exacting displeasure. Never mind. As next of kin, the claim of Miss Denham together with her brother must remain firm. There would be no concern on their part.

Still, the weeks came and went, and Lady Denham doted on Miss Brereton. Her "little discovery," it was implied, was not only apt, but the very solution for her oncoming age. Discomfited, Esther Denham mulled over their situation, pondering her next steps, determined to intensify her advances.

Until a conversation with her good aunt caused her of a sudden such dismay as to apprehend treachery.

"Dear Aunt," she had commenced one day, "you were much the talk of the gala. The young ladies from over the County, despite their sparkle, could not approach your own elegance. Beside your own gown, even my London import caught no eye—and I must willingly proclaim its perfection in pale lilac crepe, its embroidered silver to match its sash—and in a design I myself oversaw with particular attention to the month's fashion!"

To this came the rebuff, "My dear, I don't wonder at it. With Grafton House's most extravagant offering and a dressmaker accustomed to the satisfaction of royalty alone, my appearance was bound to be awaited by the select here in Sussex. Were you to observe the afternoon parade of the most solicited beaus and belles in Bond Street, you should encounter none to match it. Be assured, dear niece, even in the confines of our countryside, we do not lack. *We* need sacrifice nothing of our former grandeur. Rather, we may boast as well of *our* elite society as *our* taste!

Miss Denham heard; and quite suddenly it seemed to her that the Lady's words shifted the fixed zodiac into another constellation! Little might her brother have recognized this, or if he had, little would he have wished to take in its full import; yet for this sensitive attendant, it appeared with blinding clarity. No turning back was possible. They, her own relations, Esther Denham saw, must anticipate no further relief from that quarter.

Desperate measures were required for such a desperate hour. She must study their reversed situation. Still, scarce an alternative had presented itself heretofore, until the evening of the ball at Sanditon. Brought to her notice there were the gentlemen newly come from London, Mr. Sidney Parker, in the company of a notable friend.

The former, she had encountered all too frequently. Despite her own considerable qualities and accomplishments—pronounced excellent by all those who knew her—she went virtually unesteemed by this young man. With no difficulty, therefore, had she settled early on that he was undiscriminating, deficient in what constituted taste, thus to be dismissed as of little account in the ranks in good society.

Upon this occasion, however, with his reappearance beside a most fashionable associate, Lord Collinsworth, another prospect opened to her.

Alerted, the young woman had watched them from the moment they made their entrance into the festive room. First, she took note of the newcomer's stature, his well-formed and lean figure, his gentlemanly bearing; his graceful address. In his carriage alone, she discerned consequence. If ever there was one born to ease, it should be he. Next, she fell to studying the design of his apparel. That, too, was a revelation to the stylish Miss Denham, and what she saw fixed her opinion. Here was a man of some account!

Was not his the epitome of London-tailoring? Such smart country dress! How true the forest green of his frock coat with its gilt buttons, velvet black collar, and those fetchingly combined with the light drab of his kerseymere breeches and their drawn-in waist. Such dash, she knew, was to be observed only at the better clubs in The City—his figure stood too smart for provincial eyes.

Surely, save herself, no one present, could mark his distinction.

Nonetheless, within minutes the room was abuzz with talk of this stranger; nor were there lacking the particulars of his fine family, and his position as eldest son and heir to an ample estate in the North.

Miss Denham directed herself promptly enough towards the gentleman. Far too long had he been detained by her aunt, as if there was no other power capable of separating them. She made her approach determined to be that one, and waited beside them. Her aunt's eye must, at last, acknowledge her presence. Once introductions had been effected, the resourceful miss held him for more than a moment's converse.

Her rescue elicited gratitude; with a tactful glance, he thanked her, "Some ladies can truly work a miracle. One must be prepared to admire."

A felicitous beginning, which sped the young lady's thought forward. She pursued his further engagement.

"I gaze with astonishment about me," he had persisted. "To grace us tonight, your young women here in Sussex do themselves step forth as from a Classical vase. Your sisters and you in fine Greek drapery—seated upon Grecian chairs, and comporting yourselves with such splendid dignity. If I have ever imagined to myself the Ideal—ah, Miss Denham, this evening, I see before me the very *picturesque*. Strive to approach it, we may seldom alas, do we succeed."

Moving skillfully now, displaying her faithful adherence to the antique style, a dress cut high over the bosom, its full back, its bows of ribband from waist to the bottom of the train; gesturing lightly towards her turbaned headdress, completed by ostrich feathers, she protested, "Sir, we can not expect to equal your own standards of fashion; still we do what we can. Some of us do not allow our taste to fall behind, our allegiance to London, you see, prevails. We make it our business to be *tout-au-fait*."

Something surprised, the gentleman regarded her with a quizzical look. Curious she certainly had made him. And into his expression, she read enchantment. It was a moment! Miss Denham conceived then and there her diversion to the plan for her future. A man of property—a lord, hence of considerable consequence. Better still, a someone whose immediate response to herself spoke of potential.

Her mind danced forward, as a young lady's will. No more to pursue the arduous wooing of Her Ladyship, a thankless course, and moreover, demeaning. She need no longer entrust herself to a path in vain persuit of a goal ever-receding.

She could look elsewhere; she would strike out on her own. Over the years, had not these young people's desire for Lady Denham's good will been in expectation of her brother's assumption of his *rightful* place? And was she not ardently laboring to secure *his* fortune? Even, were their aunt to bequeath *all* to him, would Esther not continue to be beholden to that sometimes ill-advised and inept Edward? To depend on the largesse of such a fellow, albeit her own brother—that were too bleak a horizon for a woman bereft of means.

Before her rose a finer landscape. She saw a more practicable and level road toward gentility. Lord Collinsworth it must be who should provide her direct way. Enterprising, Miss Denham had ever been. Instead of their return home to Denham Park, she advertised her own plans to return to their quarters in London. The gentleman, courtly enough, offered his promise to attend her and her brother, immediately upon their arrival there.

Further rumination that same evening reinforced her resolve, as she paused to scrutinize her aunt's penniless cousin, Clara Brereton. That the creature had succeeded to ensnare the affection of Sir Edward, came as nothing new; lately, however, the girl's demeanor had altered, until exhilaration itself had begun to shine through. There was in her such a radiance, one that emanated only from the lively sensation that one is admired, valued, prized, even loved above every other.

Was her brother bewitched? Who could tell what tomfoolery he had given himself to, what rash promises might he have made?

In truth, precious little had passed between that pair. But for a Miss Brereton, such had been her deprived circumstances, she counted herself grateful for any notice. Expecting almost nothing, she embraced whatever her portion, no matter if grudgingly offered. If attention from that lively gentleman had its origin in his passing fancy, were it his mere diversion, she would make of it what she could. Were matters, in short, such as might turn by chance into true love, a lifetime of true devotion, she must attempt that happiness.

No such humility for a Miss Denham, herself, who instead looked no farther than to have the openly admiring, elegantly bred Lord Collinsworth.

Esther Denham was never one to embark upon any scheme that Esther Denham could not secure; or, for that matter, was she one to abandon her aims. Urgency now fortified her resolve to act. Indeed, the die had already been cast.

Part V

TWENTY-ONE

As was her habit in these sunshine days, Miss Heywood walked out early. All was then genial, the air softened, the blue of the sea a fair place to rest the eye upon. About her was a splendid stillness, for at that hour few yet stirred. Even so, to her amazement, on this particular morning, it was there among the moored fishing vessels that our Charlotte came again upon the latest addition to their colony, that lady feted and fussed over at Sanditon House.

Quite alone, Mrs. Emmeline Turner was to be seen threading her way through outcroppings above the sand of marram grass and tall sea buckthorn flowers. Her eyes cast down as though preoccupied, she seemed unaware that anyone had appeared within her notice. Yet, as the two came face to face, Charlotte saw that she could *but* make address.

"Accept my apologies, good Mrs. Turner," began she, "I do see your thoughts are far away, and want no voices from a pedestrian intruder to call you back. I will wish you good day merely, and continue on my way."

Mrs. Turner, however, in all civility assured the young woman of her recognition, begging her stay her steps. Was she not that same miss of her recent evening at Lady Denham's, who had been so brave to rescue her from tedium, and brought them all relief?

"Dear Miss Heywood, you can not rush away," was her plea, "I am glad to see you, and appearing yet more delightful in this morning's fine light. Do you take the early sea air so promptly? I myself have not failed to do so every day since my coming into Sussex. Indeed, I am certain—

that of all the cures we hear touted—though this should hardly be an opinion I would circulate widely at Sanditon—only the simplest can serve us. Thus, do I, like the rest, repair to the shore, whatever the weather! Never mind all those intricate formulations set forth by our best medical men, our Dr. Relhan and our Dr. Russell, or, for that matter, *any* other of their eminent colleagues. It is nature, I am convinced, nature alone, that opens its arms to my condition; it is nature that fills me with hope."

Here, she raised her head to breathe in the briny air.

Charlotte Heywood looked upon the lady appreciatively. "Yes, I do note it, Madam, how altered is your complexion even since our first encounter. Already, you seem renewed! Who knows, but that the sea and the Sussex sunshine sparkling upon it shall not prove your ministering angel. This light most certainly cheers one, it so enlivens and inspirits. I find my contentment just to walk over this blessed strand, and readily give myself to its magic. But then, our good Mr. Parker instructs us with his descriptions of those new-wrought harmonies between our body and its hidden depths, so eloquent he is in his reporting of the feats of restoration he sees daily. Yet surely, dear Madam, your own ailments cannot be of such a magnitude as *their* sufferers claim to possess."

The lady laughed heartily. "Indeed, child, despite our skepticism, his extravagant claims could prove accurate! Just think upon our own mood. Is it not altered by this innocent excursion? And does it not fix the case? Alas, while we ourselves could have little understanding of its turbulence, *we* are enmeshed ourselves by the forces of the universe! And we ought to obey them, or, so it would seem, for the sake of our health. Let us then oblige ourselves to do so. Our calmer minds may then follow our poor bodies as they must. So must we hope." She paused before continuing, as though to reassure her further thoughts in the freshness of the breeze.

"But Miss Heywood, how admirably did you speak out for me at Sanditon House. And how surprising is your comprehension of the hazards of artistry. Understanding in one so young, does, I confess, delight me. Few, who themselves do not do battle in the arts, so much as conceive the difficulties with which one contends—that constant exhortation to woo what is in these years idolized as "the greater public." Ah, such a legion of worshippers of novels designed only to please, and yet worse, to cajole! To be captive to readers who will never permit themselves the burden of thought, but desire only to be soothed, and lulled into sweet satisfaction. As their applauding to a contemplation of life—it is a vain hope.

"Nowadays, that is the reader I am urged to seek; such are coddled in London literary circles. To indulge these will soon drag us to a sorry place, I fear, a society bereft of refinement *or* civility. Then, too, Miss Heywood, I need not harp upon the daily obstacles to imaginative ventures ever planted in the path for those of our own sex. Our small voice, if at all welcomed in the marketplace, is heeded seldom, however grand our hopes for achievement."

Charlotte heard this lament with considerable interest. She was fascinated by the lady's display of candor. Little accustomed was she to serious talk, or meditation on any subject; certainly not here at the seashore. And, coming thus so freely from one informed.

To be noticed by this remarkable lady, and in this complimentary mode, delighted Charlotte. So agreeable was it—let it be granted here—our heroine was instantly won over.

While protesting that her words at Lady Denham's table had resulted merely from having heard such extravagance spoken—and confessing her impatience with exaggerated meaningless glorification—she modestly disclaimed any bias of her own. She hoped to be thought of an admirer, a reader; yet never more than a *dilettante*, nonetheless.

"It *is* true, she explained, "that though my family has never been so fortunate as to enjoy those many advantages easily assumed by urbane society—its reading and debating clubs, picture galleries, concert halls and pleasure gardens—we have, even so, found our country solutions. You see, Mrs. Turner, it has ever been my good father's fundamental conviction that an Englishman's first duty is to elevate himself above vulgar ways, to avoid boorish thoughts—to rise beyond what he calls, *bumpkin behavior.* His own belief—and he sees it to obtain alike for man and woman—runs that cultivation of an informed eye, ear, hand, and mind must be always foremost in our education.

"Thus, have we—we many young Heywoods—been given every encouragement toward learning. Our diligent parent has provided us with books to the purpose, and, with them, so much stimulation as to keep us industrious and dedicated. For, in my family, dear Madam, it is the custom always to read aloud our books, and amongst us all.

"You can imagine the consequence. There was never a lack for converse with my brothers and sisters at home. We stood, not ready to study only and appreciate, but question and always to argue what we heard. Sometimes, when recognizing nonsense, I confess, we could not help but laugh aloud. Yes, Mrs. Turner, for little could escape *our* notice, there were so many of us together! Whether it was in the histories we perused, romantic or Gothic tales, travellers' journals or philosophical treatises, we must have our say, disputing with one another often. How I did love," the animated young lady now concluded, "such evenings at home! I ranked them above any other amusements. There it was I found a sense of myself and a way to view the world."

Charlotte paused, abashed. Theirs was but a chance encounter. She feared she had a spoken too plainly and too long.

Mrs. Turner felt no such compunction; indeed, she welcomed these spirited recollections from Miss Heywood. Engrossed by her depiction of her life at Willingden, she would know more.

"It is my turn to admire your pursuits," she offered. "What happier company for the acquiring of cultural refinement than one's own family? No, my dear, that is never to be regarded as the property of sophisticates exclusive to London. I commend your estimable father. As for whatever diversions your education may have lacked by its seclusion, artful works remain in place; they shall be available to you as you choose to seek them. Miss Heywood, you are young yet, and will, I hope, encounter a great many people, enjoy beautiful places, and take pleasure in adventurousness when you are ready."

Encouraged, Charlotte persevered, pursuing her first thought.

"You see, Mrs. Turner," she said, "I had once assumed mistakenly that those who read broadly must prosper through greater understanding. In that I was mistaken. Since I have come into the society here at Sanditon, I have discovered that this is infrequently the case. Reading in books, the many and various portraits of good and evil as are recorded, *may* offer wisdom, discernment, and perhaps the power of judgment—but who is to say what we ourselves can take from them? Even Mr. Richardson's genius, for example, assures no such benefit. His villains seem so alive, they preoccupy; to some young men even seem heroic models. His world does so intrude, Madam, that one can hardly surmise from his telling what it is to suffer the saddest of experience."

Mrs. Turner understood her at once, and laughed. But, of course, she thought it as well to say nothing to mock the notions of the preposterous young man so subtly alluded to. Yet charming did she find Miss

Heywood's puzzlement; more so, her earnestness, and concern.

The ladies walked on, conversing comfortably. Upon parting, they determined when to meet again, appointing the bright hour before the dippers brought their charges down to the water, or the town began to stir.

Thus they did, encouraging an easy friendship that suited them both entirely. Mrs. Turner continued eloquent not only on subjects related to her own work, but upon her particular favorites among books, and her love of the poets; always, she found in Miss Heywood a mindful recipient for her every contemplation.

The days passed, the older lady's mood was heartened by her new friend's eagerness to listen and to learn from her; while she herself was struck by the lively intelligence she saw before her. It is true also that she was much affected by the young person's so very warm anxiety for the welfare of her affectionate hosts.

As for Charlotte, this chance acquaintance proved the happiest diversion she could have proposed for herself since leaving home. Spellbound by the distinguished lady, she was grateful for her attention, and grateful to attend her. Each recounting by Emmeline Turner—whether of visits to theaters in the West End of London, to artists' studios in Covent Garden, or her frequentation of meetings with other writers at coffee-houses—seemed to the country bred Miss Heywood the dearest stuff of her dreams.

The beauty of the fair Sussex coast that had captivated her upon arrival made the more lustrous by delightful talk with Mrs. Turner; what greater pleasures were there to be had?

Still, one morning, Mrs. Turner related some local news she had heard; and it gave rise to alarm in Miss Heywood. Apparently Mrs. Turner had been visited the previous afternoon by Lady Denham, who honored her with the important revelation of a development of some consequence. It should, she had said, particularly interest Mrs. Turner, that the lady announced greater designs for Sanditon's expansion.

"We have long wished, Mrs. Turner," had her Ladyship begun, "to provide splendid, truly elegant lodgings for our distinguished visitors, already growing in numbers. I am proud to say that our Waterloo Crescent, promptly to be embarked upon, will inaugurate that plan. Since I have assured Mr. Thomas Parker, my coadjutor, that no sacrifice can be too heavy for the purpose, he has consulted his bankers as well.

There is to be no delay. We shall have quarters to match Cheltenham, to equal Brighton, certainly, to excel anything proposed in upstart Brinshore." Mrs. Turner had attended carefully, yet heard all of this in some confusion. Had she not, too, she asked Miss Heywood, only lately noticed vacancies within the ancient town? Was construction for shortages not then something precipitate? How might the need for lodgings be so much increased?"

Charlotte listened to these words with some perplexity. Large investments in building had indeed been spoken of during the short time Miss Heywood had been a guest of the Parkers; but always Mr. Parker demurred. To be sure, he had countered, his own interest in the making of the most wonderful Crescent was as intense as her Ladyship's. For him, such a project was, alas, the Waterloo that must inevitably follow upon the triumphant construction of his own Trafalgar!

While the gentleman's fortune, his land, his family heritage were ample enough, and could comfortably serve himself and his family's daily need—even, could it maintain his old properties while he himself was absent—still, its reserves were sorely taxed. Well he knew, that in proposals for speculative development of a larger enterprise, there was vastly more at stake, sums he could ill afford. Already, had he contributed generously in the restoration of the Assembly Rooms and the erection of the Circulating Library. Charlotte wondered what it could mean, with his assets so constrained, to push now upon his budget like this?

In quieter moments together, an anxious Mrs. Parker had hinted at her fear of overextension; even, protested to her charge that such an ambitious undertaking was a worry.

"I often think," she had confessed, "about our old surroundings. Why, you yourself saw the vegetables from our kitchen garden, Miss Heywood, how fine they grew there. We do not surpass them even here at the shore, no matter how we do strive; they do not seem near so sprightly somehow. That was a simpler life we led. Our Trafalgar House is so much more grand, more suited to Mr. Parker's tastes. I do suppose that in years hence, once the saplings come to their growth, our own prospect promises to equal Lady Denham's fine position."

"To be sure," she paused, checking herself in such futile contemplation, "all that was before Mr. Parker dedicated himself to the cause of benefitting our health and happiness. We ought not question his wisdom in these matters."

Upon hearing Mrs. Turner's report, Charlotte sighed. She must wonder, what good would come of extravagance continued? Lady Denham, she knew, was transfixed by her ambition for their seaside wonderland. Nor would she rest upon the completion of Waterloo Crescent. Sanditon *must* have everything; a theater perhaps, or a concert hall; certainly, the delights of a pleasure garden. Everything must contribute to its prominence among society's elite. Her position, her fortune, her very person, depended upon that emergence.

Were the whole of the Parker family then blind to the hazard of the situation? Would none speak out, to save them before it was too late?

Charlotte wondered where it must end.

TWENTY-TWO

So preoccupied was Sir Edward by his determination to fulfill the momentous mission he had undertaken on behalf of his aunt, that he took little notice of his sister's own enlivened countenance during their journey up to London. Had he attended at all to her prattle, he might, have detected a chirp in Esther Denham's delivery; this, the effect of an exhilaration over Lord Collinsworth's anticipated call. Little could distract the adventurer from his errant purpose; barely upon arrival at their quarters in Ryder Street, he was off again on his way to Piccadilly.

Soon he could be discovered amid the crowds milling at Brooke's. He felt sure of a distinct assortment here of gentlemen; select society, ministers to the Crown, even, it occurred to him, the Prince himself, together with his royal circle of immediates. Available, too, at this establishment—unlike Boodle's, Wattier's or even White's was an abundance of credit; withal, a genteel distance in the billing. Among such advantages, this idolater of the fair sex counted a still greater titillation. For there, to be gazed upon—to be encountered at play—were the most fashionable ladies of the Club.

The presence that very evening of such persons as Lady Archer and her daughter, together with Lady Buckingham, secured in those about him a decent gravity of manner. Still, conviviality was the rule here. It was preserved, even as the serious business of gaming proceeded apace at three tables set out in the Queen's Drawing Room. Whatever the play chosen—be it faro, macao, jeu d'enfer, blind-hookey, or hazard—and however large sums might there be exchanged, Sir Edward knew *these players* were up to any reversals. All was civility in their settlements. With respectable company such as were there assembled, where was there meanness to the sport?

He felt certain of finding among this group those people of taste he sought, to whom he might expatiate upon the excellences of Lady Denham's Sussex retreat, extol the virtues of "immersion into the deep," exalt the latest cures, and cry up the properties of the salt sea water over the inland variety, such as the chalybeate spring of Tunbridge Wells, or the waters at Bath.

Within the hour, he was comfortably engaged and whetted for gaming. He sat at table amongst eminent company, his own inclination mounting, his fascination with deep play in evidence, as he mused over each turn of the cards; best of all revelling in that moment when his canny move carried off the wager's cash upon the table!

Calculations firm, Sir Edward's was a cool manner and a sure hand; what he saw in the expression of his fellow gamesters was the ease of such triumph. This was temptation indeed for poor Denham. Almost, at that moment, the young man had been turned from thoughts of his arduous errand—the rescue of his community's enterprise—toward the smoother, surer rewards he saw before him.

Just then, Lady Archer addressed him, "And are you, Sir, among those bitten by our mania, who worship only the demon of play?"

Upon hearing her, he was something taken aback. To be thought a gambler merely! Bitten, incurable? Never. His breeding, his devotion to study, his achievements, his erudition, all his heroic nature rebelled within him. Always had he conceived himself as nobler of mind, of mettle greater; for he was such an one never to succumb to common excesses! The *man of feeling* was brought sharply to his senses.

Quick as he was to protest to the lady, that his was no such predilection—most certainly not he—Sir Edward continued altogether genial. Of course, he could laughingly confess to *occasional* pleasure at cards.

"My own delights are many, Madam," and raised himself to exhibit his fine carriage, "I have been known to make a trifling wager now and then, and even will admit to certain skills in that quarter. Yet, I choose to look instead towards nature for the true wonder and for a glorious reward. For example," and as he spoke he bowed to the Lady and her daughter, "I devote myself to the admiration of beauty wherever I find it, and *that*, even now I see before me. In truth, if I might claim for my own any demon, dear Madam, it would surely be my worship of womankind."

The Lady listened to the handsome young flatterer as he ran on. "Indeed, my character, I find, is prone to enslavement to the Ideal. There, my imagination takes fire. I am ever compelled to seek out wisdom in poetic creation. Thus do I remain an ardent reader, bound to the intricate music of that Scotsman, Robert Burns, and the faithful disciple of the dashing Lord Byron."

"But, dearest Lady Archer, if you speak of pleasures at sport, when it comes to that, nothing truly engages fancy as much as the excitements of the turf. There can I find superb inspiration—not only in the green splendor of the outdoors, but in the most admirable beauty of exquisitely bred champions. Besides," said Sir Edward, lowering his voice, and looking confidingly at her, "the stakes encountered are not so high as in tonight's play!"

The Lady had by now taken his measure. She leaned back in her chair and peered through her quizzing glass to view this person of such decided opinions, and so ready in their expression.

"You are fortunate indeed, Sir" she declared, "for in this very room is the only knowledgeable gentleman of all of London. He is himself the owner of some of the finest running horses of the kingdom." She turned towards a rather frail person of middling size at another table, to call him to her.

"Mr. Dawson," she announced, "you see before you an admirer of horses, an enthusiast of exploits on the turf. He takes small interest in our own little amusements, despite his winnings tonight! I regard this something of a pity, to be sure," added she, addressing herself for the first time to the silent daughter who sat beside her, "for we take delight in the presence of decorative young people, do we not, Isabella?"

The solicited Mr. Matthew Dawson slowly approached, ready to inspect our gallant.

"Denham? Denham, did you say? Never heard of the name," was his curt dismissal. "I know no such breeder, your Ladyship. Nor do I recollect him visible at Epsom or Newmarket."

Turning to the gentleman himself, he saluted him impatiently.

"A regular attendant at our meetings upon the turf? If so, Sir, how curious it is that we have not found you there? Can it be that your enthusiasm seeks out the new fads—those steeple chasers, who lately run wild over the countryside for extended distances. Madness, I assure you, lately imported from the Irish, where tradition counts for nought, where the horses are fat, their riders encouraged to jump our gates, and despoil our gardens in their gallop through every property. Perhaps, it is this lunacy you prefer for your equestrian sport?"

Sir Edward respectfully demurred. He would explain that only as an admirer of beauty did he speak, and that of the perfection of the traditional meet, those graceful, flat racings between the finest of lines. How well he remembered the splendor of *Sultan*, the glory of *Eclipse*. They had inspired his youth! As often as he could—and such was no great claim— he must make his way towards those remarkable champion animals. And even when he could not, he took his turn wagering upon them at Tattersall's in Hyde Park.

"As I see it," he intoned, "there is purity, imagination, even art, to the practice. To breed champions, to choose the mares to foal them, to watch the eager colt emerge, see him stretch and grow in the pleasant heath or downlands into an exquisite specimen of horseflesh—what greater pleasure than such, the feeding, the development, the exercising, the long wait. To look upon a yearling and witness his breaking; and further on, to behold the fine two-and three-year old thoroughbred perform. How fine the swiftness of their movement; how rare their staying power in the run. Just to contemplate a four-mile heat without the hint of a breaking down was in itself a joy."

"Surely, Sir, this must prove the most elevated of pastimes. Even, it could be thought noble, for I am told that the Regent—at least when not wholly absorbed in the elaboration of his colossus at Brighton—boasts of his own grand specimens. They are his pride, even while the Derby continues a preoccupation for him. Yes, noble, indeed! I do envy you the enterprise."

Matthew Dawson heard the young man's passionate recitation. It softened him towards him; and the two continued in an exchange of knowledgeable chat for some while, before Denham could allow himself to come to the point.

"Yet, I do confess to have wondered at those continual reports of sad decline at Epsom. How it has grown reduced in these years, even subject to the most chaotic practice. There are, I hear it told, neither lists nor barriers at these races, where the onlookers—and lately they are said to be not always of quality—find themselves encouraged to gesticulate, to shout aloud, to induce general hullaballoo! Are such doings not a scandal? Do you not yourself see them objectionable?"

Just so! Purely a descent to chicanery, and more," said Dawson. "It is become a trial to both horse and breeder; it is a mockery of the races themselves."

"Would it not," ventured the young advocate finally hitting home, "be opportune then were such majestic enticements available at a wholly new site, to seek some other location, altogether? I speak of a future for racing upon a course nearby the coast's most spectacular views, in the vicinity of an engaging society recently emerged, at a seaside haven in the county of Sussex? This choice region is already upon everyone's lips; it is the season's best discovery."

His listener was confounded by the suggestion; yet quite ready to hear more.

"Epsom is a shambles, indubitably," confessed Dawson. "Indeed, Sir, such runs as we see on race days through Fleet Street in the vicinity will not satisfy any gentlemen of quality. But—at such a remove, I wonder?"

His poetic interlocutor countered, "How might you doubt such an ideal attraction as Sanditon, good Sir? It combines with the lure of the sea, the possibility of miraculous cure through the bathing holiday? Even now, its esplanades stir with sparkling potential, its Waterloo Crescent is well into construction, magnificent lodgings to house its many newcomers. And, think, it is situated closer to London even than Brighton or Weymouth! With a fine new turf, a glorious run upon a course of such promising aspect with, a sea wind to speed the animal along—be assured, London, Sussex—all England—will come looking for the prizes."

The gentleman stared at Denham, who stood delighted with himself and his oration. Fortunately for the success of his argument, just then a familiar figure approached. It was Lord Collinsworth, the same elegant person carried to Sanditon by Sidney Parker. He had that moment arrived and taken up his customary place at table. Denham saw renewed possibility, and acted upon it.

He alerted Collinsworth to his presence, and had barely greeted him before he resumed where he had left off, steadily pursuing his claim.

"How auspicious to find you again, Collinsworth, and so lately returned from the very place I just now cry up to my companion."

Presenting Dawson to his friend, he bid *him* report more exactly upon Sanditon's extraordinary position over the sea, the graces of its upcoming society, and more.

Collinsworth, though taken by surprise, was up to the task, and not unwilling. Yet Dawson, in truth, needed no introduction for him. The young Lord, with more than passing acquaintance with the world of thoroughbreds, recognized this notorious figure about London, one he had encountered before this.

He ventured merely a judgment of what he had seen, "An enchanting township, advantageous in its position. A fine beach, and every summery breeze of the southern shore. I'll warrant, you'll find there as well the best dippers of any spa upon the Coast."

"Ah, but Denham here," interjected Dawson, "proposes a racing course for the vicinity. He would see it become a center for the sport. What do you say to that, Collinsworth?"

"To be sure. What better locale for gentlemen wagering upon best of breed? A desirable notion, no doubt of it."

Dawson thought a while, clearly taking notice. He looked pleased to hear him. The prospect of developing such a turf could not but appeal. With the presence of eager company to support it, it enticed him.

The project hatched, Sir Edward left in triumph. What could provide for Sanditon's future more securely than development of a fine racing course in its reach? Would it not bring enthusiasts to its shore?

Eager for his evening's gaming, Collinsworth turned his attention away, but not before inquiring briefly after Miss Denham's well being and offering his determination to call upon them before long.

To a jubilant Sir Edward, nothing could be more agreeable. As he now conceived it, this evening's labor had been successful in every way. His industry in the interests of Sanditon was barely begun. His thoughts were turned forward and set upon the coming Assembly at Almack's, where he hoped to gather in for their society the best of this year's crop of London heiresses.

TWENTY-THREE

With distractions mounting so about her, Charlotte's hours of leisure were fewer with each passing day. Already, she knew, she had gone too long since dispatching her last missive to her family. She sat to the purpose:

Dearest Papa, she began,

If I have not in these weeks been very exact as to my letters, I depend upon you—you, before every one else, gentle Papa—to grant me patience. In the while, I ask but one further mercy, that you give reassurances to my sweet mother, to all my sisters and brothers—to the whole of our family— of my continued welfare and indeed eupeptic state amongst the Parkers of Sanditon. Explain to them, this much at least, of my current neglect, that truly, there is cause!

For hereabouts—and I willingly confess to it—along this coveted coastal haven, with the gentle breezes and its translucent moistness of the shore, land where the air is so favored, scented with just that delicate touch of salt mixture to give it divinity—and where even the vasty deeps do present a peaceful current to all comers—each moment's delirious business, every frenzied impulse to take the plunge, diverts your most dutiful daughter from her proper attentions to her dearest family. Alas, she too begins to wonder, hardly to know anymore, what ought to be thought seemly.

Sir,—and I do ponder upon it—what might be thought of your own pilgrim set here within this greater world? How, in effect, could yourself make her out amid these brilliant practitioners? Indeed, when every minute of the day or night, and all about, there are such great stirrings, and exorbitant degrees of energy expended—all in the cause of securing health! And these, so invested, that the new regimens outdo for variety, and change, every former remedy!—What might you say to it all?

For myself, I do yet find the whole of it inspiriting. How heartening to see fervor in man and woman, young and old, in those who suffer but the mildest of complaints as well as those who must endure frail and sickly. Equally, do they charge towards their rewards—a fitter body, a reformed spirit—and longer life. So far away from the distraction of the fouled City, it would seem, such tonic exercises guarantee them greater moral aims and, moreover, convince them that they can then permanently forswear disorderly or illicit conduct upon their return!

Staggering it is, at first, to contemplate such efforts; yet I vow, something wonderful, miraculous even. Still, the mere contemplation of such goings on proves distracting. Thus, dear Papa, do I make my case—to excuse my own lapse; for as you can see, such antics are lately become almost my preoccupation.

Just the other morning as I returned to my sun-filled room upon the hill at Trafalgar House, I encountered a scene that must serve to instance my meaning. There before me was the youngest brother of our new-found friends, my good hosts, Mr. and Mrs. Thomas Parker. Arthur Parker is a gentleman of some twenty-one years, whose former exertions, it would seem, were severely limited, and whose exposure to any provocative circumstance during the whole of that short lifetime was virtually non-existent.

To my view, Papa, the fellow might be deemed rather an invalid, although to look upon him, you might never so much as suspect it. God knows, to me he appeared robust enough upon his arrival here. One would have surmised that, until recently, it was his own excess of appetite which contributed his vast girth. Certainly, it left me no doubt that his never-ending complaints issued from that burden alone. Yet, this early of a morning, here before me stood the young man, and he, in the fantastic process of being led by the dippers to his frigid renaissance.

You will remember, dear Papa, I speak of an individual who but a fortnight ago would not venture out of doors were there a hint of a breeze, so possessed he was by the certainty that some attack of the lumbago should render him powerless. The same gentleman who, when his close guardians; the Parker sisters arrived in the neighborhood of Sanditon's salt laced air, had stood in fear for his very life!

Even so, after the very first light of dawn, and full in the nippy air, he now appeared all readiness, barely clothed and in highest expectation of an icy plunge! All for the sake of adjusting a newly-found harmony between body and sea. And why? Merely to suit this new faith!

His immediate address was bold—to inquire regarding my own inclinations. Would I not myself have courage to take up the challenge? Did I not wish to improve my state?

"Dear Miss Heywood," was the cry, and this delivered with a zeal akin to that of a singing Evangelical, "If you do not partake, you are remiss in your duty to yourself, and to the health of your spirit! You too must come to know that pleasure in the whipping of the waves! The sea, you will soon find, offers you qualities: its brine, its brisk temperature, and above everything its magnificent turbulence."

"Consider, dear lady, even though it may act as extraordinary threat to one's being—to confront the violent waters in jeopardy, to be swept under, or struck by the full force of its swell—ecstasy! Yet, in the marvel of the here and the now, all this is without risk, without the loss of one's footing! Ah, the sensation of peril, and all the while, miracle of miracles—it is but counterfeit danger truly—for faithful attendants stand in wait, prompt to rescue. I tell you, Miss Heywood, a new spirit is born of it. Dramatic modifications create prodigious upheavals in the body, stir nervous fluid in the organs to bring forth your true energy. Thus is it that you gaze today upon a stronger, fitter, worthier man."

What response could I make, dear Papa? For I remained stunned altogether. The perplexity of his sudden alteration! To be so exposed to such violent means to health and well-being! There seemed little to account for it! Yet this much I will acknowledge. The Arthur Parker I now looked upon was something more animated than that lethargic laggard I had first met at Sanditon. And, when all is said, who am I to doubt renewal in any man?

So you see, Sir, I am witness here to revolution, of a sort. There may be no armies or gunpowder, but our coastal soldiers must be accounted as valiant as any who serve upon a battlefield. You may count upon it, they are survivors of the strictest of regimens, who then—wonder of wonders—show visibly the stronger for all their pains!

Unlikely it may seem, Papa, but there is more yet to this hearty tale. Other crusaders follow Arthur to take up the course as well . One among them is a timid young person, a certain Miss Augusta Beauford. She is the elder of two sisters in the care of a Mrs. Griffiths, who makes her daily appearance in company of her various aspiring young ladies. Of frailer stock even than her contemporaries, that ingenious miss shivers through the whole of the process, yet seems willingly to return to fight on undeterred, with the first light of each day.

One must presume that such devotion is to the interest of strengthening her constitution. Yet, Papa, I cannot but wonder, after all, if it is that improvement she seeks, since this young lady during that ordeal gazes down the beach toward the gentleman's own station. Had I not noted a partiality between herself and our own Arthur Parker, I should never have thought to doubt her motive.

You will, I trust, not mistake my meaning, dearest father, for in the bathing cure there is no intermingling. The ladies continue their regimes always remote from any that the vigorous gentlemen embark upon. Yet, many a curious party, will in the process—for why not?—study the comings and going to the beach, perhaps to manage even a salute in passing. So, in encounters upon the Terrace, where discussions persist upon the efficacy of their cures, those who have partaken may finally succeed in voicing their passions. How tirelessly they review their morning's exertions during the leisurely strolls of the mild later day! How self-acknowledged in their achievements! Such compliments, as "transformation," "metamorphosis," are much pronounced by them, in an unlimited enthusiasm. They seem transported. I find it jolly enough to watch their flirtatious exchange. Better still, to witness in them Arthur Parker's emergence. For, with our recent loss of more presentable prospects to interest the young ladies—such as Sir Edward Denham, or Mr. Parker's other brother, Sidney—who lately dispersed to their commitments in the City—Arthur has found himself promoted to the forefront of Terrace chatter. And, since Mrs. Griffiths' charges have themselves had been instructed in their social duties, they quickly seek out what quarry remains.

Arthur certainly thrives in the attention. I warrant that for his adult life not a word that young man ever spoke among his good sisters was ever attended. Yet, here he stands, upon any evening, heroic against the kind breezes, discoursing broadly upon his research, his innovations, his private path to renewed vigor. All this, solicited and applauded by eligible young ladies. Is it any wonder that he flourishes? I would but add that notable already is a more decided bonus: the clearly discernable narrowing in the gentleman's waistband!

But by now Papa, I have delighted you long enough with news, outlandish conduct, and, I do freely confess it, the most idle conjecture. Let me turn instead to the best of my encounters, to report upon a lucky meeting here at Sanditon, and one that has resulted in a friendship that I do cherish. Since the arrival from London of Mrs. Emmeline Turner, who is native to nearby Lewes, and who has lately returned in hope to restore her own calm along her childhood's seascapes, my own enjoyment in Sussex, though already ample, has grown prodigiously.

She is a figure of some literary distinction, whose name, I know must be familiar to you. Nor can I doubt that you will applaud my having made such a valued acquaintance, for she is most private. The lady's fondness for walking out at the early morning hour, together with my own inclination to the same, brought us together for these regular exercises.

In its course, came the delight of conversing with a learned, temperate, and wise lady. How can I describe the privilege to have encountered one such as she? We talk upon any subject, without reserve; our discourse has no boundaries, we delight in the contrast of colors of sea and sky, in the taking a survey of the stars in their course. We range over every possibility, books she has written, the novel she now labors upon. Her learning introduces me to works she enjoys, and even it provides me with some new volumes she has carried here to Sussex.

In this lady's company, it is as though I were back with you again for our evening reading—and all that I have missed from home. Here in the open air, in the sea's light, does our contemplation run on, for as we go briskly upon the strand, so we take further delight in extending the reach of our minds.

Moreover, Mrs. Turner is intimately familiar with these shores. She points out the special peculiarity of each fissure in the cliffs, and shows me every hidden turn into the secret coves. We study the sea birds as they fly over us, watch porpoises leap up from the blue. Each day do we venture further on in our investigations, as eager seamen just come ashore from a long voyage. This wild coast appeals the more by her tutelage.

Only yesterday, as we emerged into a space new to us, we came upon a cave cut into the sandstone rock cliff, and were curious to see within. We stepped through its high arch, and gazed into the darkness of what might have been a passage into a deserted tunnel.

All about were wooden tubs, some scattered inside the cave and others hidden outside behind the shrubs. Good-sized they were, and seaworthy; and we wondered at how the bare-legged local folks who labor over the sand to gather their cockles, sea slugs and crayfish were served by them.

The fishermen were respectful enough in response to our inquiries; but would tell us very little altogether. Even so, we could not help but become aware of activity all about us. There was an eagerness to keep us in ignorance of their purposes; indeed, they seemed to wish to send us on our way again.

Mrs. Turner turned me about immediately, expressing a wish to see us from that place as fast as our legs would carry us, and we took our leave. Only as we recovered the distance to our own Sanditon cliffs, was she ready to speak of what had seemed strange to me in that cove.

"I have heard of the trafficking on our shores," she offered, "and the dangers of this industry. To stumble upon it thus, in broad daylight, is more than I could have foreseen. Yet, dear Miss Heywood, it seems that we two have managed to do just that."

So you can see, dear Papa, unlike our quiet Willingden, there is much of curiosity, and of intrigue, to be found along these shores even as one stirs out. Such as can not be imagined among the gentle hills of our peaceful farming county. This strange, open, ever shifting shoreland, each day uncovers for us adventures, even mystery.

To my sweet family, I now send my love, continuing to trust that this finds you all well. I dare now demand prompt reply from Willingden. There must certainly be a greater supply of you ready and willing to accomplish that task! I, too, promise no further delay in answer. And will write again with word of my pioneer doings in this unpredictable world beside the open sea.

Your very affectionate daughter,
Charlotte

Postscript: Alas, I have just learned of Mrs. Turner's imminent departure. Too sudden it is. She must to London, she informs me, and that, immediately! I am overwhelmed by her kindness, Papa, for she has offered to take me with her!

She calls it "high time" for my introduction to so many things she feels my education now lacks.

"Indeed, Miss Heywood, you ought to come. Let me show you the City's riches, put on display for you its wealth. Just to stroll with me to the galleries and museums, walk in the parks, spend evenings at one of its theaters, will make up the difference."

Dearest Papa, shall I take her invitation up? Might I go? And would you not consider treachery itself my leaving Sanditon, after what I only just now have written? Perhaps. But, even so, please write me soon, and send your permission.

Part VI

TWENTY-FOUR

*E*ver a fancier of the finest specimens in horse flesh, and more particularly of that nimble, galloping sport wherein such champions excel, Lord Collinsworth was enticed by the fortuitous encounter with Sir Edward at Brooke's. Indeed, his daily London rounds too often consisted, it seemed to him, of a ceaseless struggle to overcome propriety and boredom. This unexpected promise of the potential for yet another locale for amusement—a dazzling course of thoroughbreds visible upon the hard white sands of Sussex—much enlivened the avid sportsman, posing for him a delightful alternative, and even, perhaps, an extended program.

Persons of ancient family like himself seldom rise early. But this day, despite himself, he would make the attempt. It might hasten the completion of vital errands in Bond Street, where he was currently immersed in that perpetual challenge confronting fashionable young men—the maintenance of exactitude in attire. If Collinsworth had long understood that to cut a figure in his presentation was essential, especially he had come to appreciate a more subtle characteristic of *his* social set: to attract attention by one's dress merely, was the supreme mortification. He had made foremost *his* practice, to ascertain his own natural impeccability before venturing forth.

Unlike the dandies now peopling London society, whose pretensions to grandeur were founded exclusively upon the brazen statement in their clothing—an ilk, who were established and sustained through display and sham alone—Lord Collinsworth comprehended, that he, an aristocrat born, required no such ancillary. Wherever one turned—at the smartest engagements, whether the openings at Drury Lane, a select evening in Brighton, a dance at Almack's, or, lounging at the turf in Epsom—the beau was encountered by the dozen. In these unquestioning days, he yearned for distinction from their kind.

To conclude affairs swiftly today was thus his aim, to make it a point, before proceeding, of looking in early upon his good friend Sidney Parker with his news. The hope was that this gentleman would accompany him and make their presences felt in Ryder Street.

Parker was indeed to be found at home; but when this young man was alerted to late developments, he showed no surprise. In Sidney's view, Denham's early appearance in the City, or, for that matter, his command at the gaming tables were news hardly unanticipated. Something other, however, was the revelation of Sir Edward's prompt success in enlisting to his purpose a well-known London horse breeder for the watering place. This intelligence did give Sidney Parker pause.

"Does this gentleman then," was his incredulous query, "propose to remove his own stables all the way to Sussex for the running of horses?"

When Collinsworth gave his assurance that just such was the scheme, the discovery put Sidney into a perplexity regarding the advisability of it. He doubted its soundness; and could only wonder at the interest of the sportsman himself! Even to contemplate such a plan troubled him, though he asked himself why that should be? Only later did he dismiss his anxiety with a characteristically skeptical shrug at the extravagance of the proposal.

"Sir Edward Denham's grandiloquent manner has won him over? A remarkable achievement! But depend upon it, Collinsworth, such racing enthusiasts are not to be duped. Denham may be earnest-minded, dedicated in the presentation of his case—and, I will confess it—as a man who wholly believes himself, he is the sort not to be contested—yet in the company of a shrewd breeder of champions, a keeper of running horses, and moreover, a dealer in large sums, there could well be more to it than we suppose," he continued, "such a canny fellow must have other views! Denham has made a conquest, for the moment. Who knows what may yet come of it? As to the practicability of the notion, one thing seems clear to me; here in London little credit will be given it.

"Indeed, Collinsworth, think upon it—Why build another, with the whole region already so well-endowed with sporting enterprise—with Epsom, Southend, Newmarket, nearby Lewes, and above every other, Brighton itself, available for our sportsmen's diversion? Does he propose to lure the Prince from his favorite haunt, and turn him eastward towards a new downs, miles away in our undistinguished, unheralded Sanditon? The very thought," he smiled, "of founding grand entertainment in my brother's teetering society? What sense can be in it? Does he foresee mon-eyed men from the town, the nabobs and stockjobbers, our newest gen-try, stuffed complete with their money of paper, and all variety of upstarts visible since the war's end, running after in pursuit? I confess, I am astonished. What can be the meaning of it?"

Surprised, Collinsworth listened to this recitation all silent. What had seemed to him simply an inventive design to extend pleasure, a prospect of innocent recreation in a distant country locale, had caused Parker apprehension. He had known nothing before that could so perturb his friend.

He himself foresaw no harm arising from the enterprise. But then, few were Collinsworth's notions of the entanglements of commerce. To an heir of fortune and property, such concerns were unnatural.

"Come, Parker," he intervened, "surely, there is no cause for your con-cern. If that spirited fellow Denham can work a miracle, while you your-self need not be bothered in its creation, why not accept it? A fine turf down there in the salty air can but enhance the reputation of your broth-er's land speculation."

Sidney heard his good-willed, naive friend, and allowed himself to be eased. "Perhaps you are right, Collinsworth," he said. "My brother's ven-turing has never before appeared to have a serious nature to me. Who knows but that I may not have taken the true measure of what expansion is moving through the countryside in these altering times."

Here he left off, determined to let the matter take its course. The scheme might be ill-advised, even unsound, but Sidney could not pretend that its very conception—a partnership between young Denham, that inept example of aesthetic, unworldly sensibility, and one of the shrewdest of London touters—was a charade not to be cherished, a diversion even worthy of the price it might exact.

With that, the two made their call in Ryder Street. They had not been unexpected; and certainly, once Miss Denham had learned of her broth-er's chance meeting with their friend at Brooke's, she had scarcely stirred from their quarters. Collinsworth himself seemed prepared to pay his respects to the attentive Miss Denham; but upon arrival, they found themselves greeted by Sir Edward, who was this day more animated than ever they had yet known him.

His jaunty salute began, "Ah, Collinsworth, here amid your London confederates, so elegantly attired, so unlike our former country mode. As for you, Parker, without question, always the dashing presence wherever you choose to appear."

In time, Esther Denham made her entrance. With the gentlemen already seated, she knew the moment when her superb carriage should be viewed to advantage. Thus could she assure that her appearance be the principal subject of their discussion. With her hair fashionably dressed, herself bedecked in fine white muslin, elegantly worked down the front, with pea-green ribbon full round the bottom, and below that, her white slippers just visible, the picture was irresistible.

Of course, the gentlemen did not disappoint. They rose, admiration itself. That Sidney Parker had chosen to accompany her awaited guest surprised her, yet only for a moment before she rallied in gracious welcome.

"How delightful, Lord Collinsworth, to find you again within your proper surroundings. And, dear Mr. Parker! In truth, much as we do love our Aunt Denham and gladly follow her dictates, she *will* find her pleasure at *such* a distance!" She then took another turn about the room to demonstrate the back of her gown. "It *is* distressing to remember how frequent must be our journeys away from civility."

This afternoon at least, her brother could permit no such cavil. He would talk but of the excellence of Sanditon, its blessed situation, as of a paradise emerging. Yes, he assured them, it shall take its place in history. With *his* turf established, it would be favored by the best of London company, elegance to suit the finest of tastes.

Now, in a spirited show of modesty, Sir Edward added, "Mr. Parker, you shall credit such a recent triumph to your own sister, Diana! She it was who fixed solidly the urgency of action, and charged me go forward! She, who dispatched me for Sanditon's envoy. Truly, it is a woman who understands nuance. You—we all—must be grateful for her acumen.

"Our new breeder's ambition for the locale is admirable. Once the racing stables house his choice stallions, he has little doubt that other of his sporting cronies must hasten to join him. Soon, there will be a Riding School opened, answering to the pleasure of every nobleman whose son accompanies him. He intends also to make claim immediately upon one or another of the nearby public houses for all the visitors. *The Pelham* or *The Rounder*, I make out, which ever proves closer to the beach, to give over for our carousing sportsmen. As I remember it, at the *Pelham*, the landlord is a betting man, ready to receive every addition to his clientele."

Little cooled in intensity was Sanditon's champion, who had single-handedly overseen the process by which his Aunt's colony must take fashionable hold.

All this while, Miss Denham had not lost a moment to engage Lord Collinsworth. Baronets like her brother, she knew, were frequently to be found in their circle; only occasionally would a decorative gentleman of his rank see fit to appear at an assembly or at country balls. Newly re-examined by this alert lady, he qualified as an object of greatest interest. She fluttered with admiration; and promptly expressed her eagerness to learn more of his family, his ancient properties, and their management.

"Surely your duties must require your own absences from London? Need you not, Sir, yourself attend to your family's estates, and look to their maintenance for some long part of the year? How very inconvenient you too must find these departures."

"You are indeed perceptive, Miss Denham. Yet my family bears a constant concern for the proper improvements of our lands."

"To be sure, it is the current mode, Lord Collinsworth. They too must favor the glorious Palladian architectural embellishments and landscape redefinitions."

"Improvements for their surroundings are ever in their thought. In these fashionable days, how might they not be overtaken by the enticement of romantic notions. My dear Miss Denham, they cannot be expected to resist the desire, that they, too, can repose themselves upon a 'rustic and a ruined tomb' during an afternoon's walk about their estates?

"I confess that I do suffer their ire because I am disinclined to share in such enthusiasms. To my mind, there are obligations more important, Miss Denham, which must take precedence for one of noble family! My loyalties are, you see, fixed more firmly upon the maintenance of standards of propriety! In London, for example, I need make a show, periodically at least, with my fellows in the ruling body at Westminster, before it is the hour to visit at the *Change* to look to our family's financial interests."

"You must agree that there is in London far more to distract and elevate, and all that which makes us worthy of position. I, for one, no longer take pleasure in our uncouth country pastimes. I willingly abdicate to the rougher sportsmen their fox hunting, their shouting contests among the lower beasts—their cockfights, their bear- and bull-baiting. London sport is of another standard. It is refinement itself, the only thing worthy of the gentleman's interest. Rules, as specified by the sporting Clubs—whether it be the Pugilists, Jockeys, even among tennis ardents—rules set forth and strictly adhered to. Decorum! I cannot imagine if there can be a more suitable preoccupation for those properly bred."

Miss Denham was gratified to hear such views; they spoke to his position of eminence.

"I take your meaning," she responded, "and do heartily commend your distinctions. So many of these coarse times seek merely to please their appetite. Your own diversions are spirited. They associate with discrimination, imagination, and genuine elegance. Such standards, Lord Collinsworth, in a nobleman's sport, are certainly everything."

A flattered gentleman countered appreciatively. He must perforce take up his charge in the country; yet until then, "I find myself far too engaged in my own preoccupations, though one day, I suppose. . . ," and left off."

This last, she found suggestive enough to bow her head, in acknowledgment of his meaning. Their encounter had delighted her, his cordial response boded well; it was encouragement itself. Now she was in London, she could hope they meet again.

Such satisfaction as Miss Denham thereby received might have been diminished considerably had she been aware that her brother Edward's effects upon young Parker sat not at all agreeably. The recital of his sister Diana's engagement in the selling of Sanditon's virtues made him uneasy; it had accelerated his own alarm for the future of that already ailing community.

These extravagant designs for construction of luxury suites; the crying up of a new theater; and now, a racing establishment—and in the hands of a London breeder? Was that progression not something questionable?

Sidney recognized in Thomas Parker a dedicated man. Sanditon and its success was his very life, virtually equal to the health and happiness of his family. Yet, perhaps his good brother was moving now in a set too fast to benefit him.

He recalled that alarm he had seen in the lovely eyes of young Charlotte Heywood weeks ago, when she attempted to alert him. Miss Heywood's fear was for the perils of their recklessness. How perceptive her concern for his family.

It was, in truth, he who had been unobservant, who had seemed uncaring. He felt mortified. He had allowed such follies to proceed unchecked too long. Sidney Parker comprehended of a sudden that action was needed. With the like of Sir Edward and his misguided sister, Diana, in command, how might Thomas Parker's dream not end in wreckage?

He could no longer sit by to watch while his dear, foolish family was left in its ruins.

TWENTY-FIVE

S idney decided that the task, urgent before any other, must be the prompt solicitation of a physician for his brother's community. Or, if it should prove difficult, he thought to seek out a reputable apothecary willing to take up the formidable assignment. As Parker conceived it, the responsibility demanded of such a gentleman not only proficiency in the medical arts—or in the dispensing the latest concoctions; but that he be a someone versed in, and open to, such current innovations in the cures fashionable at seaside communities.

He would make haste towards Harley Street, where, he had been informed, an eminent practitioner of the vocation, one William Hallett, might oblige him. Were he himself unavailable to undertake such a position—given its great distance from London—yet he might he provide Parker educated counsel leading to that competent man who could.

London's light this day seemed remarkably brilliant. There was a lifting breeze in the streets to fill him with hopefulness. Since he had come to resolution concerning Thomas' peril, he felt the strength of conviction; even, a resolve surprising to him. He would not slacken in his effort. Before it was too late, some attempt at least *must* be made to turn back that flood of folly at Sanditon. Despite the complacence and flagrant uninterest so manifest in Thomas' arrogant associates, some recourse for emergency must at once be established through importation of a doctor for the town residents.

The gentleman in question had agreed to his visit, welcoming him cordially enough; but in the hour following upon Parker's explanation of his particular errand, Hallett's tone altered appreciably.

"Ah, good Sir," he began, gravely, "how little can you know of the mischiefs, the detriments engendered by all the casual approaches to our art running rife in the provinces? These strange theories and bizarre speculations, the neglectful heedlessness shown towards proven practice? Your worst fears are in no way idle. Already have I seen innocent lives fall victim to runaway enthusiasm. People hobbled, lamed, broken! Reports come to us of the charlatans to be found in one or another spa or seaside resort. These clever tacticians are too frequently ignorant; or, worse, grossly oblivious to legitimate symptoms, to every medical sign of oncoming disease, and bodily deterioration. Yet their transfixed adherents take counsel from such saviors; and they grow the more desperately wild as they read their condition for themselves! In their fervor, they can only be likened to newly-made sectarians, those fanatics of past times so given over to blind devotion."

"My own concerns have grown deeper each year, Mr. Parker, for all the many miserables entrapped by these quacks. That persistent nonsense put forth among the earnest believers—especially by the most revered of their advisors—remains unconscionable. Only consider the simplest of questions, 'What can air, drinking water, and sudden immersion into the sea on chill autumn days, or, and worse in icy winter, accomplish for the severely ailing? Would they not do better surely, to seek instead a good fire in the cozy, restful indoors?

"There can be no doubt of the hazard. The more I do ponder upon such practice, the more I see in it the evil of our times. Surely, you too must have observed it? Will you believe me, when I say that the revolutionary dawn of this new century, with its recognition of the Rights of Man, was brought forth with another, wholly preposterous, notion: I mean, man's right as *self-medicator!*"

Mr. Parker could not but smile at this.

"You may laugh, Mr. Parker, call it nonsense, dismiss it as rant, but, think upon it: not so long ago, air and water, and even the light of the sun were not in the hands of the physician to dispense! Only with the new century came this fantasy. Now, each man is so free to choose his fate, that the air and even the morning light are embraced as a new liberation! And, in truth why not? Are they not there to be taken just as they are found! Alas, as Dr. Buchan himself has reminded us, with such license comes the rub—for indeed, calomel, bark, laudanum and more, are there also for the taking! All ready for indiscriminate, unrestricted employment—for applications unprescribed by the honest physician! In point of fact, Why should a free man trouble himself with authority, with science, or allow any such restraints as knowledge and experience?

"Good Sir, to my continual dismay have I witnessed an otherwise sensible patient turned from traditional remedy, and seldom to his benefit. Whether the complaint be a roaring noise in the head, a scorbutic eruption, or the onset of deafness, the desperate will go forth. They think to alter their fates in the frozen sea, by fantastic vapors, through the frenzy of total immersion. Shock and fright, to bring calm and health? The sheer folly that pervades, the delirium of those regimes! Why, the most successful of such retreats take on the aspects of carnival. No, there can be no science in it, I assure you!"

"But, Sir," pleaded Sidney Parker, his discomfort growing, "surely there must be *some* restorative effect to these natural phenomena, something wholesome? Could not a brilliant physician of your command undertake to set extravagance at bay, and use through moderation what there may be of good in such run-away experiments? Someone like yourself must try to bring sense to these folk!"

"Not I, Sir. I would not challenge the mania," said the gentleman, but looking now upon earnest young Parker's dejected expression, Hallett bethought himself and called to his assistant in the next room.

A slim, youthful figure entered. It was a Mr. James Porter, who had only that moment returned from attending a failing patient in their offices below.

"I believe our visitor must be of especial interest to you, Porter," began he. "He comes to enlist help for a seaside community possessed by those plunge and fright cures, those mad correctives we hear of as so much the deadly fashion. And I know you, Sir, to feel those same misgivings I myself entertain."

Mr. Porter listened to a recounting of Sanditon's climate of nonchalance, its unmindfulness of medical eventualities, and he too was incensed, the while betraying his rage in a west country burr. In the expression of his opinions, there was scarcely any delicacy.

"Nowadays, there can be no inch of coast free from this latest plague upon Englishmen, nor without a supply of candidates to populate them. Do you not speak of those congregations of effete ladies and gentlemen, whose prime urge is the display of elegance, who think only of prancing about in grand style? Vain creatures, breathing the fragrance of nature in the wishful projection of recapturing their youthful beauty, and its once perfect health? Or, more particularly, hoping to snag a rich husband for their dowered daughters?"

Porter's contempt encouraged Parker to press his brother's need. With as little mention of the specific of recent developments as he might manage, he explained that numbers were expected to join the founders and pioneers in the Sussex retreat. Surely, he argued, those ailing unfortunates must hope to rely upon one such as himself, whose calling was dedicated to the preservation of life!

Would Mr. Porter, he pursued, not think upon the matter, and consider the potential for resettling himself into a worthy practice among them?

Porter looked towards his senior before making an answer. The older man showed no hesitation, "Were I your age, Porter," was his counsel, "I would see it my duty to address such regimens. Take up this cause! Young man, I myself promise you every support from London, when complexities arise."

Thus was it settled. James Porter determined to seize this opportunity promptly.

Emerging from these offices, Sidney Parker was both heartened by the success of his mission and, in his own sportive way, already in anticipation of the potential entertainments to be derived from the entrance of this outspoken Devonshire provincial among the Olympians of Sanditon. He mused happily over the image of crusading Mr. James Porter's arrival, and his reception by Lady Denham.

As he went on his way, in high spirits, he noted a carriage drawing up before him. To his amazement, out from it stepped none other than the lady herself he had most recently encountered at Sanditon, Mrs. Emmeline Turner. In her company, moreover, was a companion at least as familiar: that discovery of his brother Thomas, Miss Charlotte Heywood!

At once did he make his presence known, cheerfully offering assistance.

"Can this be?" was his greeting, "Are you the very same as I did encounter altogether too briefly during my late excursion into Sussex? So surprisingly discovered in London? I wonder at my fortune in this chance meeting." His pleasure, revealed in his enlivened features, was altogether genuine; it enhanced his bearing as he proceeded, "But now, I assure you, I am at your command."

Mrs. Turner and her friend had indeed arrived but the day earlier. They too were amazed to find him, standing hale and hearty, a contrast to the succession of elderly frail gentlemen departing from their visits to their physicians.

Mrs. Turner cordially responded.

"Is it Mr. Parker, truly, of that fine family of Parkers in Sussex? Well met! As you can see, before continuing so in the country, *I* was required to leave our Sanditon friends to take consultation with proper medical authorities. That, alas, and to answer to urgent London business. But *you*, Sir,—ever so much the man of leisure, why might *you* have abandoned us at the shore, when it was just becoming so glorious? You did disappoint us."

"Madam, in truth, I am unable to claim a logic in my comings and goings, which are as well dictated by frivolity as by restlessness, I confess it, by tedium itself. Notwithstanding, at this very time, there is new purpose to my presence here, even urgent cause. Distressing intelligence has come to my attention, and it alters my course, not for myself alone, but my family too. This very hour, have I been engaged in soliciting for Sanditon's security, by providing such comfort for residents at the seaside, as you yourself now seek, to make their cure more feasible."

He paused to gaze at her companion. His look encompassed her London transformation, her stylish attire, and how it became her.

Though Charlotte had not dared more than a nod in his direction, he directly addressed her. "You did chide me, Miss Heywood, not long ago, to think better of my brother's situation. How perceptive was your care even then! Nor could you have dreamt how prophetic it would prove! Belatedly, do I look to regularizing Sanditon's deficient medicine. My eyes, once opened, see now that that shifting scene must be put right. Too long has our new Arcadia floated in dreamland, without attention to reason or even common sense. It has, I fear, been drifting towards misfortune, and may bring us to general destruction."

He checked himself, for he had already said too much, too heatedly. It could be hardly expected to settle Sanditon's woes here on a London street. Recovering himself, the young man inquired after their own good health.

Mrs. Turner replied that her aim in this return was simply to report upon her own progress to the distinguished Mr. Long. She would demonstrate the revived state of her health—the effect of air and rest. It was to that end they were hastening.

"Be assured, Sir, that your concerns for Sanditon are apposite. Miss Heywood and I do applaud your intervention. Do we not, Charlotte? We have ourselves thought of little else. We must hear of your progress. Will you not come to call upon us at our own lodgings in Sloane Square, where we may talk at leisure? Even, if you will, to plot Sanditon's rescue? We may at least think how to salvage something of that *best of all possible worlds.*"

For Mrs. Turner's engagement, he was altogether grateful. After glancing at her young friend for some sign of approval, he bowed, promising to come to them soon.

Those compliments which profusely followed—Mrs. Turner's unqualified admiration for his person, her generous assessment of his character—will be recorded here without apology. Yet it was her conclusion, "I must wonder at this change in the young man. Our Mr. Parker seems suddenly quite determined, do you not agree, Miss Heywood? He could be taken as a fellow with new purpose," that startled Charlotte.

But neither need we linger upon her own confused impression except to notice that the sensation she felt at this moment, in her unexpected re-encounter with the truly puzzling member of that flawed, ever-phantasmagorical, fond family, was something visible in the high color of her face.

Part VII

TWENTY-SIX

With what wonder our heroine greeted her new surroundings! She had dreamed, but scarcely hoped for a stay in that teeming metropolis. This, because of Willingden's considerable distance from it, and isolation from that great world. Charlotte recollected her dear father's strong disinclination for London's frenzied pace as a barrier that made such a prospect remote to her. Now, suddenly she found herself in the company of a distinguished friend, with the city's many pleasures at their disposal.

Those first hours after her arrival, as their carriage proceeded through its streets, and she felt herself deafened by the uproar that swirled about her, and distressed by the hawking, shouting voices—such strenuous energy of the vendors on every hand—the press of humanity that engulfed them—these sights that astonished her, perplexed, and left her gasping. Hardly could she have imagined such a variety of life, as she saw displayed on all sides.

Coming as Charlotte had, fresh from the empty, open shore, and, before that, as an innocent acquainted only with such benign beauty as was to be seen on the footpaths and byways of their beloved Sussex countryside, with its tranquil landscape, gently rolling fields, its modest country houses, she could have had but the least presentiment of such a scene.

Upon this difference our Charlotte reflected now, with some mortification. Despite the comfortable certainty in her own young life, despite every confidence in her family's ways, despite diligence in study, that exposure to "experience," only through her books—she discovered herself in no way prepared for such a spectacle. Never had she felt more the simpleton—a wide-eyed country girl suddenly at large.

Confessing the whirl of her thoughts under such impressions to her hostess, she found Mrs. Turner unsurprised; rather, something diverted. In courtesy, she contained herself, lest she betray her amusement.

"Dearest child," she said smiling, "be of good cheer, for here is my very purpose in bringing you to London. You must know how entirely I have commended your efforts, all you have taken from your reading. Yet, think upon it, what can truly convey this city but its very self? All our imaginings of the greater world are merest conjecture, are they not? They come to little enough. Our sight needs extending, our senses stimulation, if we hope to comprehend the world as it is, and so full of complexity."

"I speak not only of the London you see exposed in its daily whirl, such intense motion, with its sordid revelations; but of much more. I would that you consider as well its wondrous features—its inventions, its sophistications, its immense achievements. Dear girl, was it not after all, our wise Dr. Johnson, who told us most aptly that none of us can have so much as attempted life—not, at least, a thoughtful one—until we have set foot in London? And, then there is the poet Wordsworth's exultation as he views the city from Westminster Bridge, that 'earth has not anything to show more fair!'"

An awed Charlotte Heywood attended to her mentor. Her solicitude and civility touched her, and she responded warmly.

There was no time to be lost. The very next day, Mrs. Turner commenced her urban education for her protegeé. She would take her from their lodgings, towards a show of London's finery; and first off, towards the scene of construction of that latest wonder, Regent Street.

Miss Heywood's own inclination, once having acquainted herself with Mrs. Turner's sitting room and the ample collection of books in her library, was to retreat to read there, insisting to her hostess that in no particular would she permit special attentions. The preoccupied lady, who must needs attend to her pressing commitments, should not be distracted by Charlotte's presence.

Mrs. Turner promptly dismissed any such nicety. "Nonsense, child," was her response, "I warrant that there will be leisure enough to return to isolation when you shall have retired once again to the country. Here, you must allow yourself all those splendors about us—in the very atmosphere which reflects the glories of our epoch. Why, our London can, I do assure you, defy the memory of Nineveh and Tyre! Victory after victory are celebrated in our bold facades and sweeping vistas."

"Moreover, I myself shall attend to your first views of the environs, and oversee your examination of those colonnades-to-be at John Nash's Crescent, some already standing in brilliant whiteness, to coax upon you proper admiration of such grace in the grand sweeping turn of the street! Such sumptuousness shall present itself, I promise you, as you have not yet dared to imagine."

Mrs. Turner engaged a carriage for their excursion. Since the day was so fine, they could take later their stroll, as she would wish it; here, there, everywhere. First, to marvel at the shops, filled as they were with sparkling wares; to examine the silks and satins and every article of elegance and fashion upon display; to pause and wonder at all, so arranged with the greatest symmetry. At the silversmiths, they should gaze, awed, upon the gleaming plate in rows, so plentiful and ready for arriving ladies and gentlemen. There was wealth to dazzle Miss Heywood on their walk that day. So much, that she was speechless. She saw in these squares little poverty, and no hint of the squalor which had unsettled her upon her first sight of London town.

Miss Heywood was entranced by her afternoon, excited by the bustle, the carriages, the endless commerce through all these passages. She felt herself aglow; but determined to keep her countenance, to offer little comment; in short, to be discreet in every observation to her friend. She understood that she had been introduced to a world in which she felt as an ignorant as a babe newborn.

Dear, attentive Mrs. Turner spoke to her charge of finer arts to be explored; pleasures associated with taste and imagination; not merely those to feed the appetite. She reminded her that her efforts had but begun! Forthcoming were visits to the galleries, to the opera, evenings of music, and certainly, attendance at the plays then current at Covent Garden, Haymarket, and Drury Lane. To seek out everything that would engross the best thought in her young friend was her intent.

"Just consider, Charlotte," she delighted, "the prospect of standing before a Reynolds portrait, or sitting in attendance to the sublime sounds of accomplished musicians in concert. All this lies within reach; it is here to be sought out, and find it you shall."

And while the weather continued agreeable, Mrs. Turner would initiate her young lady still further. This time, in the joys of ambling through the fashionable pleasure gardens on every side. The city was indeed one of parade—the whole of London seemed determined—whether it were diversion at Marylebone, Vauxhall, Kensington, or Ranelagh—to see, and be seen, and in all its finery! It was to Ranelagh that they repaired on a balmy afternoon, for as Mrs. Turner confided to Charlotte, "Ranelagh is so much preferred in these days, and best, it is closest to our quarters in Sloane Square."

As the crowd gathered on that day, it seemed that all London had made a similar choice. So could they saunter, admiring, enjoying, inspecting the smartest dress of the ladies and gentlemen promenading there.

Charlotte rejoiced in the setting itself, the glorious color of its verdure and elaborately planted flowers. To look upon the damask roses, the pinks, the stock, some purple, some red, was sufficient excitement for her. And before them was much more: our visitors were greeted by jugglers, equestrian performers, strolling players, and, all the while, the musicians played in the bandstand of the vast rotunda.

Contented after much pleasant *divertissement*, the ladies made their way towards the exit. There they were again surprised, coming upon yet more familiars from their own favorite Sussex post! So soon after their encounter with Sidney Parker, how curious it seemed to Charlotte to discover Sir Edward Denham. He, in company with his stylish sister, the *mondaine* Miss Denham, and, notably in attendance upon her, none other than that dapper gentleman, Lord Collinsworth, who had only recently been presented at Sanditon by Mr. Parker's brother!

That group was itself startled at the coincidence. Here, together? to reunite with their country acquaintances amidst London's most elegant! It was a circumstance that would but result in something of a flurry.

Fortunately, Miss Denham could show her mettle. She tripped forward to greet the ladies, with a displaying welcome that added new dimension to her character. Here in her own London, and beholden to no one, Miss Denham exceeded in her civility, her condescension. To the like of country-bred beings, who must certainly find themselves perplexed at the sophisticated circumstances about them, she was salvation itself. True enough, of Mrs. Turner's capabilities, she felt secure—but what of Miss Heywood? How *she, all innocent*, must feel her difference! The knowing lady would provide her counsel, acquaint her with the subtleties.

Animated in the presence of her admiring gentleman, Miss Denham hastened to restore for Lord Collinsworth what was surely a scant recollection of "those ladies," up from her aunt's resort.

Compliments followed, saluting the elder lady's eminence, before she devoted herself again to our heroine. "Why, Miss Heywood," began she, "how unexpected to discover *you* thus at leisure at Ranelagh! Even to see you continuing, my dear, amongst us, and all the time looking at ease as one who belongs in London! La! Does she not, dear Lord Collinsworth? You might almost think our Miss Heywood born to such a promenade!"

She paused deliberately to peruse the young lady's costume, circling her the while, "I myself, this very day, should have worn my tambored muslin had I not considered it unwise to endanger it. You must learn to mind here the thorny roses, you know. But, then my dear, you may be easy. To this good lady's tuition, you shall now add my own. Error need menace you no more. If we put our minds to it, we can instruct you together as to appearance and nuance in etiquette too. I expect progress of the swiftest; for intelligence such as your own, nothing can want."

There was a moment of silence. Who could hope to equal Miss Denham's generosity of spirit? Its extravagance, however, took Lord Collinsworth something aback. With the greatest cordiality, he now turned to both ladies. "A wonder to greet you here," began he, "but then you too, perhaps, Mrs Turner, are enlisted to salvage our favorite resort? With your prominence and wide acquaintance in London, this must be of benefit to Sanditon surely."

Mrs. Turner, nonplussed, made no reply. So for some moments, further converse ceased between them.

Until Sir Edward took charge, with an inquiry into their own satisfactions at Ranelagh. He would hear, how long they had been within the gardens, how carefully they had studied its intricate composition, and the magnificence of its design. "Had they not," he asked with affect, "felt its picturesque embrace of the countryside? And so wondrously, here, in very heart of London?"

That gentleman felt himself liberated by his démarche from Sanditon. Disencumbered from the necessity of dancing attendance upon his aunt, indeed, no longer within the presence of the commanding lady, he felt his spirit rise freely once more. His demeanor, always forthcoming, positively radiated *bravado*.

Addressing himself directly to Miss Heywood, he explained, "Just this week have we commenced our regular attendance at the best of assemblies. How I should be honored to call upon you, Miss Heywood, and dear Mrs. Turner, to favor us all—Miss Denham, Lord Collinsworth and, myself, with your company at one of them."

Charlotte, again embarrassed by this importuning gentleman, deferred, explaining that she could but follow her hostess's direction in such affairs, adding as graciously as she could, that Mrs. Turner's many engagements made such a prospect unlikely.

Young Denham turned his appeal to the lady. He must insist upon it!

Mrs. Turner herself had stood by through all of this, entertained by the self-satisfaction of the gentleman, who was even more confident-seeming than when she had seen him in Sussex! Glancing at Miss Heywood, she slyly whispered, "Surely, a festive ball is within the purview of your London studies, Charlotte? And we can not, can we, do without dancing?"

Charlotte smiled. In the interests of thoroughness alone, she acknowledged that Mrs Turner requests could not to be denied.

The pair left Ranelagh Gardens with the waning sun, even while the orchestra played on, and ladies and gentlemen still rambled idly.

To Charlotte Heywood, how might fashionable London not seem all gaiety? For a person cloistered all her life, the delights of the interlude staggered. And in these heady days, whatever our young heroine concluded privately of the true desirability of its entertainments, or its way of life, her own stunning exposure to London left her profoundly silent and full of thought.

TWENTY-SEVEN

When Mrs. Turner's young Sally delivered into Charlotte's hands a letter from her father in the morning, she was startled to learn of some delayed intelligence from home. The missive, dispatched earlier to Mr. Parker's Trafalgar House, had gone astray; but with Mrs. Parker's kindly redirection, it found its way to her in Sloane Square.

Mr. Heywood's was a brief note. He was aware of his daughter's concerns about her brother Henry's welfare, and would promptly inform her of his son's arrival in what he designated as that "hothouse of vice," while at the same time conceding a fortunate acquisition there. Not only had Henry found adequate living quarters, but a good situation for himself as well! His son had, in effect, provided assurance of a safe establishment within London!

To have news of him came as relief to Charlotte; her first sensation was of joy. Yet in the same instant, she knew she must fly to Mrs. Turner in hope to obtain her consent to seek him out; for she could not rest before she had visited Henry that very day in his lodgings.

"Good Mrs. Turner," she began breathlessly, "I have only now learned where he is settled. I do not imagine that he himself has any suspicion of my own presence here in London. What cheer such a discovery could give him, what satisfaction for us after so long a separation! I freely admit that he is, of all my sisters and brothers, my most favored! For we are almost of an age, you see. And we grew together so closely that we could act in concert, as one, never opposed for a moment together; we smoothed the other's hurts, soothed each of our own injuries. We could even make light of our family's travails, and turn away adversity. Dear Mrs. Turner, once you have come to know him, I feel confident that you too shall see his jovial, superior spirit. In every particular, he is a laudable fellow."

However unprepared the lady was to discover young Henry so close at hand, she was gladdened for her charge. Considering the circumstance, she became something pensive, "He has, you say, elected to come to London, to make his future here? That forthcoming, country-bred lad you describe? A curious enough notion, to be sure! However, I shall salute him, and, on your account, as many others of your relations as should wish to come among us! Should they resemble their dear sister, they must bring with them to this great city—that singular, rural, Heywood *esprit*."

Mrs. Turner, this afternoon, was occupied with the business she had come to execute in London, and unable to oblige her guest by her company. Nevertheless, she would not delay her friend's excursion. The kind lady saw the child's disappointment at the thought of delaying until the morrow, and encouraged her proceed on her own. As it was yet early, she might make the carriage available to Charlotte before setting out on her own errand. Only, when she reviewed the *situation* of Henry's rooms, written down for them by Mr. Heywood, did Mrs. Turner express some anxiety for Charlotte's safety.

"I could not be easy in this! To enter that quarter at *any* hour of the day! And you, a stranger to London ways! No, I fear you can not manage this search upon your own."

Ringing for her man servant, she insisted, "I will see you are attended at all times in *that* neighborhood. Upon my instruction, Poole will keep close by your side, and only after you have embraced your brother may he leave you. Your Henry must take care to see you safely home, of that I will be certain, although, now I think on it, even he can not yet know London's hazards. Caution must be exercised! I can not be content until I know you secure each moment."

A grateful Miss Heywood offered her solicitous mentor every warrant: she would proceed with care; she would not stay long; she would return Poole to his mistress when once she was before her brother. With Henry's good help, her return was assured to perfect safety.

So did she set off to seek him. The journey itself was not a long one.

Still, as the carriage proceeded eastward towards their destination in Langham Place, the sights about her were little enough appealing, the tumult and clamor oppressive, and the startling outbreaks of violence unsavory. Even so, Charlotte felt only exhilaration. Her eagerness to meet her brother again gave her ample courage.

Having arrived near his dwelling place, she discovered the scene there scarcely encouraging. They passed through alleys, down narrow lanes, along rows of stands; all was warrens and dark shops where artisans sat at labor. At last, Poole identified the very structure they sought.

With that good man's assistance, she stepped from the carriage only to find herself standing in mud to her ankles, and, moving forward from it, surrounded by more soggy mire yet. Sustained by the anticipation of soon greeting her brother, Charlotte took little heed. She made her way through the unkempt corridors, and climbed to his garret door.

The look upon poor Henry's face as he opened it was of an agitation such as his sister had seldom seen upon that winsome countenance—a succession of expressions to make her laugh and weep at the same time. First, a retreat into disbelief; then a consternation; and that, followed by perplexity. Could it be? was the question in his eyes, his surprise having rendered him helpless. Yet, for the young man, no vision could have been more heartening than the sight of Charlotte. He gave a cry of joy as he comprehended that it was no apparition that stood before him. Their embrace was warm and long, their unchecked chatter gay and heedless of the time that passed; and it continued, thus. Only the recollection by Miss Heywood that poor Poole patiently awaited further instruction just outside her brother's door, could interrupt their mirth.

Henry rushed to bid him enter, but the steward, satisfied by the success of his mission, declined, turning the care of his charge over to the young man, and made his hasty return to his mistress' service.

They two were able then to talk at their leisure. So much was there to be said, so filled with event had their lives been, and so long ago did it seem to the pair since their last meeting at Willingden!

While her brother had attended to Poole's leave taking, Charlotte glanced about the room. There was little more than a bed to be seen, and beside it a chair. It pained her to find her brother in such reduced circumstance. Yet she said nothing of it, for his good humor, his enthusiasm, were just as they had always been.

"Dear, lovely Charlotte," he cried, "to find *you appearing* so at my door here in London, is clearly more miracle than reality. What can have brought you from Sussex? I can scarce make you out in all this finery!"

Charlotte told of her new friend Mrs. Turner's generosity; explaining her fortunate circumstance, and marveling herself at the turn that had brought them to London. But, why should she dwell upon her own remarkable situation? She would, instead, know the particulars of his own.

Only then did Henry make reference to the shabbiness of his quarters. "No matter, dear sister," was his confident dismissal, "I do not intend to rest long here."

Somber, he continued, "How little are you yet aware, Charlotte, of the many alterations in our own Willingden in these latter days? Why, the nearest of our neighbors, Sir Godfrey and Lady Marlow, and even young Fraser, so newly-come into his properties—and who only lately rang with talk of convention and decorum, of a determination to sustain the importance of his position, of service to the farming families dependent upon him—all have abandoned us! These friends have packed their bags, taken their ladies away to the seaside, towards the City, towards the Americas! We know not where. They are not alone. Wherever we turn, there is prodigious migration!"

"The meanwhile, our own father broods. He sees coming ruination only. As strangers enter in his county, he stands confounded by their ignorance of our ways, he despairs over 'improvements' in the vicinity. Little peace has he now.

"Charlotte, I confess to it: I have come to see only the decay of all that once was. And it has made me resolute in my search for another circumstance, a different way of life. Wrenching though it prove, to myself and to all our dear family, there is no other course. So much is changed, Sister, with the war's end and the Corsican no longer threatening. A demon is loosed right here among ourselves! Our trade is stagnant, and provisions scarcer and costlier. Empty stomachs move the most decent among us to protest. I can not think how we might prosper in the country as once we did!"

"Charlotte, need I tell *you* with what sadness I ruminated the matter before coming away? The more I thought, the less could I fathom a solution. What, after all could London become for me! I myself, a country boy given to outdoor pleasures?"

He now laughingly turned to his sister. "How curious are the workings of fate! Dear, sweet girl, you will remember that from my boyhood, my entire devotion has ever been to the best of country sport. Had I had my own way, were we not so much engaged in the service of our good parents, I should have ridden out upon my stallion all the day, from the early morning to the setting of the sun, whatever the weather."

"Then too, you must recollect those times when our dear Papa himself took us several Heywood brothers up to view the sight of the running horses at The Derby? Ah, the wonder it did create in his sons! From that first vision, I for one, vowed to follow those favored champions in their triumphs upon the course. You yourself watched in some impatience when I scoured newspaper reports and posted sketches of steeds from the cuttings reporting their victories."

"Nor could I ever get enough of the sport. Consider, Charlotte, my worship of the old champion, Highflyer, and my devotion to Noble, and of all those brilliant Derby descendants who made us proud. Beautiful runners they were, the choicest any equestrian breed can produce. None has excelled them, not before, not thereafter, and Epsom has seen no such grandeur since! Such a show was it then, that Derby lists, embossed with patriotic names for their specimens, the *Admiral Nelsons, Wellingtons* or *Waterloos*—never equal their like!"

"Yet, Charlotte, in its own course, my recent turn of fortune has brought new hope. Here did I come seeking to London, with not so much as a friend to look to; yet even so, came upon that very man to provide for my own future! A gentleman of some stature he is, who like myself loves great horses; but possesses the means to pursue their breeding—unlike myself!"

"Dear sister, and it was all so simple. Knowing not where to turn, or how to proceed, I found my way to Tattersall's at Hyde Park Corner, just that I might stand in the square with the sportsmen milling about of a Monday following the Derby."

"Around me were enthusiasts of all cuts, whose high spirits and lively talk, whose admiration for the animals they followed, was a balm to my hungry spirit. The hum that day was of a current favorite, the extraordinary *Smolenko*, and of his miracle run on the course. As I listened there, several spoke eloquently of the superiority of their own lines, and the hazards of the enterprise. Others argued for constancy in the rearing and caring for the beasts; they lamented the lack of educated hands in such cultivation."

"There, with those settling accounts and exchanging sums, was one honorable gentleman, whose devotion to his horses seemed of the most extraordinary. It determined me that moment to engage his attention, and express my wish to serve him by bringing that knowledge and passion I feel for such horses as his own. If I could but tell you, sister, of my true delight at his warm reception to my overture; better still, of his subsequent interest in learning of my Sussex origins. In short, after considerable talk between us, was I engaged thereby in the business of breeding horses!"

"Charlotte," he concluded, "It is the very thing for me! Hardly could I have dreamt, that in leaving my own country, I might find its pleasures once again. Such has been my extraordinary luck. He is the very employer to provide me responsibility, a gentleman thoroughly devoted to the breeding of champion horses!"

His sister was at once amazed and cheered to learn of such prospects. To have found congenial occupation in London and in so short a time was itself triumph; but to do so in following his country skills was little short of miraculous.

Both sister and brother might have persisted happily in their chatter, had they not observed the lowering of day. Charlotte, much heartened, would now return to Mrs. Turner, the while assuring her brother that his prompt return at Sloane Square was expected, where he must be acquainted with that eminent lady, her hostess. With that, Henry escorted her back to her quarters in Chelsea.

TWENTY-EIGHT

*F*ixed firmly upon his unrelenting quest for a sturdier constitution, Arthur Parker set his sights on a discipline he had never before so much as contemplated. Only such regimen, he felt, could purge him of the wretched lifelong burden, a millstone he had borne for as long as he could remember. His new routine meant, not only spending extended periods out of doors, it required a far livelier pace than his sedentary ways; it was such that he must foster agility, and learn to move his limbs to accomplish these higher aims. Yet, so happily did it serve to advance him over the weeks, that the glaring sunshine, and the sea air, for all its cutting draughts, had begun to lose their terrors for our eager acolyte.

From such preoccupation, moreover, he had grown detached from the counsel of his devoted, solicitous sisters. During daylight hours, in fact, they seemed to see *too little* of the young man, who had been until recently *too much* in their view! No longer did their ample, sluggish brother bundle himself up and lounge at his post by the fire. Young Arthur, it appeared, reexamining his position, had redefined his accepted notions of comfort, of satisfaction, and most of all, pleasure.

Can it then be wondered, that while the gentleman's larger, lustier self seemed to wane, the Parker ladies' unease for his welfare should wax but stronger? Sweet, open-natured Susan, for one, was bewildered by his regular absence from sight. She asked after the wayward Arthur, and when she did finally, come upon him each evening towards sunset, she would discover him curiously elated, if something weary. He had, he explained, so much to accomplish, and, from the sound of it, far more to say, too, that concerned his day's adventure. The very appearance of their *invalide* dazed his poor sister. She must allow for this much, at least: now on view in Arthur was an energy revived, a speech enlivened, even an unaccustomed confidence in his delivery. Exhaustive did she find such exchange; still, she herself could only marvel at his transformation.

Miss Diana Parker, on the other hand, was herself less receptive to Arthur's metamorphosis. She grumbled aloud over the improbable reversal. Soon enough, her objections took a more serious turn. *She* must fear for her once placid brother's well being. What was before their very eyes, she insisted, seemed like a man bent upon the destruction of his health! With that, she warned, its inevitable conclusion must be somehow in their own demise.

Was it not after all, his sister Diana who fully comprehended his congenital infirmity? She, who had coddled him through all his grueling bouts; she, who had nurtured his debility from infancy? Consider his rheumatic propensity—time after time, the anguish he had suffered in its throes—and this, in truth, was to overlook his general susceptibility to the disorders that pressed in upon them from every side. Diana could be in little doubt of it. These childish notions, his outlandish flailings, must, succeed in undoing them!

"Do you not," said she, addressing her timorous sister, early one morning, "apprehend what hazard he lets loose upon us? I can not think what has seized our boy! You concede, Susan, that despite his substantial aspect, our once biddable Arthur is frail within. Aye me, and as for his spirit, we know him to be weaker still. This quackery, these latest panaceas and cure-alls, though not unlike any we have superintended in the past, will be the death of us. Recall sister, his passion for *tar water* remedies and clysters, for boluses, for draughts and juleps, which, though in their way, may have served to restore him—for the moment anyway.

"Yet surely, he must be made to remember our solemn pledge. Why, dearest Susan, can he have forgotten that we had together long since vowed to forsake the whole of the zealous medical tribe, together with their apothecaries. To my mind, their wild designs can only bring us disaster the sooner. Ah, sister, his latest scheme, and here, in this treacherous sea air, shall take off the pair of us along with him, and that, handily."

For a moment she sat pensive, absorbed in her weighty meditation; to continue with a sigh, "I have long since recognized it, Susan. To have dislodged ourselves, come all this way from our secure quarters in Winchester, was not merely a misjudgment, it has transformed itself into error of some magnitude. I quite assure you, were it not for poor Thomas's own desperation, and my strong conviction that I alone can truly recover his situation, I should never have allowed us to venture it.

"And now, you see, what dire result has been wrought! I blame myself, that our poor Arthur will soon be only a skeleton of himself! Alas, our nursing chore will have then but begun. Worse, dear sister, I sense my own debility rising with every moment. You know how I suffer from the spasmodic bile? I can feel it stirring!" The poor lady pleaded almost tearfully, "What can Arthur *mean* by plunging himself into this madness that already beleaguers our befuddled elder brother?" All this doctoring, regimens, elixirs!

Susan did not entirely understand what should be the nature of their impending calamity; yet to her she must solemnly concur. She never contested Diana's judgment. Her sister's wisdom was ever evident, its superiority plain.

Besides, for the moment, there was little the sisters might do to alter the course of circumstance as it advanced upon them. Arthur's crusade for his own rehabilitation commenced with the dawn of each day; either with a precautionary dousing of seawater over his head by the dippers who awaited him on the strand—this, to insure less shock in the icy proceedings that followed; then, a brisk climb up to the Terrace, difficult though the ascent continued. With every morning, he showed himself as undaunted in adherence to the rigors that challenged him, as once he had been unmovable in his resistance to contemplate them at all.

In those bracing hours, there was movement all about. When, to his own surprise and glee, in the distance of the open shoreline, he made out among the scattered young disciples clustered about their guide, Mrs. Griffiths, one particular young lady, he must pause and give his attention. Miss Augusta Beaufort, in her own devotion to salubrity, was always there in the brilliant light to be admired. Her approach to the bathing machines, her notable assortment of bathing garments, which varied at each appearance, her flannels and wools, suitably thick enough to keep her cozy, withal so loose-fitting as to avoid the definition of her slender form, would have graced a more elegant scene.

The lady was not insensible to the curiosity of this idolater. In her alluring attitudes, her accidental waving of arms, the reticent movement of her head, she made sufficient, if scant, acknowledgement of his steadfast regard. The mere hint of her own inclination resolved Arthur to whatever arduous morning exposure. He was now a dedicate, and devoted.

Nor may we, at this juncture, allow it to go unremarked that even as first revealed, when the hero now emerging had appeared at his most indolent, when he was pronounced a "malingerer," Arthur Parker was never immune to the charms of young ladies! And it will not have escaped the diligent that, following their arrival at Sanditon, his attentions to our own Miss Heywood had been scrupulous. Consider his offerings then, his preparation by the fire of that special creation of his own: buttered hot toast.

Before destiny had captured him, in those first idle days, when he had wandered across the Terrace in a sorry state of illness and exhaustion, even then had he considered the extra exertion worth effort, if only for a sight of that graceful lady, upon her lofty perch, together with her stylishly clad sister.

For Miss Beaufort was indeed that she of the sounds divine, which emanated from their quarters above the promenade, she, the miss of the ethereal harp. And now here she was, each morning appearing to single *him* out, as if drawn by his new intensity, her admiring eye engaged by his movements.

Afternoons, in encounters at the Library, at the shops, or strolling on the Terrace, the two sauntered among their colleagues, inspecting the fashions, giggling with their companions, declaring their sophistication, and, all propriety, conversing with one another, acolytes of their common faith: regeneration, and health.

Such discourse as theirs could while a way an hour or more, as they relived their experience, recalled the trepidations of their "first plunges," protested the brusqueness of their own respective dippers, or reviewed the suite of wondrous bathing attire displayed by the lady. In short, their talk rehearsed each step in their progression to recuperation and rebirth!

As Miss Beaufort's awe at Arthur's adaptation persisted—just to observe him imbibing such quantities of seawater!—her approval of his achievement in so a short a time flattered and heartened. The gentleman could walk proudly, replete with self-gratulation.

"You alone have truly comprehended my plight, Miss Beaufort," was his confession to the receptive lady. "*My* battle with the coats of the stomach is more defiant than any here dare claim! It is, you see, the biliousness of my nature that plagues. Little use to deny it. I am fated to struggle against such effects. I do so as valiantly as I know how. While some of us, dear lady, are blessed—my brother Sidney, for example, knows not one day together when he does not awake as certain of his fitness as the one that went before—indeed, some enjoy ease, they can breathe without thought, they will swear that well-being is for any living youth—whilst I, through all my childhood needed strive against adversity, and that merely to live!"

"My good Sir," returned the tender-hearted miss, "I do not doubt it. In this world, there is scarce regard for the sensitive, and seldom for any whose delicacy of person is buffeted by a digestive disease. Such as we are *the* most put upon! Even so, do you not find it a remarkably *suitable* frailty? It is one I am proud to own to! The artistically inclined, Mr. Parker, understand this power of the nerves. One need only to have been asked to perform for the pleasure of friends at the frequent social assemblage," she said blushingly now, "to know how fearfully can our nerves intervene, how they direct their ill effects to the stomach? Why, for myself I need but think upon such moments, when I must rush to the salts to revive! Faint as I grow, I may *not* succumb! To run mad, that is conceivable, but swoon never! Not I! Like yourself, I'd persevere against every assault as fiercely as I can, for that is my nature. Yes, good sir, you have my closest commiseration for our devastating ailment."

How she sensed his need! Arthur revelled in the loftiness of such understanding; her tone was emollient to his chafèd spirit. Her discernment it was that gave him courage to enter deeper into tales of lifelong heroism in his combatting the suffering of by his invalid past.

"To have endured such maladies as some can not imagine has been my portion. Why, the simplest of daily pleasures may render me susceptible to violent response from my body. Once, when troubled by the whitlow in my middle finger, for example, by merely following my apothecary's prescription to drink mallow leaves and fennel seed, the mildest of concoctions, I was poisoned. Ah, to wake in a fright, to find my arms incapable of movement! Such has been my fate."

"In you, so perfect of form yourself, so slim, such frailty of body might well be assumed; while, ample as I may appear, I am seldom regarded susceptible or even worthy by the world at large. To tell it true, though I have ever felt its piercing look upon me, its scorn for my debility, none, before this, has seen my sensitive nature. Your kindness to me is priceless. I shall be ever grateful for it."

His gaze was all adoration. What welled in Arthur Parker was perhaps even more than gratitude to the sweet lady.

TWENTY-NINE

Word went widespread through Sanditon, of the establishment of offices by a Mr. James Porter. The energetic young doctor had presented himself to Mr. Parker immediately upon his arrival from London. He bore greetings of his "dedicated" brother Sidney, and offered a recital of the desperate importunings—the many solicitations and urgent pleas to take up the challenge to tend the ailing in Sussex—in short, an account of Mr. Parker's determination to engage a reputable practitioner in service of their invalid community by the sea.

Thomas Parker was himself taken by surprise, so unexpected was this application; but joyful for his brother's concern on their behalf. It had been Mr. Parker's purpose precisely from the start. He wished to provide Sanditon with a proper representative of the profession. Only minutes after his introduction to this gentleman, the doctor's sober demeanor, his knowledgeable speech, his commitment to his science, his sentiments for better health and more natural regimens, fixed him in Thomas' good opinion; he deemed him satisfactory for the post. Yes, Porter's application to devote himself to their cause suited him; he urged the scientist to take up promptly his duties among their several afflicted and aging residents.

"Now you see, my dear Mary, our former efforts were not in vain," he crowed. "As for our Sidney's penchant for showering us with the ridicule of his humor, it is but diversion for a fanciful spirit. The playfulness of his youth, and of little import! See how vigilant he remains for our peace of mind and for future harmony. Loving he is, withal, and thoughtful too; now, he has accomplished what we ourselves could not! All was meant to be as we planned."

Hastening to call upon Lady Denham with the news, he intended to convert the skeptical lady.

"You must, Madam, regard this appearance as a godsend, though its means present themselves in the offices of our Sidney. Consider, at what an excellent moment the gentleman comes to us! How he is in time to serve those many attaching themselves to Sanditon. I estimate a want among our newcomers for expert counsel as only he can give. Though I know you reluctant to welcome any that clan, because you do suspect the worth of their profession—and why should you not, when at such proud years, you relish your remarkable health, and all without their intervention?—you must not doubt, that as our enterprise continues to prosper, we are ensured to receive a variety of contagion, agues, and what not; and they, sufficient to keep the medical gentleman wholly occupied."

The lady's approval, if grudging, did come. "Take care, good Mr. Parker," was her gruff caution, "to see he does not pounce upon the efficacy of *every* remedy. They often do, you know! I can not, you understand, permit the benefit of my milch asses to be contested. No, not Sir Harry's finest milch asses. I promise you, Sir, I for one remain a steadfast positive believer in the positive property of their milk, which is pure nectar, and heals the frail. I *will* persist in my care for those who like myself comprehend its intrinsic worth, no matter who presumes to oppose us."

To be sure, in the Sanditon of these days, there was renewed bustle. What with the sustained disorder, the noisiness and construction of the Crescent in progress, workmen encountered upon the Terrace at all times of the day, much too present in the full sunshine during their labor, the general impression offered was one of development, of industry, of change. There were strangers to be encountered, their continued arrival prompting various knockings upon doors, queries as to the availability and location of lodgings. There was the certainty of enlargement, above all, in the expectation of the population that must result as the splendid structure, soon to be Waterloo Crescent, filled up.

More still. With the introduction of a certain Mr. Matthew Dawson, a dapper Londoner, a novel attraction was evident. Together with his several associates, immediately deemed personable, and sufficiently affluent, he was busy with, preoccupied in, the search for every kind of accommodation, to suit both his men and his beasts.

With so much astir, Lady Denham beamed, dismissing further concern for Sanditon's progress. Mr. Parker could watch the ferment about him with pride, if not always with perfect equanimity. Notwithstanding his financial worry, this sparkling vision of community moved forward incontestably.

Clara Brereton was among those heartened. Private intelligence had alerted her to their imminent prosperity. That missing favorite, her most attentive friend, had in communications to his lady-love been characteristically his best self. Each of these missives nourished her secret hope. One letter commenced:

> *My very dearest Miss Brereton,*
>
> *Of my successes in the great city, I shall not boast, as their effects are soon to be displayed to you in ways you will hardly guess at! Triumphs, good lady, I can only call them triumphs. Each one following hard upon the next to bring all to fruition! Know this: henceforth all is altered, good Miss Brereton, since distinction only, and a future of consequence, must be my portion. You will understand that with my genius for such intricate business demonstrable—there can be no lack of prominence—for I am marvelled upon daily even by men of business here, all our emerging magnates of industry.*
>
> *This much alone am I ready to confide, dear friend, for surely it represents a poetry of its own, and I know you, especially you, must cheer when you learn the exquisite simplicity of my means! Having soon after my arrival, had the good fortune to encounter in my searches a distinguished man-about-town, and gentleman of parts, a horse-breeder and racer of reputation, I would woo him come join with us. Before such urging, I had thought hard upon it, and put forth instead the most unlikely of enticements to bring himself, together with his horses, to the fine turf of our Sussex; in short to settle him nearby our sumptuous coves.*
>
> *I sought to beguile Mr. Matthew Dawson first with the lore of the sea, to titillate—to pique his curiosity with the romance of our shore, make him privy to the exciting diversions to be discovered— the nighttime visits with the seamen to be found owling on the sand, the nocturnal parade of swinging lanterns to lure innocent vessels, the daring climbs in darkness by tubmen in flight upon the cliffs surrounding Sanditon. Lady, I could have myself have been our inspired sonneteer of the scene, a valiant versifier of the night—a Byron*

of our outer shores! Moreover, the allure of intrigue did not find him indifferent. Seduced by all he heard, he was in my power. It wasn't long before I gave my blessing to his proposal to build anew, and grandly, there in Sussex.

You shall soon enough see the upshot! Within reach quite suddenly now is my Aunt's precious dream—and all, by my hand, become reality. Sanditon's future secured! Such success, my dear lady, and how might we think other, is not the result of cold commerce; it springs from poetic artistry, it is a victory of the true imagination!

And sweet Miss Brereton, I have just begun; for I do see vaster designs. How can you doubt that my own efforts on Lady Denham's behalf shall be rewarded, and amply? Freed from former cares, I am at last to be the destined man of position! As for Denham Park, I shall maintain it in a style it never knew, even while my good uncle thrived there. Of course, when such elegance grows tedious, we have ever the possibility to slip away to the charm of your cozy hideaway—that of my own little cottage orné at the southern shore! Nothing to interfere with ease, not whilst my superior worth is recognized by London's best. What then, dear Clara, can you think of now, to keep us apart? I shall yet carry you off to Timbuctoo, or, to exotic isles still unseen. Await me. My work for the good of our coastal haven nears completion. We two shall devote ourselves to those feelings given alone to mortals, "with less of earth in them than heaven." I will not be long from you, for I am, more than ever, yours.
etc., etc.

It could not be denied. Her capricious hero had effected conspicuous turnabout. Signs were everywhere, as breeders and race enthusiasts arrived. They were to be found in the Library, upon the Terrace, and at the county's inns and gathering places. Mr. Dawson, having spread the word, even before his own appearance, of the soon-to-be-opened course for thoroughbreds, which should be a place to rival London itself, had in fact brought about such anticipation.

Shopkeepers talked of little else but doubling their stocks of wares. Mrs. Whitby at the Library had already gone up to London, in search of cunning notions and tidbits to suit the most stylish newcomers. As to the innkeeper at the Terrace, he was to be found always consulting with his cooks, and scurrying to ready his best rooms.

When the Inn filled up, others had to make their way to modest accommodations wherever they could find them, and not always within the upper new town. They could hardly expect quarters of elegance among simple townsfolk; but it did not seem to discourage these persistent comers. At the neighboring establishments settled upon by these gentlemen, the talk to be heard now was exclusively the language of the turf. It was indeed the only conversation.

Despite comfortless sitting rooms in the often gloomy surroundings of such peripheral establishments, these followers, Londoners of every sort, took little notice of such inconvenience. They put up with anything to find themselves situated at Sanditon, sustained by their passion for the competitions to come, the fine animals to be discovered, examined, and observed in trials, every excitement of their favored sport.

Lady Denham applauded all such busyness; she regarded it as dedication to the splendor of her own locale, a confirmation of her abiding faith in *"her"* Arcadia.

"As you see, my good Mr. Parker," she said, "however we may choose, we can in no way avoid due recognition from the world. It *will* come to our gem-like discovery. How might it not? We must be sought out! Who, on this coast, can compare with its natural blessings? Not Brinshore, to be sure!"

Mr. Parker, witnessing the ceaseless activity, was not so easy of mind. He was fretted by its altered tone, its coarse sounds, its dashing pace. In truth, the newly-come sportsmen little noted Sanditon's natural phenomena; its health regimens for that matter held no interest for their kind.

These gentlemen's eyes seemed fixed upon other matters, most prominent among them, proper billeting for their horses, and a concern over the dampness in the atmosphere, its frequent changes of temperature, and the wind and storm blowing up unexpectedly from a suddenly violent sea.

Nor were they to be encountered among the regular early morning dippers. If they went down to that fabled shore, they seemed wholly embroiled in negotiation with commoner folk, seeking out boys for the feeding and running of their horses, and for their attendance in other daily chores.

As for the most prominent of these visitors, Mr. Dawson, his passionate involvement with everything pertaining to local affairs had shown itself instantly. There seemed no limit to his curiosity about the life of Sanditon's sea-going men. He would rehearse their tales of heroism, hear again their contests with the ocean, study their disasters and triumphs. He pursued the smallest detail of Sussex lore, and showed deep interest in the fishermen's ways, their routines, news of their latest arrivals and departures. In truth, no limit could be found to *his* vigor in their purpose.

Most curiously, his study extended to round-the-clock observance. For this gentleman, the night's work seemed as fascinating as the day's, its industry at least as worthy of attention.

His investigations included the types of ship in port, its square-sailed luggers, its fishing boats, the row boats, and even the caulked tubs. Nothing escaped his questioning, even to the roughest, rudest—unruly seamen who unkempt and newly-landed from the Continent, or from long, arduous voyages over the vast seas. He talked with these and with the look-out men posted atop cliffs to signal the approaching ships; he befriended the batmen and the bodyguards, listening to their tales of narrow escape from the Excise. Cozy in their caves, he even sampled the tea brought in from the tubmen's runs.

He became their familiar; trusted, aware of their baits and their freights, privy to their account books. The gentleman's studies were all in the best grace; he made no exchanges nor carried away from such meetings any wares. Mr. Dawson, through his continuing generosity—the various supplements he would introduce to keep all content—had made himself a welcomed presence wherever he ventured.

All this while, news of his larger enterprise for the good of the country had spread rapidly. The town's good will was added to his repute. As work proceeded upon his running turf, the London breeder had also become a confidant and ally. His nocturnal wanderings seemed an eccentric diversion, as his intimacy with the villagers was enhanced. Thus it might have continued—so long as Sanditon's fortunes prospered.

Part VIII

THIRTY

In the interim, Henry Heywood had impatiently awaited a moment of leisure, before presenting himself in Sloane Square. He was eager to look upon his sister in her exalted London circumstances. Her mentor had long been something of a heroine for him, and he wished to make her acquaintance.

For this distinguished lady to have taken up his dear Charlotte hardly surprised him. There was that in his sister's spirit—a joy at discovering the world—which combined with a fanciful power to express what she alone could decipher of the bizarre doings encircling her this past year and more. How might she not attract a brilliance to burnish her own? No, he did not fault Mrs. Turner's choice of companion: it spoke to that lady's discernment!

What did impress him was Mrs. Turner's having so liberally offered to provide Charlotte with the magnificent privileges of the metropolis! This seemed something extraordinary—for it demonstrated a singular generosity. He well remembered how, during their growing up years, in their cloistered rounds at Willingden, together they two had pined for a mere taste of London. Here she was before him now, with the city at her command.

Emmeline Turner greeted young Heywood as she might an old friend, with a cordial informality that set him at ease. There could be no stiffness between them. Charlotte, at their side, stood radiant as she observed his unassuming, gentlemanly manner of speech with her friend. The lady had already heard much from his sister of the young man's adaptation, concerning his prospect, and hopes. She could but offer compliment upon his progress and wish him all success.

His natural deference, his modest demurral, together with his wish to return all converse back to her own—*true*—achievement—was charming. Henry talked eagerly about how his family had celebrated it, at home in evenings both mirthful and yet moving. He continued feelingly to describe what good company her creations, her *chefs doeuvres, Ethelinde,* and *Celestina,* had been, of how much they had meant to them. Such praise could not have been more welcome to the author had it been delivered by her particular favorites, Mrs. Radcliffe, or a Fanny Burney.

Their thoroughly agreeable exchange was interrupted by a knock at the sitting room door. Sally entered to announce that gentlemen had come to call; they were waiting her pleasure below. Mrs. Turner read the name of Mr. Sidney Parker from the card, and he was promptly, accompanied into the room by his excellent friend, Lord Collinsworth.

Young Parker entered in notably altered spirits. Unabashed, he assured himself of Miss Heywood's presence in it. Meeting her eye, he seemed heartened, and immediately turned to their hostess. The elder lady, always gracious, directly opened their exchange.

"Good Sir," queried she, "and is your scheme to dispatch a medical examiner to your brother's ailing colony already accomplished? Will we see Sanditon enabled as *the* locale for our healing? I look to discover it a haven for natural improvement of health. One must guard against the representations of quackery. Sanditon ought to promise that even the frailest can be certain of reputable practitioners. Don't you agree?"

Sidney Parker offered his reassurance. In the hands of Mr. Porter, a man dedicated to his oaths, he should know little doubt. There would be little danger of untoward incident now, no losses exceeding the laws of human necessity. No, no, he had, and he was certain of it, secured the place from charlatanism. Better, he added, he had intelligence not only of that gentleman's arrival, but of the warmest welcome received from residents lately settled into the Sussex vicinity.

If Mrs. Turner—her own health intermittent—was comforted to learn of this enhancement, she could also remain something incredulous. Of Sanditon's redemption by such scant means alone, she kept a skeptical reserve.

"And do you then, Sir, carry a full budget of restorations for that enterprise? Can you contemplate a complete recovery? While your earnest young scientist may undertake to treat the body's many deficiencies, and heal every failing of our human constitution, even to the discouraging of its dissipation, have you considered Sanditon's ungovernability?"

He seemed taken aback by this last.

"Good Mr. Parker, what of the obstreperous and the intractable among the incoming? Think upon their imagined illnesses, their wilfully induced fantasies, the unruly tendencies of more than a few to fear and hysteria. How will you hope to touch upon such woes?"

"Madam," laughed he, in the usual manner of his nonchalant self, "you do indeed ask much! Your demand is not for relief, but deliverance! I do not aspire to miraculous transformation, to alter the course of events, nor yet to challenge such faddish trends. And most certainly I am incapable of impeding what is deemed, by the new men of our century, *progress.*"

"That lies more within *your* reach. Much more possible through those journeys of epic intellectual discovery by your good heroines—in their ardent quest for the inner life. Among *your* artifices, such wonders, realizations, comprehensions, alterations, are indeed to be anticipated, even awaited. You choose to uncover the best of man, and woman too. You mean ever to influence and to improve. You offer hope for the future even for those most put-upon. Do not mistake me, dear lady, my own admiration for such endeavor is boundless. Yet, here in the observable world, among our common humanity, can we suppose such marvels? In the world at large, one seldom chances upon such fables come true."

The seriousness of this exchange had long since resulted in the defection of Lord Collinsworth, who promptly led young Heywood across the room, where they were absorbed in livelier, happier talk of current champions at Epsom. The gentleman was contented by young Heywood's cordial response to his inquiry into the nature of his new position.

Even so, Mrs. Turner demurred not. She found herself affected by the brooding philosopher manifest to her in Sidney Parker. Not only did he understand her broad concerns, but spoke to them, and spoke well.

"Clearly, Mr. Parker," she persisted, "there can be little hope of putting back into the box what Pandora has already loosed? What began with the conversion of a peaceful fishing village and its surrounding farming community into a watering place, has moved into a more fantastic sphere—that of a pretentious and feverish artificiality obsessed by health! Who shall undo that questionable accomplishment?"

"Why, dear Sir, the very conception of Sanditon must be suspect. As for the people who flock to it, surely, are they not those who would fly from themselves, away from the active world and into a reclusive sensibility?"

The lady paused, amused. She would recall how in the course of her own brief stay even the small talk never so much as touched upon the weather, so preoccupied was it with each whiff of discomfort, yesterday's ailment, and the minutiae of the moment's ache.

"No, my friend, though your cheerful brother may have dreamt of an ideal community, what he has got for his pains is a sheltered harbor for *invalides* on their interminable pilgrimage to salvation! In itself, unsurprising. How might Sanditon not attract the indulgent, the detached, the rootless, the irresponsible? Perhaps, they of "feeling," who seek out total immersion, prefer total obliteration in their delusion? Ah, good Sir, I do commend you for your late attempts and wish you well. Yet I must wonder, what, at this hour *can* alter the course of such excess."

A silence ensued as young Parker moped. Nor had it escaped Mrs. Turner's notice, that the customarily animated Miss Heywood, though herself attentive all this while, had been less forthcoming than was her way. Seldom had she seen Charlotte remiss in her courtesy; she sat now and offered little.

How might the lady have guessed the cause? The silence of our heroine was simply the result of Mr. Parker's manner upon entering that room. To have been openly sought by this gentleman startled her. Her color rose; head down, she awaited the calming of her bewilderment, and the return of equanimity.

From that first moment, she had seen in Mr. Parker no levity. There was this day a seriousness, a gravity to his demeanor, a tremor, as it were; and what looked like his determination to speak of recent rumination, of his own altered views. In truth, not only had his worries for his brother's position and his family's future weighed upon him; but, there had welled up in him an unease, a sense of disenchantment with his own state. The malaise had persisted for some days. No matter how he tried, he could not divine its source.

In some despair, did he finally speak his mind.

"Dear Mrs. Turner, your fears are akin to my own. I cannot think about my brother's investment in Sanditon without trepidation. You must understand, his whole heart and mind are committed to its survival and success. When I consider how many now strive for easy wealth, I can only wonder. How might *he*—simplest of men—compete with such? In his situation, those who *do* answer to his bid may well be the indolent, the indulged and self-complacent, those you have condemned as diseased not in body but in spirit, I pray that my hopeful, sunny brother will not be destroyed in the business."

Charlotte felt the distress he suffered. His impassioned feeling played over his handsome face and touched her deeply. She was urged to defend him to her friend.

"Come, dearest Madam, surely you must hold out some hope of succor for the ailing unfortunates of Sanditon?"

Turning to the dejected gentleman, she added, "Greater harms at the hands of true charlatans might threaten such gullibles as they. As for my generous host, Thomas Parker, fear not, Sir. If his Grand Speculation has become more than a game of cards to him, and exceeds all prudence, still I cannot think him so very foolish as to forfeit the fine achievements of his own, and your forebears too, in its name. *His* dream of community, of health, and good living is not dedicated 'like the others to profit alone. And for all Mr. Parker's wish to see his Sanditon flourish, he is likely to jeopardize neither the security of his wife and children, nor your poor invalid sisters and brother to the cause. His character is true. He is as tender-hearted a gentleman as any I have known."

Sidney Parker savored her words.

"He is merely seduced by the idea of this moment, fallen victim to notions, to the winds of change churning us about in these unsettled times. Like modern men, he glories in the future, adulates progress; the while, turning his face from past generations and his worthy antecedents."

Seeking approval in his eyes, she concluded, with her natural sanguinity, "Your brother, Mr. Parker, is surely the most charming to contemplate of men, if not always one to inspire confidence. Who knows, prospects for our blessèd coastal colony may grow yet, even as we speak. If not, he must soon enough see his error, and come to distinguish the possible from the fantastic; even, recoup the advantage of the old system, and content himself once more in that excellent way of our country life.

Now he has your good intervention, Thomas Parker will find his rescue with time, and that, with or without the leave of Lady Denham."

As he listened to Miss Heywood, the warmth of Sidney's gaze never relented. How exquisite she did appear to him in her earnestness! Her loyalty to her good host came before all else. She seemed devoted to the prevention of his threatened loss. Clear-sighted, sensible, she was fresh air itself to his jaded spirit.

And might it be here suggested that Sidney Parker had in these latter days suffered from his own ailment, that most disquieting of afflictions, love? He saw that he had been indifferent to the madness encircling him. *She* had parted the clouds, introducing a ray of sanity, where before there had been no light. He had walked as in a maze, even contentedly, until her luminous person showed itself. It was now, at this unforseen moment, that the secret nature of his own unrelenting pain grew clear to him, just as its beautiful remedy sat beside him.

All this while across the room, the other gentlemen had talked of diversions in the city, their picks at the running turf, their chosen champions and the current predictions. He dearly wished to still the turbulence within him, and welcomed Lord Collinsworth's advertisement to the young man of London's fascination, together with a caution about her inevitable disillusionments.

"So many come to us with hopes, and as often good skills. Within a short time, however, they exhaust their funds, and are obliged in disappointment to return to the country."

Of Henry Heywood's good fortune in meeting with like-minded gentlemen in London, he was therefore admiration itself. It was only with the young man's impending removal to his native country, to take up a post with the builders of a new course in Sussex, that Collinsworth finally made an association; upon which he professed himself astonished.

It was true. Not two days prior had young Heywood received Dawson's directive to come to them in Sanditon. The construction upon the site of the course was nearly complete, and his services demanded by the champions of the stable.

Hearing the name of his new employer for the first time, that Lord Collinsworth cried his surprise.

"Mr. Matthew Dawson? One and the same? Are you then in the employ of the man whom Sir Edward Denham has convinced to take into Sussex his running horses? Are you to soon join the group at the southern coast?"

"Indeed," responded he with enthusiasm. "I have just had word of the development in the vicinity. There is a vast excitement over the newly-arrived venture. Any number of facilities are expanded to house the influx. We shall soon, Sir, be the equal of Epsom, I assure you, a competitor to Doncaster, Brighton and Southgate. Mr. Dawson regards the prospects open, such possibilities as make imagination seem poor."

By this Sidney Parker was brought back to presence of mind. Hearing Collinsworth's considered opinion, every anxiety for his brother's enterprise arose once more. Was Thomas Parker's fate held in the hands of gamblers and adventurers?

Lord Collinsworth went on, "Sir Edward Denham is jubilant to have acquired such a prize as a brand new turf and the attendants that it will bring with it; but as to Mr. Dawson himself, young man, I will not vouch for *him*."

Sidney would learn more; yet thought the better of it, because the ladies listened as well. Only after he departed with his friend, could he quiz him upon the character of this man.

To hear such news of the gentleman's reputation came as an unfortunate revelation. As he now could conceive it, there must come a reckoning. It was a matter of time before disaster leveled all.

Reluctant though he was to leave London, he knew at once that even to entertain hope to stave off the inevitable, he must away to Sussex. And that, instanter.

THIRTY-ONE

Our dedicate to whim and its celebration, Sir Edward Denham—
not unlike those poets of pleasure whom he adulated—could
himself hesitate no longer. He too must fly to Sussex, on purpose to fix the lady, that dearest object of his ardor, Clara Brereton.

Long enough had he anticipated this prize. From their first encounter,
he had had little doubt of the quality of supernal ecstasy. For then it
was, that the daring plan by his visionary self had been determined upon.
The angelic Miss Brereton—a picture of perfection, wherein grace and
spirit discovered themselves united to worth, and manners equalled the
understanding—was still there for his taking.

It is true, certain obstacles presented themselves. The difficulties were
such as had required devices of the most subtle. This hero had risen to
the purpose, fortunately, even to the catch for their own Sanditon a
school of London's sophisticated. How might he falter in asserting his
claim? No matter the consequence, whatever the cost, such pleasure was
meant, must be his. Yes, he would see to it that she have him. Nothing
should stand in the way.

Only consider, this was a man euphoric in his passion, made for revelling above all other men in the very spirit of life! And how easily could
our young baronet find himself the equal to—nay, a cut or two above—
Wordsworth's own portrait of an Arcadian personage; *of more lively sensi-*
bility, more enthusiasm and tenderness than is supposed to be common among humankind.

Young enough, sufficiently deceived, and having until now himself arrived at nothing resembling a serious business of life, Denham could persist in cherishing his *radical pleasures*. He luxuriated from day to day amongst strong feelings, resolutely attached to the fair sex, owing an ungovernable reverence for womankind. Thus could he continue in his fancy the *dangerous* man, emanating squarely from the realm of great story and poetry.

Even so, in these last months, it must remain something of a question exactly *whose* seduction had been accomplished? Dare we submit that in fact it may have been his own?

The bereft Miss Brereton's situation, the role she had accepted in her coming forward as Lady Denham's handmaiden and companion in Sussex—an attendant subject to her crochets and twists—may have summoned up every dastardly scheme he might command; indeed, her beauty, her haplessness, cried out for the inventive Lovelace; but then, who might have supposed the actuality?

Surely, there could be no hint of wiles or stratagem in this simple lady. Yet if there were, can they be wondered at? After all, the young miss, ever at risk even amongst her kindly, yet needy, relations had long since recognized the prospect of want. For survival alone did she cultivate an innate shrewdness, demanded by a birth as unfavored as her own.

Clara Brereton's devices were unrehearsed, if disingenuous. They served to beguile her intended into that state most unlikely for him: matrimony. Sir Edward Denham must have his way with his lady, and in the end, what could details signify? With Sanditon's circumstances now triumphantly altered, why not through wedded bliss?

To Sussex to seek his lady love, and to secure her, did Denham hasten. Her life there, her position with his aunt, was of little account; what mattered was their happiness, if necessary, their happiness even in union. Upon this score, the gentleman had relieved himself of any prior concern. To whom could his aunt's position and money now fall, if not himself? With her Sanditon so chosen of all coastal resorts to be *the* place to parade, his standing with Lady Denham was confirmed.

Looking about him, as he made his entry after the too long journey, he saw such a prosperous stir—it seemed as though overnight—fortunes must be in the offing! Their haven had indeed caught the spirit of the day. He observed no bills in windows, nor notices. In so short a space of time, a few miserable fishing huts and smugglers' dens had been exchanged for structures extensive and elegant as to be fit to accommodate even the greater families of the kingdom!

As his carriage made its way towards the sea, he heard the exhilarating sounds of industry, espied workmen engaged in new constructs on the hill. It was when he reached the peak of that health-breathing incline, that he could make out below a newly-cleared running turf, innovated and overseen by his own Mr. Dawson, and from that vantage, the glorious, open ocean. It was an inspiration he exulted in.

Sir Edward hardly recognized his former surroundings, so enlivened did they seem. So many more had come to the quiet shore, that it fairly teemed. As he proceeded, the sites he looked upon demanded closer study. Passing the Library, for example, he could admire fashionable ladies idling before it, though he recognized not one. Around them were other newcomers, gentlemen, themselves freshly arrived from London. Upon the Terrace, could he espy some familiar faces from White's and Brooke's—sportsmen, speculators, those indurated gamesters. How lofty his little Sanditon had risen in the public's estimation!

Such ferment confirmed to his own efforts; he knew jubilation itself. He pictured his dear aunt's pride in his achievement, and could further envision himself her savior, infallibly her true, her rightful heir. Yes, circumstance was decidedly turned to favor him. Before the day was out, he would make his way and declare himself to Miss Brereton.

At that moment, however, another familiar figure stood before his carriage, "Good Denham, how I do welcome your return," was his call. It was Mr. Matthew Dawson.

"I have awaited an opportunity to display the progress in this glorious country of your inspired invention. Soon, our enterprise must be designated the finest of racing courses! I warrant you, the downland freshness of Sanditon is somewhat distinctive from the smoky haze never absent from posts like Epsom or Newmarket. Moreover, there shall be a pleasant shade among the pines for our spectators. Our turns of running turf will be so gentle, so graduate, that our champions will display themselves in all their beauty as they course. Here in Sussex, you do proffer breezes to delight the most elegant of society's sportsmen. And such already is the anticipation of society's comers, Sir Edward, that the sky itself opens its blue arms for our upcoming meet."

Denham's pride was unbounded. And if the thought of his own pressing business remained, it was but momentarily. "Dear, sweet Clara," thought this gallant to himself, "your patience must endure a while longer." For how might he refuse his friend, whose manner was cordial, invitation irresistible? Could a few hours more be of import? The lady was virtue itself; and, she was his alone. A pang of regret passed swiftly through him, and vanished on the instant.

Promptly was he led down towards the wide open ground to look upon every advantage in the course, its cunning construction, its splendid exposure to wind and sea.

Already the space bustled with grooms walking their studs upon the broad clearances, restless from the trials of their difficult transport, the troubles of the road, the arduous journey down to Sussex from every point. After leaving their home counties with animals as fit as any, they complained to all who would hear them of their darlings frighted by a van or cart, their balking upon stony paths, threatened by unlooked for injury. Such fears gripped them at every milestone. To all their mutterings at their tribulations, Denham did faithfully attend.

Undiscouraged, Dawson remained cheery. He had decided upon a venture here upon the Southern coast, and with it to attract every breeder to this remote village, together with followers of the turf from all of England—and it would bring success! In addition, he had found ample incentive here.

Addressing himself to our knowledgeable young baronet, he now confided, "And how might you have guessed that your own dissertation upon the lore of this land, could thus have altered the direction of my affairs? You alone, young Sir, have been the instrument of my making full acquaintance with so much that is promising! Settled here with my stable, I have had leisure to walk out to the inhabitants, sit with fishermen, drink tea with your locals—tea of the finest, Denham. In a whisper, he continued," Tea, yes, and it run in here by this bay. Young man, I shall make you privy to such industry as you have never conceived. Beneath your very eyes."

He paused. "These are jovial, daring venturers in moonlit coves. Their skills outwit the Excise at every turn. Brave men! Free-traders! Thieves, you would say—yet honest thieves. After all, they steal from no one. Accounting to the Revenue? Denham, what is more of an abstraction than that? Indeed, I care nothing for it, *they* risk their lives with each attempt. Just to look upon the gibbets hung everywhere for the gazetted among them! Come with me this very night to the caves, Denham, and you shall witness this wonder, if only in their industry, the fervor of their activity. Perhaps, who knows, you yourself may even be engaged by their daring? As for my own inclination, it has been answered by these remarkable, cunning fellows."

What could more pique the transcendental imagination of our fantast than this? He promised to be with them at nightfall.

Immediately then could he be off to seek his beloved, to throw himself at her feet. The tender scene, were we inclined to depict it here, must easily have matched the most affecting out of this gentleman's stock of grand opera.

"Miss Brereton," his rhapsody will have commenced, "you are divinity itself! Fate alone can have placed you here amidst mortals, and but for my sake alone. For are you not the stuff dreams are made of?"

A pause should now have ensued, that necessary only to adjust the gentleman's posture to suit his deliverance. The cavalier *must* be on his knees before reciting the lines extracted from *Epistle to Augusta*, newly set out by the bold Lord Byron, and put to memory by our suitor:

> *I can reduce all feelings but this one;*
> *And that I would not,—for at length I see*
> *Such scenes as those wherein my life begun—*
> *The earliest—even the only paths for me—*
> *Had I but sooner learnt the crowd to shun,*
> *I had been better than I now can be;*
> *The Passions which have torn me would have slept;*
> *I had suffered, and thou hadst not wept.*

The unfolding of that dramatic presentation need be extended no further. Let it be delegated to a higher imagination, with the confidence that nothing lacked in this performance. Missing was neither a depiction of inflamed early desire, nor the agony suffered in constant delay. Sir Edward's declaration was, in short, altogether worthy of the intensity of his passion, and a credit to his seductive powers.

Suffice it to say that same afternoon concluded the business, its lady wooed as any storied heroine could have dared to hope.

Sir Edward, flushed with victory, left his lover, prepared to meet any chance. Confidently, he made his way to Dawson's own quarters, to keep his promise. From there the gentleman would escort him into dim regions, and introduce to him to the wonders of the night.

For once darkness was descended upon the beach, another, quite distinct, world revealed itself, such a panorama as he had heretofore been innocent of. At this hour, the shore had not merely become a place from which to view the sublime power of the elements; but a great deal more. The caverns about them came suddenly alive, as in a grim theater. The labyrinth and maze of alley ways, rude natural arches, cells and chambers seemed endless. Their passages were narrow, obscurely lit, indeed, kept in their darkness, lest they be noticed from the open sea beyond. As he was led up stone stairways hewn from the very rock, deeper into the depths, he descried shadowy movement.

For this quixotic gentleman, the place was a living stage. The ever-venturesome young baronet was the more inclined tonight, he felt himself newly empowered, to enact his boldest imaginings.

The fascination of shipwrecks had always filled his boyish imagination with scenes of pain, pathos, and mourning for lost souls. At this hour, he was to discover actual heroism. Scurrying from secret tunnels were the tubmen, setting upon their excursions in such little wooden vessels, paddling out in formation to the waiting ship, like so many obedient soldiers; others, up above, their lanterns flashing from the deserted cliff-top, or lolling in details to take their turns.

Dawson, this while, continued in high spirits, for he would acquaint his friend with the importance of his discovery.

"There is much, young man, to be understood, and even more to profit from on these shores," was his offering. "But a little patience; you shall see for yourself."

By now some couriers were returning with their night's haul from a ship lying beyond the harbor. When these heavy-coated figures began to unrobe in the blackened night, Denham saw them corseted about with packets. The daring lads were done up so ingeniously, that their freight could neither be noted nor detected by a casual eye, nor yet be touched by the salt of the sea.

Sir Edward watched in wonder as each unpeeled his treasure. He saw bundled and wrapped parcels of the finest Indian teas, Eastern spices, and even some casks and little barrels of distilled spirits from the Continent.

The susceptible young adventurer conjured up from this further intrigue. What other in this whole scene was there *but* the triumph of good, of right against wrong? He saw their cause: the oppressed, resisting callous authority! Here was the just man's reply to harsh laws, imposed unfairly upon those whose voices went ever unheard! What else *could* he think? Our champion surely would enlist himself in their cause!

To think, here was all this secret allure, hidden riches rising from the sea itself. Such work was nothing if not daring, and together with Dawson, he would now dedicate himself to it.

THIRTY-TWO

Less felicitous was Sidney Parker's return into Sussex. For within those days, an odd circumstance had shattered the rosy picture we had lately seen.

The circumstance was precipitated by Sir Edward himself— and though on his part it arose from a deed genuinely open-hearted —our new partisan of free-trade had, inadvertently, and by his charitable act, succeeded in initiating an inevitable denouement.

What the eager Denham managed all by himself to do was to shake to its foundation our newly-thriving community, and put its very existence as such into jeopardy. A bright center of fashion and health, it was menaced now by an attack upon its reputation, its own rectitude assaulted! For, the Excise and Revenue men were obliged to take particular measures!

Returning to the caverns of intrigue the next evening after dark, Sir Edward had come upon a sorely-injured lad from amongst the group of landed tubmen. The poor young fellow sat moaning pitifully. In the course of his duty, he had suffered a fall, and broken his leg. In the struggle to elude pursuers, he had somehow managed the frantic scramble up the ropes strung from the steep cliff surrounding his post.

Seeing him wounded, it induced in Denham a heroic concern to succor him. He took it upon himself to find medical care for this suffering soul. He had lately learned of the committed young doctor brought down from London. He would convey the lad secretly to Porter's rooms in Sanditon town.

Despite the lateness of the hour at which the two appeared before his door, the furtive nature of their coming and their subdued manner, Mr. James Porter was his dependable self. Without a word, he saw to the emergency at hand, swift in his proficient resetting of the fellow's injured limb.

"Perhaps, young man," commented he, as he assisted him to his feet, "you will undertake no further antics with your foolish comrades by dark. Surely, other than the bravado of a wild dare and the dangerous climb, there can be no profit in its accomplishment? Nor, I assure you, will your leg for some good little time to come allow you such agility as the feat requires."

Upon the hearing of this miserable prognosis, the suffering youth was reduced to tears. He protested, his livelihood was thus lost. Then he told his melancholy history—his return from the Wars, the loss of former prospects for employment in his own community, and revealed how he had come to find himself in this night's aleatory situation.

For all his short time in Sanditon, Mr. Porter had already been solicited by several young fellows, with one or another injury of the kind. He had been puzzled over these night-time antics. Astonished, he heard him out, learning how ubiquitous were these contests. Only now did he begin to glimpse the incentives for all these climbs, not least their increased frequency. Was it not to be associated with Sanditon's new influx of Londoners! The very numbers of youth now tempted to defy the law could but dismay this honest man of science.

Rather than upbraid the pitiful patient hobbled before him, Porter confronted his companion—who from his appearance, at least, must be a gentleman.

"Is this poor chap in your employ, Sir?" demanded he. "And what sort of honest work might you call this for a veteran soldier of His Majesty? How long will you suppose may he escape the wrath of the Excise or else the Protective Guard?" Shaking his head, he added, "I assure you, Sir, he will be unable to serve his family, clapped, as soon he must be, into the cell of our local jail!"

Denham had offered no explanation for the circumstances of the young man's fall; instead, he had presented himself with some dignity, as Samaritan, doing a service in behalf of a stranger.

"Patience, my dear doctor," was his response, "you are new to the ways of our Southern shore. How little do you understand of us, our struggles against unjust measures, and our tenacious defiance. Forces that threaten from afar should be valiantly opposed. Oppression is the lot of the good people of Sussex. Why, in former times, when the owlers plied their trade from these shores, even our ancient poet Chaucer sang of their hazards in his *Tales*.

"You must see, that we suffer unnatural imposts upon the sources of our few pleasures in life. Call them luxuries? They are not! Every just man among us has ever fought, and must always struggle to see such taxes contained. You look upon one among many. These young men are the vehicles to rectify outrageous exactions upon us. I assure you, our young venturers do fine work, making their daring rescues of precious cargo, and, dear Sir, with little harm to any being."

"No harm, you say?" the doctor cried, having lost his patience. "When their employers take all near at hand, ready-trained youth, in defiance of the law, to labor at night, shifting huge loads of 'goods'? For a few shillings they risk life and limb, as you see here! Such as they have gained a lawless passport throughout the land; these are the unscrupulous, keen to make fortunes, encouraging tubmen and batmen, bribing the Revenue, convincing even the respectable to condone their crimes! All your romantic aura is a mockery. Do you praise viciousness, and violence against the Blockade?"

"Come, good Sir, will you justify such madness by preaching rebellion? By calling up pictures of winking lanterns, broached casks, and clandestine midnight gathering? Have you no idea of what has already come from ruffians such as these, here in the past in your own Sussex? What of the disasters brought by the Hawkhurst gang and their brutal like? In your own vicinity! Their heinous exploits are recorded all over the Southern coast, as far away as Cornwall. Nothing but murder, ruin and chaos follow in their wake."

Denham heard him in silence.

"You must see, Sir, that no benefit accrues to those poor souls who run to fetch contraband. Instead, only overseers, offering little more than money, profit while, taking no risk. A bloody, ruthless trade, nowhere resembling the pursuits of freedom you think it. Certainly, not work in the service of the commonality." He concluded bitterly, "Such delusion as is yours, I warrant, will see the end of our England altogether!"

Even so, the earnest doctor, compassionate toward the tubman he had served, kept his confidence. He spoke to no one of their night-time visit.

To his chagrin, however, he was sought out by the Excise men in their hunt for the man that had given them chase some days prior. When they queried him, he found he could not lie.

Thus commenced a disastrous sequence of events. Within a short time, far more was to be revealed. During that same moonlit night, the Guards, attempting to intercept a cutter coming into the shore, had boarded her and met with ruffians armed and ready for them. What followed was pandemonium. Word soon spread that several in his Majesty's service had been badly beaten by those "honest thieves of free trading," who were but defending their stores of "precious tea, tobacco, silk and lace."

That night's mayhem disturbed the peace in that vicinity—a discreet silence that had lasted for decades—to the general benefit. Rewarded for their cooperation, the Revenue had traditionally ignored the sporadic occult activities of their more enterprising townsfolk.

The sudden provocation by ambitious newcomers, on the other hand, provoked officials to pursue the matter. They *must* protest their humiliated, abused men. Soon enough, did the Guards pounce, not only upon locals employed in this traffic, but even pressed the cavalier Londoners now expanding and augmenting their operations!

Such was the upheaval that greeted a resolute Sidney Parker upon his return. He had come in expectation of difficulty, of the discovery of troubles, but he was not prepared for this latest shock—the enterprise of Sanditon now threatened by collapse.

Families were to be seen gathering themselves up for departure; some fearful for their daughters, considering the proximity of "marauders" in the port. As to the wary London gamesters, they were unwilling to be entangled with His Majesty's Law; many were departing post-haste. Notoriety came soon. A report of the incident in the *Morning Post* brought attention to "those questionable intrigues newly come to light at a certain bathing position upon our Southern coast." It commended sterling efforts on the part of "our Protective Guards to root out the culprits from the many innocent pleasure seekers and respectable visitors, just lately settled into the fashionable development."

Such exposure did not augur well. He found his elder brother Thomas in consternation over the fate of his settlement. True, Mr. Parker could take comfort in Sidney's arrival. His reappearance was propitious, and touching; it argued for continued devotion to their welfare. He saw his young brother to be in earnest, determined to help him.

"Dearest brother," he mumbled, dejected, "in these late developments we must read a portent. I fear for our Sanditon. I confess it myself. For the first time, I despair for its prospects. More than ever I welcome your counsel, and do rejoice in your commitment."

As to his coadjutor, Lady Denham, nothing consoled her. Much might she have countenanced; but this recent turn left her for once despondent. Her reputation; her standing in society; her claim to propriety—all those efforts to improve her situation in life—were dashed. Even after her attempts to ennoble it, this glorious locale, in which her first husband's estate once dominated, was now demeaned by scandal and squalid circumstance.

"Think upon *my* position, amid such goings on," moaned she. "That I should be in association with a criminal element! Why, surely the very notion that I might have fostered such lawlessness is without precedent!"

In truth, there was more to be feared. How might the Lady ever speak of her new designs for Waterloo Crescent, How, indeed, might a substantial investment be recovered? She committed herself to the contemplation of ruin.

"What is to become of us, Mr. Parker?" was her lament. "Nothing but departing guests, commerce exiting with them; rooms vacated, notices everywhere; even, the loss of takers for my precious asses' milk!

"You must know," she added, turning to Sidney, "that my late Denham's asses were only just come into their proper appreciation. We should soon enough have observed among us many an invalid restored, reinvigorated by the miracle of my milk."

Mild-mannered Mrs. Parker lamented to Sidney, but her plaints were more closely addressed to her husband's own disappointment. His dreams for their progeny, she saw now inauspiciously imperiled, and she feared as much for their health as their prosperity. Might they ever consider the possibility again of her children's growing up within enclosed circumstance, in such a depth as that "hole" in the windless valley which had been their former home?

It need be confessed, however (though she herself had little wish to divulge such inclination), that on her account, she had never delighted in those open gusts or the piercing damp prevalent at Trafalgar House; she would in point of fact welcome a return to their ancient, cozier shelter. Besides, were not vegetables there more plentiful for the better part of the year?

Sidney listened in sympathy to their plaints, striving to give reassurance to his poor family. Perhaps, most extraordinary, notwithstanding every other grievance, was the effect upon his good sister Diana of Sanditon's approaching decline. She told him, in no uncertain terms, of the affront which she had suffered from these preposterous threats to its respectability.

Since that time when she had taken up residence, assuming a vigilant duty to act as Thomas' protector—and despite her worries for her own and Susan's welfare, together with those anticipations of Arthur's necessary demise—she had found in her removal to the shore some distinct advantage. One such as she could not have dreamed! What had, in fact, come with her remove hence was an admirable enlargement of the capable lady's sensibilities!

Always had she sought to benefit her peers; until now never sojourned with so many, like herself, ailing and in need. Amidst such fellowship, she had come to know a more precise pleasure: that of daily intimacy with souls in pain. The lady had discovered more ways than ever to serve, and rewards equal to any she had experienced in the management of her feeble sister and young brother.

In her enthusiasm, her loyalties shifted to favor Sanditon. There had come particular dedication to life at the sea, and to its healing properties, along with an even more unique distinction: her own ascendancy to the rank of expert in the management of the gruff custodians of the bathing machines. Every new arrival attempting their wonders must seek out Miss Parker before risking a plunge.

"I do serve only as I can, dear brother," announced she with her usual reserve. "Yet it is with a devotion none can equal. Since I too suffer, I myself the better feel every ague as it is experienced."

Then, pleading for his help, she urged, "Dear Sidney, now you are come to us, you can be of service. Our restorations here *do* have their vital effects, they cannot be interfered with by matters of mere commerce in the township! Imagine, unscrupulous elements would undermine such good works as I now do? Calculating despoilers are they! To my mind, that must include both Revenue minders together with their more criminal challengers!"

"What matters, dear brother, is healthful, clean-thinking ways. We have found them! You need only look to their general malfeasance, dispose of it, and be about your business once more."

For his part, Sidney Parker hesitated not to promise every exertion. He may himself have been in a quandary as to what might reconstitute a Humpty Dumpy fallen from grace; but, as always, there was nothing for it when dealing with his peremptory sister than to listen, and obey.

Then too, his new imperative must fortify him for the task. Like a reluctant Hamlet, he should take arms against a sea of troubles and rescue them all. And if our Sidney Parker remained facetiously dispassionate, still proceeding, half in jest—he must concede this much at least: for the sake of Miss Heywood alone, it must be ventured.

Accidental lover that he was, he also remembered that to the brave alone belong the fair, and how, lately, had he resolved to conform himself to that judgment. Indeed, the notion now made complete sense to him.

THIRTY-THREE

Susceptible young men, however vexed by a violent passion, will rarely be possessed by it. It is the clear-minded, those in command of their persons, who by resistance to love's frequent allures, exhibit true strength of character. A pledge from one of these reticents is the more intense, if finally obtained, and certainly most to be valued.

Among this estimable lot must be counted Sidney Parker ever since he had submitted to his attraction for Charlotte Heywood. Moreover, it was to her remarkable sufficiency, her unaffected, naturally confident self, that he was to show his unwavering devotion; better still, commitment.

Particular demonstration of his new fervor came during the day he learned that among those netted by the sweep of the Protective Guard was an unknown, unassuming newcomer to Sanditon, a young horse-breeder and handler, in the employ of Mr. Matthew Dawson. It was reported that grave accusations had been levelled against one Henry Heywood, for his participation in recent forays upon the beach, as well as at sea. He stood accused of the heinous felony of defrauding his Majesty's Revenue.

Heywood's protestations of his ignorance of such crime, even any awareness of those activities, were loud. He maintained, so preoccupied had he been with his equestrian charges in his brief time at the Sussex shore, that he had never left their presence, other than to seek his own nightly rest. His pleading was ignored. He remained, held in custody, while the authorities determined what was to be the fate of the culprits caught up in the recent disturbances.

How bewildering Parker found this. He could not but wonder why, with so little evidence of Heywood's involvement, he was counted amongst the accused? Upon making inquiries in his behalf, he soon discovered the true circumstance behind that detention. It seemed, although Heywood himself had not been taken that night, that special intelligence was offered the Guardsmen concerning the fellow's guilt. It was a testimony by his formerly trusting employer, who now declared himself most discouraged.

This gentleman, they informed Parker, had talked freely to them; in truth, he talked liberally to all who would hear him, of how he had been terribly ill-used, and especially of his own disappointment with the lad.

"He is a mere boy," he explained, "whom I'd picked out of my goodness, confident of his honesty—for he had little to recommend him but his country rearing and enthusiasm for our sport. How might I have guessed at such weakness of spirit, such greed? Little hint had I then, for that was back in London, of the temptations thrown up upon this teeming shore. Irresistible, to a thief born!"

It was this accusation that outraged Sidney Parker. Once he heard it, there was no holding him. Charlotte's brother! To be implicated, and so unjustly, in the current debacle, by that unscrupulous schemer! Intolerable! He surmised that there must be some greater cunning in Dawson's protest, more than could be discerned at first hearing.

He speculated upon events over the last months, pondering about this preposterous denunciation. But gradually did their purpose begin to show. He found himself growing certain in his own mind. Surely, this was all a plan conceived by that conspirator himself—*before* his having launched into Sanditon's expansion. How obvious it seemed: this chaos arose from Dawson's chosen devices. Young Heywood was merely his foil.

Sidney fathomed what enticement to Dawson this distant shore held, and his willingness to come so far thus to remove himself from the smart London sporting scene. Nor did he wonder longer at the man's readiness to invest so prodigious an effort in the construction of a running course. Sir Edward's proposal had, in effect, presented to this shrewd gambler the most excellent opportunity, an invitation of such broad scope that only a strong strategist might perceive its advantages.

Indeed, brilliant, open areas close to the sea and waiting for his horses had held but scant appeal. Any notion to divert himself by strolling in its fashionable, salted air was not what had tempted him thither. For Dawson, the lure had been its snug coves and secret ports, the county's proximity to the Continent, and its potential for illicit trade. To have been so enabled to establish his own legitimacy at Sanditon, settled and unsuspected, near the free-traders of the profitable Southern territories, he would have extended himself even more extravagantly.

Parker's insight so enraged him, it altered our hero's essential mettle. It rid him of that pronounced indifference, until lately so characteristic, a defect that indeed fretted Charlotte. His anger raised him almost to mythological proportion, to that stature we must expect from a mortal destined as Sanditon's deliverer. Given the devastation he looked upon, his tolerance was now ended; his impatience knew no check. He would act to restore justice to his loved ones, and preserve everything they most cared for.

His first impulse was to confront Dawson, to demand open retraction of his slander against the young man. Bolder still, he would wrench from the villain a confession of the machinations that had encouraged so much nefarious activity in Sanditon.

On further reflection, a measured consideration urged him to reject forceful attack. After all, the gentleman had made his case too convincing. He had come lately to their shores with generous enthusiasm, in hope of founding new sporting environs for stylish equestrians. An admirable aim, to be sure; one applauded by every resident of a region so much in want of fresh commerce.

Indeed, while the gentleman himself might confess to a regret that a motley crowd of undesirables had attached themselves; and that they, drawn to this fine clime, and the prospect of spectacular excitement and elegant displays, had flocked to Sussex after him, there he might comfortably stop, and need admit to no more. That a wayward associate had accompanied him, to enrich himself at the expense of His Majesty's Excise—that would remain a distressing consequence. How might *he*— an honest gentleman—have anticipated such an abuse from one of his favored men?

No, Matthew Dawson had so insinuated himself with the Guardians, so bought his way to the community's respect, so shown himself an injured employer, that young Parker could expect none to give credence to his contradiction.

Sidney Parker contemplated next a moderated approach. He would appeal to the man's innate humanity, his necessary good sense. Surely, to make a dupe of an innocent young man, and ruin every hope for his future, could not be to any useful purpose? How might any gentleman conceive mischief such as that? Yet, the more he thought, the more he understood that such entreaties must fall on barren ground. Dawson's wider design was plainly unscrupulous. It would take precedence; and, since he himself had been the master-mind, to imply his involvement could serve but to threaten his avarice.

Yet a means to get at the truth *must* be discovered! The character of such a man must be exposed, and with dispatch. Parker concluded that it required more than denunciation by himself. Once Dawson's London reputation was advertised to all, there would follow little doubt of his malicious schemes. Promptly must he enlist his friend Collinsworth to stand with him, for that blithe young fellow had himself lately fallen into Dawson's hands; and had suffered not only from the rogue's power, but could supply the firm evidence he must bring to the provincial authorities. His friend should testify to the man's particular genius for evading the law; he could detail his slippery dealing, his ruses, and, above all, his clever evasion of responsibility for the mischief he could cause.

To present his case in defense of young Heywood before the Excise, Sidney Parker proceeded in just so judicious a fashion. He came forward to offer his charges, promising a witness within the week who should offer them proofs. They would have their true offender, the man behind the enormous increase in contraband nightly landed upon their shore.

In the meantime, Sidney dispatched those pressing family matters within his reach. His elder brother's continuing despondent state of mind was of the greatest concern. For alas, his former standing as begetter of the new paradise—his good repute, which had once defined the locale, insured its enchanted gaiety, its health, and future prosperity, had not proved very recoverable. Even after apprehension of the culprits and their prosecution, rumors persisted; the poisonous effect of so recent a scandal could not fade away.

Thus did the exodus of faddish and fickle continue apace. The loose talk, mean whispers, dark gossip, did not sit well with those contemplating their next visitation; assuredly not among the genteel or those in search of respectability. Others, further inclined to improve themselves in society (does not everything at the superior watering place depend after all, upon the choice of the very best of circles?) must now wonder too, who could brave being seen at Sanditon! As for those sportsmen and betting enthusiasts who had earlier migrated into the vicinity—especially those whose pecuniary resources would scarcely bear attention from the more inquisitive—they now felt themselves to be under authority's alerted scrutiny, and they slipped away.

The founders despaired. For some time, Sidney was loathe to suggest the inevitable. Little desire had he to confront Thomas with the full truth of their situation; although he hesitated to speak, he knew he must bring it home to his brother. Sanditon must surely decline. Thomas's family would do best to consider its own departure from the seaside, and return to their former, modest demesne.

Curious was it, that when at last he did propose their relocation, surprisingly little gloom was evidence on his brother's part. Disappointment, he did betray; yet Thomas Parker was truly a man of philosophical bent. He had seen reversal before in his life; he had been capable of dismissing dashed hope; he could entertain disillusion and defeat. The elder Parker was born a visionary; though he was a man with less judgment than imagination, his native optimism could not be suppressed.

"Good brother," mused he, "the grandest designs are seldom within our reach, even if at times they give us cause to believe them so. Sad only, is it, that our dreams are beyond us; they are but vapors in a world now quickened by commerce alone. No matter. We must pursue the Ideal. That provides hope. I take comfort that I, too, have ventured into another territory. I have tested England's changing course."

"No, dear Sidney, you must not fret for me; or for my sweet Mary," he sighed. "For we look to return to our old ways, to the familiarity of the country of our fathers, where we have ever been content."

The cheer with which his wife and her children greeted this decision, despite the severe alteration it would demand, resolved the gentleman's doubt. With no further complaint, their whole tribe were soon assembled, to set off with all their goods to make their way home.

That accomplished, Sidney's mind was prodigiously eased. Yet to be looked to was the welfare of his sisters and younger brother. While he had assumed that *they* would gladly depart from all Sanditon's turmoil and confusion, it was not to be. What came to pass astonished him.

Diana Parker and his sister Susan presented their brother with a reluctance to leave far greater than had Thomas. And this, from a place they had come to so grudgingly! How might Sidney have an inkling of Diana's latest triumph within the community?

To be sure, solicitous was she for the overturning of the rapid progress of what she now termed our "grand investment." Nonetheless, candor dictated what should have been only too obvious.

"You will know, Sidney," began she, "our elder brother was from the start unsuited to the enterprise required by the healing arts. Such business demands vigor, even to the extent of a ruthlessness of mien. Our Thomas' head was ever clouded by the pale thought of his contemplations."

"In the Sanditon I have come to serve, we never depend upon the lavish, fashionable newcomer. We do not pine for elegant talk; we need no gentility. No, indeed, not! We provide instead for those who come to be healed, the failing who seek out and submit themselves to our powers. There is work to be done, I can assure you! Whatever the fate of the stylish in our watering place, yet our accomplishments on behalf of the weak and desperate remain altogether within possibility."

Having mastered the latest skills in resuscitation, Diana daily applied them to those poor souls near-drowned in the course of their care. She was become an invaluable addition beside the bathing apparatus and its crew of attendants; an asset, the very preserver of life itself! Nothing should remove her from that urgent scene. Indeed, she felt, as did the several dippers, with their charges young and old, that her defection must prove the greatest of deprivations to their growing population of health seekers.

Moreover, already had intelligence of her contribution, her superb restoration of those something too actively plunged, and often even unconscious, come to the attention of London's Royal Humane Society. Its founder, Dr. Thomas Cogan, had himself written to honor the lady's courageous work. He would wish to award to her their highest medal, for they aimed to encourage her perfection of an art recently devised. Above everything, they admired that such daring rescues were undertaken by a woman, finding it a great wonder. Indeed, the tireless Miss Parker was valiant in her administration of vigorous friction to the sufferers. Her warming techniques continued, augmented hour by hour, while an exhausted Diana took no notice of her own fatigue. After such praise, such recognition for her agility, she had incentive more than sufficient to persist in her newfound profession. Nothing should separate her from a calling so lately revealed to her, and to which she brought such fortitude. Before long, she enlisted even the delicate Susan to assist her in this worthy art and energetic task: the complete resuscitation of the lost.

Nor could Sidney have supposed what was to confront him when he turned his attention to his brother. Clearly, Arthur's own life had turned independent of his sisters. His emergence from a shut-in subsistence was achieved. In point of fact, there was no way for him to retreat. This youngest Parker had pledged troth to the irresistible elder of his Beaufort sisters.

"Ah, dear Sidney, she has been the instrument of my rebirth," was his declaration. "She is the Muse that has inspired in me a renewal of my prostrate spirit. She is veritably my force of life." How apt, he exulted to his brother, had been her appearance before him in the very last hour of his need!

Their love's evolution had been so very uncommonly swift, their nuptial day was already within sight. They vowed to remain forever in Sanditon's wholesome air together. For was it not the drama of their meeting, in the circumstances of icy morning plunges that it had flourished? The dippers had not only brought them restored health, but their bold regimen nourished the wonder of their new happiness in one another! To them both was revealed their truest love—and in the open air! Nor might they risk alteration of any particular henceforth, in their life. Without exception, they must remain firmly planted. Since Miss Beaufort would bring him a substantial dower, that convenience, allied with Arthur's financial endowment, must ensure them contentment eternal.

Still another case was presented by Lady Denham. For her, flight from Sanditon was inconceivable. She had not the least intention to abandon the post which had been and should continue her home. Her road was clearly marked; moreover, she divined nothing but the fullest recovery tomorrow. Her head remained high and her appeals to the Guards became the more indignant. Would they then presume to endanger the renewal of the economy for their own people? And for reasons so abstract? The very notion to turn away prospects for glorious sport, merely because the vicinity might have been exposed to signs of unrest? Never! It was flatly and wholly unacceptable. Lady Denham would have none of it. She vouched that her own dear Denham—had he himself lived to witness their fuss—could never have countenanced stirring up of their daily order and needless commotion. *Some* regard was owed his illustrious family, was that not so?

Neither was the rogue, Dawson, himself idle. What with that gentleman's evidence of past intrigues, his vicious practice in the running of horses, and his chicanery in wagering, he thought it best to be off and away when Collinsworth's imminent arrival was advertised. He absconded to the Continent, where he would find haven for the time needful.

There was still more. The Guardians had gleaned from those unfortunates taken into custody the whole of this history, and so was exposed the scheme beneath his racing operations. These poor rustics had been paid, if not handsomely, yet promptly, by the London gentleman, who promised increasing rewards in good time. By his intervention, Dawson had assured them, all their wares could be forwarded to London and sold to his associates.

Despite that enterpriser's disappearance, strong denials persisted. Dawson had seen to the pleading of his cause, by dispatching to Sussex sundry persons, his own representatives from the Inns of the Court. Their subtle argument, accompanied by generous emoluments, succeeded in easing his position so far as concerned the authorities. His standing, no longer too questionable, and the affair smoothly covered over for him, he prepared for himself a safe return to his properties in the revived and flourishing society of Sussex sportsmen.

After these matters had been so concluded, Lady Denham's ambitious design was newly invigorated and resumed to its path so that it could run steadily along. With the resurrection her watering place assured, and its growth restored, she would make her own way towards prosperity after all.

THIRTY-FOUR

We have seen everything that could have been hoped for in Sir Edward's overture to Clara. His offer to marry her was something magnanimous. But after all is said, and no matter how long this virtuous lady had been patient, could such as he—a young man whose fantasy is richly fed by the paragons of libertinism provided by his books, and who is ever anxious to practice the seducer's wiles—settle into a familial sort of bliss? Are we to believe that the would-be rake makes the best husband?

Not likely. Yet, it was for just such a role that our Clara was formed. And what might not she have willingly endured to effect such a conversion to domesticity? *She* would *transform* what she saw in her beloved as the ancient urge of his noble blood, ever doomed to risk all for love's conquests. It was something he thought of as a superior masculinity. Whatever he might profess, Sir Edward was among such "sensitives," one of the *feeling* men. She dared to assume his was a recoverable, manageable spirit. Once within Miss Brereton's gentle arms, it wanted but her touch for its taming!

Having accepted nature's cruelty early, she could smile at the old moral, that "It is as much the province of licentiousness to betray a lady, as it is for the fox to prey upon poultry." To the which she would add simply, that "There is little profit in anticipation of anything other." Her proven capability was long since manifested by her triumph over poverty; latterly in her adoption by the formidable Lady Denham, for she had been selected heir to her mistress's holdings—and *such* a fine estate.

The union therefore must prove a splendid pairing. Like any other marriage (once the first months of jubilation have been undergone), not many demands should trouble it, even after life has taken hold. Fewer *yet* imposed themselves upon our baronet. Other than his wayward intermittent observation of propriety, he seldom heard his wife's dear voice in protest, as her contentment was assured.

They removed to his seat at Denham Park in the nearby neighborhood, at least when Lady Denham might spare them from more essential duty to her at Sanditon, which in her lifetime was infrequent. Clara persisted in the adulation of an unceasing attention, successfully preserving her Ladyship's devotion and dependency.

Astutely, Miss Brereton plucked from among her family in London a young Brereton cousin, to render continued service to the Lady. In this manner was Penelope, a biddable creature too, even almost as pretty as herself, brought to Sussex and given over. Miss Brereton spent some weeks tutoring the child, and imparting what information was needed to satisfy the unpredictable whims of their patroness.

The replacement served admirably. On the one side, were Clara's good relations, living on in near-poverty, with no prospects for their children; they must continue grateful to her. At the same time, her Penelope, at fourteen, awed by her rescue, would never presume to contest for her Ladyship's primary affection.

"Miss Clara," Lady Denham allowed, "I must, I suppose, make do with your girl. Be advised, you yourself can not be dismissed from my own service. Standards for house holding, my dear young lady, must be kept up. Upon your discretion I rely, to see it properly done."

To the increasing eccentricity of her aging mistress, Clara gracefully submitted. Given her husband's frequent absences in the years to follow—his unshakable attraction to gaming, and all the temptations London afforded—she found herself more than ready to endure the prepotence of that lady.

Esther Denham fared not so agreeably. Though Sir Edward's sister had set her cap for the charming Collinsworth, it was not to be. No more than herself, was the young lord at liberty to choose.

Not that this lady was found wanting. Her civility in London had quite suited his fancy. It was the constraint of present circumstance that checked him, in great measure a consequence of his immoderation at the race course. He understood it all too clearly that his proper duty as son and heir to a ruined estate compelled no free choice of bride. And certainly, Miss Denham was not the one to bring about its recovery.

This was the state of mind in which the gentleman made his detour into Sussex, to serve the interest of his friend Sidney Parker in providing testimony against Matthew Dawson. During his sojourn, he had by chance again encountered an exotic creature, Miss Lambe, met with in his prior visit, and an heiress all shyness and reserve. To be sure, that young lady, from the distant world of another continent, was under the watchful influence of a constant companion, one Mrs. Griffiths.

Lord Collinsworth was no novice. Before commencing his courtship of the delicate girl, he engaged her protector. His presence was soon accepted, his elegant carriage approved. Once the suitor and the lady assembled, it could not be long before Miss Lambe's choice of stylish garment, combined with Mrs. Griffiths's exquisite cuisine, advertised the young woman's several advantages.

The rest proceeded with such charming alacrity as might flatter any into happy agreement. His good family, his title, his estates to the North, were powerful attractions to an alert Mrs. Griffiths; hence, they should so prove to the lady's family. As to Miss Lambe's not inconsiderable fortune, secured comfortably in a distant clime, it appeared an asset invaluable. The affair was concluded promptly, with contentment obtained on both sides.

Esther Denham's disappointment upon learning of that too-hasty attachment proved most irksome. Long ago had she discerned her aunt's indifference; moreover, she saw with each season that passed opportunity narrowed. Still, there remained a portion of hope in her own brother's resolution of their interests. Had he not by his recent marriage to Clara, whom she unforgivingly designated "usurper," salvaged them? And if her feeling for her new sister was never to be warm, nor any affectionate friendship likely, the reprieve served for her present need, together with benefits suited to the style her birth had ordained for them, and which she had ever preserved.

Sir Edward and his new bride returned so seldom to Denham Park, however, she perforce must settle for her place as mistress of their fallen and decayed property. She took what solace she might in the knowledge that at least their Denham legacy should return to them upon the death of their aunt, even if it must come by way of Clara Brereton's surreptitious inheritance of it.

Since Sir Edward Denham's bride was well-habituated to that perch at Mr. Hollis's fine old house, for all its draughts, she could allow some courtesy to her sister-in-law, fortunately distant. Besides, Sanditon was now her proper home. And even after Lady Denham's death, she chose to keep that seat in Sussex.

What then of our principals? How might they have fared through all the late turmoil?

Time and distance had succeeded in separating them. Their feeling for one another remained unspoken, albeit to themselves acknowledged in their solitude.

We had left Charlotte in London, in midst of fresh discovery. And whether she lamented the departure of Sidney Parker for very long may be doubted, since there was so much to occupy her. Under the tutelage of Evelina Turner, her education might have run on happily, had not a disturbing letter from her father altered her situation.

> "*Dearest Charlotte,*" she read,
> "*We are newly informed that our Henry is taken into custody by His Majesty's Guardsmen for crimes against the Crown. We learned of it aghast. I beg your return home, to look to your mother and the youngest here, that I may ride to Sanditon to see to his welfare. Affectionately, and in greatest haste,*
> "*Your loving Father. . . .*"

Charlotte, perusing it, sat faint and motionless. Mustering strength, she went for counsel to her friend. Mrs. Turner's bewilderment was as thorough as her own. It could *not*, she pronounced, be the same young person whom she had lately met, not he who had made good connection in London with such dispatch?

Charlotte was left to conjecture. Her good brother held a prisoner at Mr. Parker's watering place? Into what mischief had he fallen? What might have brought disaster upon one so plain-dealing? Henry's was a gentle, open temperament, she knew; in every way a trustworthy, if, too trusting a lad.

As soon as Mrs. Turner could arrange proper means for her, Charlotte was delivered to her family, where she remained while they waited for a word from Mr. Heywood.

When news reached them, it came as joyful, for it told of his release and exoneration, promising his immediate return to Willingden with their father.

Again, he wrote,

> "My dear family,
>
> "I hasten to assure you that our Henry is now delivered from an injustice that nearly proved his ruination. My own protest against those accusations had come all to nothing; I despaired of the outcome. The wonder of it, is just how truth was finally uncovered."
>
> "An earnest champion made his unlooked-for all unhoped-for, appearance. This young fellow succeeded in bringing down from London proof of Henry's innocence. He introduced a gentleman, who delivered certain evidence of Henry's entrapment——by his own employer! His interest here—or so he averred—was that justice be done, and thereby to reclaim for his elder brother the reputation and good name of his watering place. You can imagine my surprise, when I learned of his name. He is a Mr. Sidney Parker, the relation of our own valued friend and kind host to our Charlotte all this long time!"
>
> "Such a tremendous feat it was! How brilliantly executed, for the young Parker was in fury. My dearest ones, due to his intervention, Henry and I are, by this, safely on the road to return home."
>
> "Your father," etc.

Charlotte, hearing this read, struggled to contain her agitation, for it brought the news of her brother's safe deliverance, and much else besides. As she watched her mother, brothers and sisters dance in a ring with glee, she herself remained oddly quiet.

That her brother should be safe, certainly was as gratifying to herself as to her family. Yet, what of the circumstance? Sidney Parker, energetic in a campaign to expose injustice? So to exert himself against schemers who would have ravaged Sanditon's hopes? Was such determination braided with a desire to rescue, to vindicate her own dearest Henry as well?

She spoke little of it to them. To herself, she would not deny that she was moved. Could it have been, perhaps even it was, something done for her sake? Whether or not, Mr. Parker's deed sufficed for an inclined Miss

Heywood's to admiration. Whatever else, her brother was now shown innocent, her family tranquil once more.

But, when, not many days later, Sidney himself appeared at Willingden, we must not pretend Charlotte was surprised; even to admit to her having hoped he should come and seek her out.

That gentleman made his visit with some reserve, ostensibly to answer the cordial invitation of her father and brother, whose gratitude had been insistent on it. Had as much as an hour gone by, before his partiality for Charlotte was understood by every Heywood old enough to notice?

Mr. Heywood's blessing followed even before discreet whisperings had gone the round of that lively, large household, indeed as soon as he himself recognized the exhilaration in his daughter's complexion. He had marvelled that such zeal as he had seen, such fervor, could be displayed on behalf of a watering place! Now, at last all was plain.

"Dearest child, he acted to save your brother's life! How might we not approve of him—we owe him everything. And, it was done for you!"

What suited our heroine the more was Henry's own praise for Parker's gallantry.

"To be sure, Charlotte, I must be grateful to him always. What I saw in him at Sanditon was such intensity! He seemed a man with never a hint of compromise. If this be what may come of love, we must admire it. When I first met with him in London, I took him for another sort. His wit, his easy charm, above everything his amused and stoical resignation, showed me then a different man. He never criticized the antics of his sisters and brothers; rather, he revelled in their odd notions, and laughed at their foolishness. And yet, dear Sister, what now occurs to me, is that you two are more like, than different souls. You, too, stand detached, an observer. Engaged you may appear; but I know you remain somewhat apart. Sidney Parker may even make you happy. What is better still, he will make you laugh!"

On the elder Parker's side this news brought equal jubilation. Thomas was especially pleased to be of benefit to the family who retrieved him from his fateful upset upon the road to Sanditon.

"You see, Mary, their rescue was heaven-sent," said he. "Moreover, most expedient, for has it not produced wonders we never looked for?"

Mary Parker's ingenuous response is perhaps worthy to be recorded here.

"It is certainly true, dearest husband, that our strongest advocate accomplished so admirably, what we ourselves never could. Charlotte Heywood has succeeded to attract your brother into the world, that he may live *with* us, not merely amongst us! Depend upon it, he will grow the better man for it!"

To those in love, every detail is precious. Charlotte had still more of news from Sanditon to learn; she would hear of each turn in that saga. She and her Sidney would scarce want for incident to subject to review and raillery, whether to rehearse his brother Thomas' contentment to live in the peaceful way of his forefathers; to marvel at Arthur's ecstasy in physical transformation; or to celebrate the newest honors conferred upon his energetic sisters, they could pass hours in genial mirth.

Moreover, they themselves continued to find new qualities in one another. *He* came away from that enforced, tedious endurance of his family's inevitable absurdity, and his restless wandering with his London friends. *She* had the singular delight to have uncovered, in unlikely Sanditon, a man of understanding, to whom she would yet show another consideration of the world about him.

Still, whatever *he* might become, Sidney Parker continued outspoken. In his satirical manner, he assured his lady that, whatever they might look upon, he would still cull those fools among them who spring like weeds in an untended garden.

He would often turn his disarming smile upon Charlotte, to add, "Yet nothing in this wide world of ours do I love so well as you."